EXILE

RACHEL MCCOLLIN

Heide,

Maybe one day I'll be as prolific as you!

Rachel

Catawampus press

Cover design by Alexandra Brandt

Cover image: © Paulbroad | Dreamstime.com

Catawampus Press

catawampus-press.com

PART ONE

CHAPTER ONE

JESS SCRAPED HER FEET ALONG THE POCKMARKED TARMAC. It felt wrong to be cooped up indoors, in this rare September sunshine. Reluctant to think about the future of her teaching job, she focused on the day ahead. Maybe she'd take the children onto the beach, dress it up as a lesson on seaside flora and fauna. She rolled vague memories of beach creatures around in her mind, knowing she didn't have enough to entertain them for as long as she'd like to be outside.

As she passed the allotments and reached the halfway point on the Parade, she heard a scream from behind the houses to her left. She froze then slowly turned, her glance scanning for signs of movement, signs of children playing.

Nothing.

Then, her heart stopped. There it was again. Unmistakable. A child's scream.

She dropped her bag of books and sprinted between the houses, reaching the dilapidated playground in seconds. Two girls – Asha and Soria, sisters from the school – stood on the grass beyond the wooden climbing frame. Their mouths hung open. On top of the climbing frame, their backs to Jess, were two figures she didn't recognise. Too tall and broad to be pupils in her class yet not grown men. They both wore grey hoodies. Stretched taut between their grips, a bed sheet.

"Oi! You two," she shouted. "Get down from there. That climbing frame is for children under ten."

They swivelled towards her, tangling themselves up in the sheet. Their pale faces, partially obscured by their hoods, weren't ones she recognised. When they managed to unfurl their sheet and she read the text daubed across it, she knew.

Go Home Skum.

She sighed. *Idiots.* She approached the climbing frame and the two girls made a dash for her. Their small hands clutched at her trousers.

"Get down now, please. There's no need to frighten these poor girls, is there?"

"Nah, nah!" one of them called, his voice a parody of her own. "Poor little girls. Children under ten. Eff off home, you parasites!"

She bent to the girls. Their houses were behind her; they wouldn't have to risk passing the boys to get to safety.

"Run home, girls. Stay inside until I come and fetch you for school."

Asha nodded and grabbed her sister's hand, dragging her as she ran. Saria looked back as they rounded the first house, curiosity beating fear.

Jess turned to the climbing frame. There was a movement to one side of her. She'd been joined by three village council members. Colin, the rule-abiding council secretary, her brother's best friend Sanjeev, and her own ally Toni. They moved to position themselves on the other side of the frame.

The boys were surrounded.

"Where's Ben?" Jess called to Sanjeev.

"Right here." Ben appeared next to her, eyeing the boys. Toni shot Jess a worried smile.

"Tell me what to do," Jess muttered, her hands trembling. She didn't need this on her first day as Steward.

"It's OK," Ben replied through gritted teeth. "I'll sort it."

He approached the climbing frame. She reached out to put a hand on his arm.

"No. It's my job now."

He turned to her, his eyes flashing. "You don't know what you're doing, sis. Should have thought of that last night."

She blushed and followed him. As they neared the climbing frame, the villagers spread out, forming a loose ring.

"Hello there!" Ben called up, raising a hand to shield his eyes from the sun. "And what brings you fine fellows here today?"

The boys fidgeted in their eyrie. One of them nudged the other who leaned towards Ben, his face twisted.

"Fuck off back home! We don't want you here!"

Ben sighed. "Oh dear. You boys aren't very clever, are you?"

The boys exchanged nervous glances. The one who had spoken – the taller of the two – answered in a low growl.

"What do you mean? We're plenty clever enough. Cleverer than you, anyway!" He pointed at Sanjeev. "Cleverer than *your sort*."

Sanjeev stiffened. Ben looked at him; he shook his head. Ben smiled at the boys and cast his arms out wide. "Well, you seem to think you've got some sort of safe vantage point up there, on your climbing frame for little kiddies."

The boys stumbled backwards; the smaller one had to grab the other's hoody to avoid tumbling off. "Yeah!" his companion shouted. "You can't get us up here! Too big for this climbing frame, aren't you?"

Ben smiled. "OK, gentlemen, you have a point. But in case you haven't noticed, my friend over there–" he nodded towards Colin, who had come to stand next to Jess, "–has taken a photo of you. Plus, you're surrounded. But we don't mean you any harm. We just want you to go away and leave those poor girls alone. The girls you so bravely scared off."

The boys shifted, drawing closer together. They said nothing. Ben continued.

"Now, you see, if you can just come down quietly and be on your way, we won't hold it against you. In fact we'll let you go and we can all carry on with our day. Yes, everyone?"

There were nods and grunts of assent. Sanjeev and Colin drew apart to make a space for the boys to pass through. Jess stepped towards her brother.

"Come down now, boys," she said. The tall one looked at her and gave a hoarse laugh. She felt her face grow hot.

Ben turned to her.

"Let me handle this, eh? You've done enough damage already."

She clenched her fists. "No, Ben. I'm the Steward now, not you. This is my job. I appreciate your help, but I think you should go. I can talk them down from here."

He glared at her. For a moment she thought he was going to hit her, something he hadn't done since his teenage years. Finally, he shrugged.

"Have it your way," he said. "But don't come running to me if they hurt someone."

"I won't," she said, fighting the tremor in her voice.

He turned away from her, glancing at Sanjeev. He walked through the crowd that had gathered towards the village centre and the house he shared with Ruth and their twin boys. As he disappeared beyond the first house she felt the anxiety flow out of her body.

Sanjeev looked from Ben to Jess. "Mind if I go after him?"

She nodded and looked back at the others. Colin and Toni were focused on the boys, while the other villagers exchanged puzzled looks. The boys grinned at her.

"Come on then, bitch!" the tall one called. "Get us down if you can." His friend snorted.

"We've still got you surrounded," she said, approaching the climbing frame. "And there are more of us. You'll be safer if you get down and leave quickly. So if you can just come down – oh, and hand over that sheet – we'll let you pass and there'll be no trouble. But if you don't, if you carry on bothering our children, we'll have no choice but to take that photo to the police." She nodded at Colin, who was holding up his phone. "And to post it through some doors on your estate. You are from the estate just outside Filey, aren't you?"

One of the boys nodded and the other gave him a sharp prod in the ribs. "Fuckwit," he hissed.

Colin coughed. "Come on down now, sons. I'm going to make some space and you can leave us alone."

"Ha! You shouldn't be here, what kind of an accent is that?"

Colin's nostrils flared. "Essex. And it's you who shouldn't be here. We don't want any trouble. Now come on, lads."

The boys looked from each other to the villagers. The smaller one had developed a twitch in his leg. People were staring out now from the surrounding houses. Pale figures, clutching frightened children and waiting for Jess to rid them of these invaders.

Colin moved further away from Toni and gestured with his hand. Jess backed away, her eyes on the boys. Slowly, the boys scrambled down off the frame and then darted through the space, pulling their arms in tight. They raced towards the village's northern edge.

Jess motioned to Toni and she set off in a slow jog, to check that they'd gone and weren't hiding somewhere. Jess's heart pounded in her ears as she waited for her to return. The silent figures watching from their houses didn't move, but the people around the climbing frame started to gather, muttering, some exchanging hugs.

Toni reappeared.

"They've gone," she panted. "Ran off across the fields."

"Thanks."

Jess turned back towards the community hall, remembering her dropped bag of books. She passed through the dispersing villagers, offering reassurances.

As she waved to a family huddled behind the window closest to her, she heard a woman's scream.

"Help! Someone, help me, Quickly!"

Ben marched away, anger stirring in his stomach. *How dare she talk to me like that?*

Clenching his fists by his sides and lowering his face to avoid the stares, he rounded the first house and paused to gather his breath.

"Ben? Everything OK?"

He turned to see Sanjeev running up behind him, his face red. He frowned; he didn't need babysitting.

"Fine."

Sanjeev stopped and bent over, his fists balled on his thighs. Finally he straightened and pulled back his shoulders. "It's not her fault, you know."

Ben grunted. Sanjeev owed Ben his life and would never turn his back on him, but last night had felt like something close to it.

"You didn't exactly stop her."

Sanjeev pursed his lips. "There wasn't anything to stop."

Ben squared his shoulders. How could he not see? His own sister, betraying him like that.

"You should have supported me. You said you'd support me."

"I did. But then when Colin said about the—"

"Yeah, whatever. Just leave me be, OK?"

Sanjeev looked at him for a few moments then shrugged and turned away. Ben leaned on the wall of the house he'd been standing next to. He was tired.

He caught movement out of the corner of his eye. A man was inside, calling to him through the glass. Wanting to know what was going on, no doubt.

He pulled on a smile. "Don't worry. It's all under control."

The man raised his arms in a question. *Who is he?* Ben prided himself on knowing everyone's name but the memory had left him today. Ben waved a hand dismissively.

Fuck off, alright, he thought. He heaved his weight off the wall and continued walking into the village.

He picked up his pace, heading for the Parade. How was he going to fill the day? Going home to Ruth was obvious, but then what? It wasn't just his job Jess had stolen. His sense of purpose had left him, too.

He was soon on the main road, striding towards the village square. His house wasn't far from the square, backing onto the sea. People would wonder why he wasn't at the playground. But his front door was in view now. *Sanctuary*.

A scream rang out and he jerked his head backwards. He squinted, eyes scanning the blank houses. In the silence left behind the scream, all he could hear was the distant hum of the sea and his own shallow breathing.

There it was again. Another scream and a muffled voice. He broke out into a run, glad of something – finally! – to do.

CHAPTER TWO

"Ruth love, we need your help." The surgery door burst open and Ben staggered in, carrying a boy covered in blood. Jess followed with Colin Barker and Toni Stewart.

Ruth dropped the medicine she'd been sorting as the panicked group crowded in. Ben was panting, sweat beading his forehead. The boy in his arms looked about eight years old and he was bleeding from a head wound. Toni was muttering to him and trying to catch his hand. Jess looked pale. Ruth cleared the medicine boxes from the table, placing her precious hoard on the floor. It had taken two months of planning to get her hands on this, to arrange last week's black market trip to Scarborough. She didn't like leaving it out in the open.

"Put him on the table," she told her husband. "Jess, can you get me a towel?" Jess grabbed two towels from a high shelf and tucked one under the boy's head as Ben laid him on the table. She handed the other one to Ruth.

Ruth gave the boy her warmest smile. "I'm Ruth. What's your name?"

"Rory." His voice was faint.

"He's my nephew. Susan's youngest." Toni was standing behind him, her hand cradling his. The boy continued to stare at Ruth.

The door opened again and a woman shoved her way in, nearly knocking Jess over.

"Hey, my little man, what's happened?" she wailed, kneeling at his side. He wiped his eyes and nodded at her.

"We're not sure, Susan," said Toni. "Ruth's just checking him over."

Susan stood up and twisted a finger into Toni's shoulder. "OK. You can go now." Her voice was hard.

Toni looked at her sister for a moment then headed for the door, shrugging at Jess as she squeezed past her.

Ruth looked at Jess. She hadn't seen her since last night's council meeting but knew what had happened. There were accusations swirling around her head, but now wasn't the time.

The boy blinked up at her. There was a gash above his eyebrow, bleeding into his eye. It was long and dotted with splinters but, she hoped, not deep. Susan knelt again and muttered into his ear. A smile flicked onto his lips and his breathing calmed. Ruth grabbed bandages, tweezers, cotton wool and disinfectant. She turned back to the table, pulling in a deep breath.

"Right," she said to the boy, her voice brighter than she felt. "You look as if you've been in the wars. I've got something special here I can use to clean you up, and then we'll take a look at what's happened to you."

She paused, cocking her head and smiling at him. "OK?"

The boy nodded. Tears were mixing with the blood, making it look even worse.

"Now, it's going to sting a bit, but you can be a brave boy, can't you?"

The boy screwed up his eyes. His mother put her hands

over his and made shushing sounds. She looked up at Ruth, her eyes wide.

"Can you hold him still for me please?" Ruth asked. "Hold his head? I don't want to get this in his eyes."

Susan stifled a sniff and moved her hands to her son's head.

Ruth opened the disinfectant bottle and held a piece of cotton wool to it. She looked up to see the band of onlookers watching in blinking silence.

"You don't all need to be here. Can everyone except his mum leave us, please?"

Ben threw a look at Jess, a look that said *impostor*. Jess was too busy watching the boy to notice. "Let me know if you need anything," she told Ruth.

Ruth grunted, not ready to acknowledge Jess's authority just yet. She looked at Ben. This would be hard for him.

Ben offered a thin smile in return and followed Jess outside. The bell over the door rang as it clapped shut. Colin followed, casting a meaningful look back at Ruth as he left. Ruth wondered why so many of them had come along with the boy.

She took a deep breath and surveyed the wound. She could hear the clock ticking on the wall above the door.

She dabbed at his brow with the disinfectant, feeling him tense beneath her touch. His mother held him still. Ruth eased out the splinters, examining them before dropping them into a metal bowl. Soon his forehead was clear except for the red line of the cut. She turned back to her medicine drawers and found a plaster which she smoothed onto it. The plaster had cartoon pictures of cats, designed to cheer the spirits of children who'd suffered bumps and grazes.

This was more than a bump, though. Around the cut, his flesh was starting to swell and darken. And there were those splinters.

Rory's eyes were fluttering open. Ruth smiled.

"That's better. Now, d'you think you can sit up for me, please?"

The boy let his mother pull him up to a sitting position, skinny legs dangling over the edge of the table in his oversized blue shorts.

She grabbed a cloth and ran it under the tap. She handed it to Susan, who held it to her son's head.

"Is it bad?" Susan asked. Her voice had lost its panic.

Ruth shook her head. "I don't think so. There were some splinters but I got them out. The disinfectant will have cleaned it up so it won't get infected. But he's had a nasty bump to the head, so you'll need to keep a close eye on him. Have someone sleep with him."

Susan nodded, her lips tight. "You don't think it'll get infected?"

Ruth felt her face tighten. "No. We'll need to keep an eye on it, though."

"Have you got anything, if it does? Antibiotics?"

She shook her head. "Sorry. They probably wouldn't work, anyway. Not anymore."

Ruth remembered how blithely she'd handed packs of antibiotics to clients in her days as a veterinary nurse. How they'd shovelled them into pets with the slightest risk of infection; dogs with tooth decay, cats with flea infestations, even a rabbit that had been bitten by a squirrel. How she'd struggled to get them on the black market on the journey here, after Ben's mother Sonia had taken ill. Now so many of those medicines she'd taken for granted were lost. If supplies hadn't been wiped out by the floods and their aftermath, they'd been defeated by the bacteria, reproducing at breakneck speed and acquiring resistance to drugs that had once been life savers.

"Now, Rory," she said, forcing breeziness into her voice.

"Let's go into the shop and see if we can find you something that will help make it better."

"Thank you." Rory's voice was pale and reedy. He slid down from the table under his mother's guiding hand and stood on the hard floor, swaying.

"Ready?" asked Ruth. He nodded and she led them out of the tiny pharmacy that now served as village surgery, into the village shop that fronted it. Pam Heston was in there, tallying ration sheets. She looked up at Ruth.

"Everything OK? We had quite a crowd trailing through here."

This shop, in turn, was Pam's dominion. She guarded it jealously, knowing how important it was to maintain control of stock, to ensure everyone got their allocation and nothing more.

Ruth gave Rory's head a tousle. "All fine, thanks Pam. Sorry about the crowd. Rory here cut his head and they were helping out."

Pam grunted. Ruth decided to ignore it.

"But Rory's going to be back here tomorrow, with his mum, so I can check him out. Meanwhile could he have a lollipop? From my rations?"

Pam raised an eyebrow. "Sean and Ollie won't be happy."

"Sean and Ollie will never know. But Rory has been a brave boy and deserves a reward."

"Hmmpf." Pam stooped under the counter, placing a hand on her back. She scraped a box across the floor and took out a lollipop, handing it to Ruth, not Rory. Pam disapproved of people sharing their rations. But she wouldn't want to anger the woman she still believed to be the wife of the Steward.

"Thanks, Pam," Ruth said, handing the lollipop to Rory. "There you are. A reward for a brave little soldier. Now you can go outside with your mum."

A crowd had gathered in the village square. As Jess emerged from the shop with Ben and Colin, a red-faced man pushed his way towards them. Michael Walker, Rory's father.

"What's happened to my boy? Where is he?"

Ben stepped forward, but Jess slipped past him and raised a palm. "He's going to be fine, Mike. Ruth's taking good care and his mum is with him. He's had a cut on the head but Ruth can clean him up."

The man paled. He looked from Jess to Ben and back again. "What? How the hell?" He lowered his voice. "Is it infected?"

"Like I said, Ruth will clean it up. I don't think there's a risk of that." She looked around the crowd before turning back to Michael. "Please, let's not panic. You'll see him very soon, once Ruth's finished."

"What happened to him?" A voice from the back of the crowd. Jess shrugged.

"Ben found him between his house and the playground. He was lying on the ground. I didn't see what happened."

There was a hush while people waited for Ben to speak. He nodded but stayed silent.

"I saw!" A woman pushed forward. "It was those thugs. From Filey. What are you going to do about them?"

The woman's face was twisted and she jabbed at the air with a finger. Jess tensed. Next to her, Ben was drawing patterns in the dirt with his shoe, his head hung low. Jess let out an exasperated sigh.

"OK," Jess said, scanning the crowd. Sanjeev, in the centre, was watching Ben, waiting to catch his eye. She looked at the woman again. "We need to find out exactly what happened. D'you mind sitting down with me and telling me what you saw, please? We can get someone to open the JP, have a cup of tea to help us all calm down."

"We don't need to calm down! We need revenge. Those kids have been terrorising our village for weeks!" The woman was advancing through the crowd, jostling people aside. Ben cleared his throat in warning, but Jess ignored him.

"Please, everyone. The important thing now is not to overreact. We all know that our existence here is fragile. If we retaliate, we'll be on the back foot. No one will believe our side of the story. Meeting their aggression with more of the same won't work." Jess could hear a shrill note in her voice.

"So what are you going to do? And why are *you* answering me, not your brother?"

Jess felt heat rise to her cheeks. Ben, still looking at the ground, smirked and stilled his foot. She waited a few heartbeats before replying, pushing a lightness into her voice that she didn't feel.

"Good question. There'll be a village meeting tonight following yesterday's council meeting. I'd rather not be telling you like this, but I've been elected Steward. So I'll be doing my best to"

"We need *him* right now." The woman thrust her finger towards Ben. "A man who knows what he's doing."

Jess forced the tremor out of her voice. "The Steward's term of office is two years. That meant we had to elect a new person."

She looked over the crowd towards the houses opposite, where the other members of the council lived. She was still in the house on the village's edge that they'd been allocated when they arrived, six years ago. The house where her mother died.

There was a movement in the crowd, people muttering to each other as they processed what she'd just told them.

"So," she continued. "We need to get to the bottom of what happened here today."

The woman was still glaring, but now her hands hung loosely at her sides. Jess swallowed.

"The first thing I'm going to do is ask you and anyone else who saw what happened to come into the JP, one at a time, and tell us what happened. Colin, can you help out?" She turned to Colin, who nodded and motioned to the woman to follow him. Sanjeev started threading his way through the crowd to join them. Ben looked up to watch his friend, his face hard.

"Thanks Colin. Sanjeev." Jess's voice was lower now. The crowd was breaking up. "Ben, I'd be grateful if you could come too. Let us know what you saw."

He looked at her, startled. Defiance crossed his face. "I didn't see anything. He was already on the ground. No one else around. Apart from Rita here." He motioned towards the woman who'd been shouting at Jess. "She was standing over him, screaming."

Sanjeev was with them now. He put a hand on Ben's arm. Ben flinched.

"Anything I can do to help, mate?" Sanjeev asked in a low voice. Ben shook his head.

Jess approached her brother. "You sure you didn't see anything else?" she whispered.

"Nothing," he replied, avoiding her gaze. Then he looked up. "What about school?"

"Oh." A weight dropped into her chest. "Er, the school won't be opening for a bit – not until we've spoken to the witnesses." She turned back; most of the remaining villagers had children with them. "Please can I ask parents to keep their children at home for a while while we sort this out?"

More muttering. This was something she'd have to find a better solution for.

"Thanks, everyone," she said. "We all need to pull together as a community on this and I appreciate your help."

She sighed and turned towards Ben, ignoring the contempt in his eyes.

CHAPTER THREE

That afternoon, the children were restless. Jess kept catching fragments of increasingly outrageous rumours about what had happened to Rory.

Finally, she decided to take control.

"Everyone," she announced. "I want us to talk about this morning."

The twelve children who'd made it into school stared at her in silence. She looked around the group, wondering about their previous lives, the journeys some of the older ones had made to come here. The children under six – more like nine or ten if you counted what they could remember – had never known the luxury of twenty-four-hour power, of so many toys they never had time to play with them all, of so much food that they could afford to throw half of it away.

"I know you've been talking about this," she said. "Asha and Saria were in the playground this morning and saw some boys from outside the village."

All heads turned towards the sisters, who blushed.

"Asha and Saria were very brave." Jess smiled. Asha smiled back but Saria's gaze dropped into her lap. "And you've heard about Rory. Well, again I was there and you'll be pleased to know that Rory's going to be fine. He's got a cut on his forehead, a bit like you did, Paul, that time you tripped on the way to the beach."

The heads turned towards ten-year-old Paul, who puffed out his chest. His cut had been more serious than Rory's. Ruth had needed to send out for surgical glue, and his parents had worn a haunted look for days afterwards.

"Paul, you were fine after a little while, weren't you?" Paul nodded, raising a finger to the faint scar above his eye. "So you all know that Rory will be too."

She sat back in her chair, waiting for questions. A hand shot up.

"Miss, will the boys come back?"

Jess bit her lip. The fear of invasion hung over the village like a permanent fog, threatening them with the prospect of being exiled once again.

"I can't answer that question, Shelley. But the village council took photographs of the boys for the police. The boys won't come back if they think they might be arrested."

The children shared nervous glances. No one here saw what remained of the police, or any authority figure from the outside world, as an ally. They were alone here, and the children knew it.

Another hand shot up. "Will there be guards outside the village again?"

Jess swallowed, remembering the attacks four years ago and the guards that had patrolled the village perimeter each night. Ben had been a junior member of the village council, and Sonia had still been alive. Just.

"I don't know, Mandy. But we're doing everything we can to keep you all safe." She paused. "Now, let's go down to the beach, shall we? Have a game of rounders."

The older children groaned and some of the little ones

looked nervous. She stood up. Getting the children outside would break the mood. She hoped.

"Come on, everyone, let's enjoy some of this sunshine!"

At last the end of the school day arrived and Jess flung open the schoolroom doors. One of the upsides of this life was the fact that none of the parents felt the need to accompany their children home from school. Instead, the kids were free to spill out into the village, some meandering home while others stopped to play.

Today was different. As she opened the school doors she heard voices outside. Every child, it seemed, had a worried parent here to pick them up. When she emerged, a hush descended. She smiled reassuringly as the children shuffled into waiting arms.

"See you tonight at the village meeting," she said, as they started to turn away, shepherding their children home. There were a few nods and murmurs of assent.

Sean and Ollie were the last to leave. As the youngest in the group Jess usually accompanied them home; it made for an excuse to drop in on her brother and sister-in-law. But today their mum was here to pick them up herself.

"Hi Ruth," said Jess, glad to see her.

Ruth blushed. "Hi."

"Come for the boys?"

Ruth nodded. She gathered them to her, ruffling their hair and kissing their foreheads. Ollie looked up at her, puzzled. She gave him a warm smile, a smile that always made Jess melt. Ruth bent to him and his brother, whispering into their ears. Ollie frowned, then shrugged as his brother grabbed him and pulled him towards their house. Jess guessed Ben was in there, licking his wounds.

Ruth turned back to Jess, her eyes lowered.

"How's Ben?" Jess asked. "I really didn't mean to hurt him, you know."

Ruth bit her lip. "We need to talk."

A lump came to Jess's throat. "OK. Come inside."

Ruth looked over Jess's shoulder into the schoolroom, then back at the house. Ollie was pounding at the front door, Sean not far behind. The door opened and a silhouetted figure greeted them: Ben.

Ruth turned back to her. "No. Come into the pharmacy." She paused. "If that's OK."

Jess trailed behind as Ruth led her to the village shop, throwing Pam a tense hello as she passed through. Once inside the pharmacy, Ruth leaned against the table where Rory had lain earlier. Jess perched next to her.

Ruth pulled a hand through her hair. "How did you get on in the JP? With the investigation?"

Jess thought back to the witnesses she'd spent the morning interrogating, the jumble of information they'd provided.

"OK. Only one person saw anything. Rita."

"What did she say?"

Jess hesitated, remembering the way Rita had looked at her. *Impostor*, her eyes said. "There were just two boys. The ones who were at the playground. They started taunting Rory. Then they hit him with something. He went down and she screamed."

She slid down from the bench, turning to face Ruth.

"Have you any idea what they hit him with? Could you tell, from the wound?"

Ruth nodded. "Judging from the splinters, something wooden. Some sort of stick. They might have picked it up on the playground, maybe the beach."

Jess thought about her trip to the beach. There had been

pieces of driftwood cast about.

"Did he tell you anything? Rory?" she asked.

"Too shaken."

"Poor thing. I hope he'll be OK."

"He'll be fine."

Jess shuddered, remembering how helpless she'd felt when Sonia had suffered from infection. How it had nearly killed her. Ruth pulled a cardigan down from a hook and wrapped it around her shoulders. The pale blue wool was threadbare, in need of darning.

"People have been asking me if they're going to station guards again," Ruth said, looking at the floor.

Jess realised that her sister-in-law was scared. Her hair was dishevelled and her face had lost its colour. She was scared herself, too. Not just of the intruders, but of the weight of responsibility.

"We're meeting tonight, to discuss it. I hope you and Ben will be there."

Ruth stiffened.

"Ruth—" Jess began.

"I don't understand," her sister-in-law interrupted.

Jess tried to keep her voice even. "Sorry?"

"I don't understand why you did that to Ben." Ruth twisted her hands together.

Jess sighed. "It wasn't exactly my idea."

Ruth said nothing. Jess reached out but she shrank back.

"I didn't mean to upset him," Jess said. "But he knew it was time to elect a new steward."

Ruth looked up. "You?"

Jess felt her cheeks heat up. "Someone has to do it."

"Ben's livid."

"He needs to get some perspective, then." Jess could feel herself shaking. "Did he ask you to speak to me?"

"No." Ruth looked nervous. "I don't understand, that's all. We're a family. We should pull together."

Jess frowned. "Pull together?"

Ruth nodded.

"I don't recall us pulling together when you and Ben moved out of the house. Left me there to watch Mum die."

Deep lines creased Ruth's forehead. "What?"

Jess waved a hand, already regretting what she'd just said. "It wasn't easy."

"You never said so."

"Of course I didn't. Ben had just been elected, you had the boys to think of. I owed it to Mum to take care of her."

"So why now? Why are you accusing me of this, after everything I did for her on the road? I was a better daughter to her than you were."

Jess's vision blurred. "How dare you."

"I'm sorry." Ruth's voice softened. "I didn't mean that. You were with her at the end, when she needed you."

"But not earlier?"

Ruth said nothing. But Jess knew she'd neglected Sonia when they'd been in London. Wasted all that time she could have spent with her. And Ruth had been like a daughter to Sonia, nursing her on the journey, risking her own neck to find medicine.

Jess wiped the tears from her face. Ruth moved away from the table and busied herself at the cupboards where she kept her supplies under lock and key. Jess felt numb.

Finally Ruth broke the silence. "You've really hurt your brother." Her tone was matter-of-fact.

Jess closed her eyes. "I know. I'm sorry, I really am. It didn't turn out quite like I thought it would. The council meeting, I mean."

Ruth's eyes narrowed. "No? So how was it supposed to turn out, Jess? Tell me that."

Jess swallowed.

The meeting had started innocently enough, the first two agenda items being purely procedural. In fact, it wasn't until the third item that anyone other than Colin spoke.

"So. Item three on the agenda." said Colin. "Election of a new Steward."

Normally Ben would chair these meetings but this time he had to sit and listen while Colin led the meeting as council secretary. Colin was a perfect fit for the role as a natural upholder of rules and procedure, a man who had been active on committees in his old life: golf club, rotary club, Neighbourhood Watch. Jess knew that Colin would resist what Ben was planning.

"Do we have any nominations?" Colin looked up from his notebook and peered through his smeared glasses.

They were in the space that functioned as schoolroom during the day and community centre in the evenings and at weekends. Tomorrow morning there would be a yoga class in here, middle-aged women heaving their way through stretches and contortions in the hope of staving off ill health. Anything to avoid getting sick.

Low-powered lights cast an ugly yellow glow on the tops of their heads. Being limited to an hour of electricity gave the meetings focus.

There was a cough from Jess's right; Sanjeev.

"I'd like to nominate Ben," he said, folding his arms across his chest.

Colin rolled his eyes. "Ben's already had two years as Steward. Surely you're aware, Sanjeev, that he can't stand again."

Colin hooked a finger beneath his collar and tugged it loose.

"Two years isn't long," said Sanjeev. "And Ben's a good steward. I think we should amend the rules so that the steward can be in post for up to four years."

Colin exhaled through his nose, clearly trying to calm his breathing. "This is not the normal process."

"Four years. No more. With elections every year just as they are now. It seems reasonable to me."

Ted Evans was sitting across from Jess. He stared across the table at his sidekick Harry Mills, his eyebrows raised. Harry realised he was expected to speak.

"This is daft!" he spluttered. "The constitution says a maximum of two years. That's a long time when we've only been here six. Some of us much less. Ben here took over from Murray when his two years were up, and Murray in turn took over from you, Colin, after your two years."

Colin nodded. "Thank you, Harry. Now isn't the time to start suggesting changes to the council's constitution. Can I ask for nominations please—"

"Hang on a minute!" It was Sanjeev. "You can't just ignore my suggestion. I move that we take a vote on an amendment to the constitution before we hold the election."

Colin's handwriting on the pad between him and Ben had morphed into a scrawl. He turned to Ben.

"What do you say about this?"

Ben shrugged. "I don't think it's for me to get involved. Nor anyone else who wants to stand for election. But I do think we should ask members what they think." He looked at Sanjeev, who nodded.

Ted was glaring at Ben, so hard that Jess thought her brother might disintegrate under his stare.

Harry coughed. "This is all highly irregular. If we're going to talk about an amendment to the constitution, we need to hold a special meeting and then elect a steward afterwards."

"We can't do that, Harry," said Toni. "Ben's term of office expires tomorrow."

Colin sighed. "I have to admit Toni does have a point. We can't be without leadership."

Jess watched Colin and thought of his brother, of the past he'd kept hidden from most of the people around this table.

Colin straightened and gazed around the table. "I move that we take a vote. All those in favour of an amendment to the constitution, allowing the steward a maximum four years in post, with annual elections."

There was a shuffling sound as hands went up, some fast, others more hesitant. Five hands, including Ben, Toni and Sanjeev. Jess shifted in her seat as Ben glared at her.

"Those against," Colin muttered, writing names into his notebook in tiny text. Paper was expensive and couldn't be squandered.

Again, the rustling sound of arms being raised. Ben was still staring at Jess, but she held her hands in her lap. He raised an eyebrow. Six hands this time, including Colin, Harry and Ted.

"Abstention," said Colin. Jess raised an arm, avoiding Ben's eye.

More shuffling, accompanied this time by the sound of Colin clearing his throat and smoothing the paper of his book. His voice was edged with relief.

"I'm sorry, Ben," he said. "But that means our next agenda item is electing your successor."

Jess could hear Ben's breathing across the table, slow and deliberate. He nodded.

"I nominate Ted," said Harry. Ted sat up in his chair. Colin and Sanjeev frowned. Toni looked from face to face.

"Thank you," said Colin. "Any other nominations?"

Toni sniffed, looked at Ben and then Jess, and cleared her throat. "Yes," she said. "Jess."

Jess blinked and stared at Toni. Panic slid over her, making her short of breath. Sanjeev was still watching Ben, who frowned. Toni was nodding, a smile playing on her lips.

Colin looked towards Jess, a mix of surprise and relief in his face. "Jess," he asked. "That OK with you?"

She nodded, her mind racing. She tried to ignore Ben's eyes drilling into her across the table. Had she just agreed to stand for her brother's job?

CHAPTER FOUR

Jess sat in the grass on the cliff top. Far below, she could hear the waves crashing down the coast from the North, but tonight's clouds cloaked the ocean in grey. Power down had begun hours ago, and now only the occasional gas lamp or candle illuminated the houses.

She lay back in the grass, staring at the clouds that dragged across the sky, watching the moon's ghostly outline break through them. The grass beneath her head was wiry and cold. She soon sat up again, digging her hands beneath her thighs. She stamped her feet slowly, wriggling stiffness out of her body.

Today hadn't been easy. The villagers were agitated, and she'd had no easy answers. Sure, they had photographs of the boys who'd been on the climbing frame. Evidence. But the police were almost as hostile towards this little community as those boys were, and had no interest in tracking down their attackers. They would have to look after themselves.

Ruth had turned quiet after Jess had recounted the details of the council meeting. Jess had tried to explain that it had never been her plan to take over her brother's job. But no one believed her.

At the village meeting tonight she'd announced they would be posting sentries, teams of two with the honour of staying up all night, blowing on their hands against the cold and trying to spot anyone entering the village. She hoped that the dark night and threatening rain would put any intruders off.

She wondered what Ben would have done today. More than once she'd tried to take him to one side, ask his advice. But he'd refused to speak to her.

They'd had intruders during his tenure. Once there was even a protest at the main entrance to the village. But that had taken its course, the villagers staying indoors and no confrontation taking place. Ben had never had to deal with a violent attack inside the village boundaries.

Out of the corner of her eye, she glimpsed a movement and swivelled round. The light of a torch was bobbing up and down to the beat of its owner's footsteps. She watched the beam, feeling her heart rise in her chest.

From the edge of the village, Ben could see the grass fanning out in front of him. In the narrow beam of torchlight it was impossible to tell if it went on forever, or stopped just beyond his feet. Beyond the cliff, he knew, was the long sweep of the beach, beautiful on clear nights but hazy tonight. Like his own mood.

Jess was out on the clifftop. He could see her silhouette, arms raised against the wind that pushed in from the North Sea. He guessed that she'd come out here to be alone or to remember their mother. Or to hide from him.

He picked his way towards her, tension tightening his

chest. The torch beam bobbed in the air before him, the yellow ellipse of light shifting over the grass.

Finally, the beam lit up Jess's long red hair. She swivelled round, squinting and raising a hand to protect her eyes.

"Hello, Jess."

Her hand fell. "Ben."

He snapped the torch off and they were plunged into darkness. The only sound was the thrum of the waves.

"How did you know I was out here?" Her voice was hard.

"Do you really need me to answer that?"

His own voice was rough, shot through with the shock of the past twenty four hours. Jess tightened her shoulders and went back to staring at the sea. *Coward*, he thought.

"What the hell was all that about?" he demanded.

She turned again. A brief, guilty image of her falling backwards shot through his mind. He blinked it away.

"You know I didn't mean—"

"You didn't mean? *You didn't mean?* What exactly didn't you mean to do, Jess? Undermine me in front of everyone? Steal my job from under me?"

She sighed, pulling up the hood of her coat, and climbed to her feet. She extended a hand towards his shoulder.

"Don't," he snapped, pulling away. Her hand froze in mid-air, then she let it fall back to her side.

He looked past her towards the sea. A gap had formed in the clouds, letting in a chink of moonlight. He could see waves breaking on the Brigg End rocks, just beyond Filey. He thought back to the look on her face in the community room, her feigned surprise last night and then her smooth assurance this evening. *Why hadn't he seen this coming?*

"You've got a nerve, Jess. I thought you supported me. You know how important this job has been to me, how much I love it. I'm bloody good at it, too."

"Ben, please—"

"No." He could feel his eyes prickling. "I expected trouble from Ted. Even Harry. But I never thought *you'd* be the one to stab me in the back."

She inhaled, a tremor in her breath.

"I'm sorry," she pleaded. "I promise you. It was as much of a shock to me as it was to you." She paused. "But Ben..."

"What?"

"Maybe it's right that the Steward job is only for two years. Maybe the village does need someone new."

"Someone new? *Someone new? You?*"

She put her hands on her hips. "Why don't you think I can do it? Why am I not good enough, and you are?"

"What?" This was new to him.

"You always let me play second fiddle."

He tightened his grip on the torch. It was one thing that she'd got his job, but another entirely that she thought she deserved it. That he didn't. *How long had she been thinking this?*

She held his gaze, her eyes shadowed by her hood. Sonia's coat. *How come she ended up with all Mum's stuff?*

She had no idea how lost he'd felt, how he'd clung to the steward job after Sonia's death. Without it, there was nothing between him and his grief.

"You're a selfish bitch, sis."

She plunged her hands into her pockets and closed her eyes.

"I'm sorry. I really am. I swear I didn't expect Toni to nominate me. I didn't ask anyone to vote for me."

He glared at her.

"You made a right mess of what happened this morning. Those boys. You don't know what you're dealing with."

There was a pause. The sea felt as if it was creeping closer, hissing in the darkness.

"Look, think what you want," said Jess. "I can't make you believe me. But I can promise you that I never meant for this to happen and I never meant to hurt you. You're my brother."

"Not any more, I'm not," he snapped, and turned back towards the village. He strode into the wind, buffeting against his body, slowing him down.

"Ben, please come back!" she called over the sound of the waves.

He dug his hands into his pockets and pushed on.

Jess watched Ben's silhouette recede into the darkness. Then she turned back to the empty night, sighing.

She froze. There was something out there, moving with the waves.

She spun back towards the spot where her brother had disappeared.

"Ben? Ben!"

No answer: not surprising. She felt her heart quicken.

"Ben! You need to see this! Please!" She flung the words into the night. When there was still no reply she started to run after her brother.

"Ben, there's a light! Ben, please, come and look!"

"Ow! Shit, Jess."

He appeared suddenly out of the darkness, the torch still extinguished, and they smashed into each other.

"Sorry," she panted, pulling away. "But please, you need to see this."

He scrambled for his torch.

"No! Keep the light off. Look out to sea."

He put the torch away. Darkness sank over them. She turned towards the sound of the waves and felt him do the same.

"What is it?" he asked.

She pointed out to sea, a hesitant finger aiming into the darkness.

"That. Right there, Ben!"

"What?" He was quiet, scanning the darkness.

"That light," she said.

Ahead of them, about halfway towards the horizon, a light was flashing intermittently. Near the Brigg End rocks.

"That's odd," he said.

She nodded, shivering. No boats came down this stretch of coast at night. There was no decent fishing any more and they had long since passed the time when those people who did own boats (and the fuel to power them) attempted to cross the sea in search of sanctuary.

"It's flashing," she said.

"Is that normal?" he asked.

"I don't know." Her voice was strained. "But I think it's morse code."

CHAPTER FIVE

"How do you know?"

"I did it at Guides," Jess replied. "Well, I had a go. Didn't get my badge but I do remember enough to know what that is."

"Which is?" He felt a gnawing sensation in the pit of his stomach. Today had been hard enough without mysterious boats signalling to them from the North Sea.

She leaned on his arm. He stiffened but didn't pull away.

"SOS. Dot, dot, dot, daash. They're signalling SOS, again and again. Pausing between each one."

He rubbed his neck. "So what are we supposed to do about it?"

"Well, there isn't a coastguard along this stretch of coast anymore, at least not one you could rely on," she replied. "So I guess it's up to us to help them out."

Ben didn't like this. He'd worked hard to create a refuge in this village, a place for people to rebuild their lives despite the power shortages and the rationing. A community that had learned self-reliance. When they'd arrived, the place had been barely inhabited, just a few other families and two officials from the council allocating houses. They'd been given the house Jess now occupied, perfect for Sonia thanks to its privacy. The officials were harassed and reluctant, and the villagers had soon taken over their job.

And it had worked. Despite the hardships, and the attacks from outside, they had drawn in on themselves and defied those who would send them back to what remained of London.

But now Jess was telling him to reach outside that bubble.

The sky was darkening, clouds thickening over the sea. Somewhere beyond the light he saw two quick flashes. Lightning. The thunder wasn't far behind.

He swallowed. "I'm not so sure."

Jess's face was pale. "We can't just stand here and watch a boat in trouble. People could be drowning."

"I know, but look—"

She raised a hand. "We'll need the boat," she shouted over the wind. Her gaze was fixed on the sea. "And people to sail it."

"What? Jess, that's not the sensible thing to do. It's the middle of the night."

She finally looked round at him. "They'll be dead by the morning. We have to help. Either come with me or don't."

It was a slap in the face.

"OK," he finally muttered.

They ran to the JP, where the key to the boathouse was kept. They hammered on the door. Jess pressed her face to the glass, peering inside to find Clyde, the landlord.

Ben placed a hand on her back. "You tell Clyde what's happened. I'll get some more people."

He raced towards his home between the village square and the cliffs, hoping Ruth had gone to bed. He started knocking on doors. Sanjeev first, followed by Colin, Toni and – reluctantly – Harry.

Sanjeev threw open an upstairs window and stuck his head out.

"What the—?"

"It's me. Ben," he called up through the rain. "There's a boat out at sea, a distress call. We should help them."

"What? It's gone ten o'clock, Ben! It's too dangerous."

"They're in trouble, San. This village is all about helping people who are in trouble, isn't it?" He wasn't about to admit that Jess had overruled him.

"Where's Jess?"

Ben gritted his teeth. "At the JP. Getting Clyde. Don't worry, San, I'm not mounting a coup." He could hear the sarcasm in his voice.

"What? Oh, OK," his friend groaned, disappearing back inside. Moments later he appeared at his front door, shrugging on his waterproof.

Ruth gazed at her shadowy reflection in the window. Ben had gone out looking for Jess nearly an hour ago. They would be at the beach, she was sure: Jess's place of refuge. She shuddered.

She wanted to go and find him, but didn't trust her knowledge of the dunes. Despite growing up near the coast, she'd avoided the beach and had never been a confident swimmer. Ben's family had grown up in cities, never understanding how the sea could dominate a landscape, how you could smell its mood changing. How the weather it ushered in could hit you with raw force.

Besides, there was no way she could leave the boys. She'd checked on them twice since negotiating the bedtime routine, quarrels and refusals mixed in with cuddles and the calm of the bedtime story. Sean and Ollie were too young and too wrapped up in each other to dwell on what had happened to Rory, but it worried her. Until now she'd often let them play in the streets between the village houses, knowing the older kids would keep a watchful eye over them. But that had changed when she'd seen the terrified look on Susan Walker's face.

There was little to see beyond the window. Hers was one of the last houses before you reached the cliffs, in a row of former holiday cottages occupied by council members and their families. So she was surprised to see a flash of movement out towards the clifftop.

She stepped closer to the window, not daring to touch the glass. There it was again. A figure, running across the grass. She froze. Ben always took the path and there weren't many others who liked to go near the sea at night. Those boys from this morning would never dare to come here after sun down. Besides, the guards Jess had stationed at the edges of the village would soon see them off. It couldn't be them.

But if it wasn't Ben, or the boys... who could it be?

A shiver ran through her and she glanced back towards the stairs. As she turned back to the window, her heart leapt in her chest. Someone was there. Right outside, waving their arms in the darkness.

She scrambled back. She wanted to flee up the stairs, to throw herself across the boys' bodies. To protect them. But she couldn't take her eyes off the person on the grass.

The figure came closer and she cried out in relief. Ben. He knocked on the window and made a circular gesture with his arm, then darted towards the front door. She raced to fling it open

"Ben! What's happened? What are you doing? Where's Jess?" She was scared, but also annoyed that he'd managed to frighten her.

He leaned over, hands on his knees, panting. His hair was

dripping. "Don't worry about that. There's a boat. Out in the bay. Distress signal. We need to get our boat out. Help them."

Her eyes widened. "What?"

His breathing was settling now but his face was dark with exertion. Behind him, people ran between houses, calling to each other.

"I'm sorry to disturb you, love, I know the boys are in bed. But there might be people injured. Clyde's down at the boathouse, getting the boat ready. He and Harry are going to take it out with a couple of the Golder lads. They're strong swimmers."

"Swimmers? You don't want anyone swimming out there in the dark. Do you know what the currents—"

"Yes. I know. But Jess says we have to help whoever's on that boat. They could be injured. We might need you, in the pharmacy."

"OK." Jess was right. They couldn't stoop to the level of the outside world, however badly it treated them. "I'll get Sheila Barker to keep an eye on the boys. Is Colin with you?"

Ben nodded. "He is. I'll sit with the boys."

She smiled. "Thanks."

Ben pushed past her, creeping upstairs. Ruth grabbed her coat.

When Jess arrived at the boathouse, Samuel and Zack Golder were busy untying ropes and hauling tarpaulins off the boat. Clyde folded them and lifted them up to a high shelf.

Jess hadn't been down here for a while. The boat was only kept for emergencies and critical trips down the coast past Hull, still impassable. Diesel was in short supply and so Clyde limited boat trips to once a month or so, giving its engine a quick blast to blow off the cobwebs.

Sometimes Clyde would have dolphins for company, smooth grey outriders whose backs glinted in the sunshine. Jess would spot them from the beach, watching them bounce in front of the boat through her binoculars. But there weren't enough fish in these waters for the dolphins to stay long. And besides, the ocean here was often freezing cold and polluted. Debris would wash up on the beach. Lengths of rope, empty bottles and cans, sheets of plastic mixed in with toys and clothes sometimes, a sight that made Jess shudder. No wonder the dolphins didn't hang around.

Harry arrived as Clyde was directing Jess to the lifejackets kept in a metal storage unit at the back of the boathouse. Now was as good a time as any to build some bridges with Ted's right hand man. Maybe Harry would be less hostile on his own.

"Hi, Harry," Jess called over the hiss of the rain. "Thanks for coming."

Harry grunted. The wind blew his hood off and he yanked it back up again, swearing under his breath. "Fool's errand, this. Why the hell we're going out there at this time of night, I don't know."

Jess drew in a long breath, remembering her conversation with Ben. She glanced at her watch. Was it only half an hour ago that they'd spotted the light? It was going to be a long night.

"We know it's not the best time to be at sea, Harry, but I guess that's why they've got into trouble. We can't just abandon them."

Harry didn't say anything, but reluctantly took the life-jacket she offered him. He was a heavy man and it wasn't easy for him to squeeze it on. Jess shrugged hers on with ease, taking her eyes off Harry to fasten it correctly.

Clyde passed between them, checking each lifejacket in turn. The Golder boys – not boys anymore, but young men –

lifted their arms for Clyde to check the fastenings at the side of their jackets. Jess followed suit, watching Harry's disgruntled expression as he waited for the final checks to be made. Once Clyde had given them the all clear, Jess spoke again.

"I appreciate your help, Harry. We need your experience tonight."

Harry grunted again. "No place for a woman, this," he said.

She shrugged. "I'm the steward. I saw the boat. I think I should go."

She placed a hand on her chest, feeling her heartbeat through the thick wadding of the lifejacket. She was more scared than she let on, and glad to have Harry here.

As a former trawlerman, he was the best placed to navigate these waters at night. He'd worked somewhere along the North Sea coast. There was a good chance he'd fished further out than they were going tonight, and in far worse conditions. She knew he was contemptuous of this tiny day-boat, a frivolous leisure craft. It would have to do.

Clyde and the Golder boys released the ropes securing the boat's trailer to hooks on the boathouse wall and started dragging it down the beach. The off-white boat floated over the dark sand. A flash of lightning reflected off its sides, illuminating the name painted in scrawling letters. *Mary Jane*.

Jess paused to close and secure the boathouse doors then followed the others onto the beach. A small crowd had gathered. In the dark she couldn't make out faces, and wondered if Ben or Ruth might be among the villagers. The crowd was silent. No farewells or well wishes tonight, just a quiet acceptance and dread.

"Hang on a minute," said Jess. As the boat neared the water she was struck by how tiny it seemed. "We don't know how many people are on that boat. We can't all go out, not if we're going to have room for passengers."

Clyde looked at her. "You're right. I'll stay here. Harry can pilot the boat, and he knows larger boats, so he'll be more use once they get there. The lads are strong – they should go with him."

Jess frowned. She didn't want Harry out there without her, and the boys were heavy. They didn't need both of them. "No," she replied. I'll go with Harry and one of Sam or Zack."

She turned to the twins. "I don't mind which one of you comes with us. You decide, quick."

Zack lifted a hand. "I can go." The pair exchanged glances. "I'm a better swimmer than Sam." Sam shrugged and took a step backwards. Jess nodded at his brother.

"Good. Now, let's get going."

CHAPTER SIX

THEY EDGED THEIR WAY OUT TO THE DISTRESS SIGNAL, still flashing across the waves. Jess pulled at her lifejacket, wishing she'd stopped to put on an extra layer. The rain needled into her flimsy waterproof, and as they left the shore the wind accelerated to a full-blown gale. They stared ahead, fixated on the light as if it might disappear. Their silence was punctuated only by the drum of rain on the fibreglass hull and the rasp of the outboard motor. Harry sat at the front of the boat, peering over the open cabin's low roof. Jess huddled on the bench behind him, her knees rubbing against Zack's every time the waves rocked them.

The light drew closer, its reflection bobbing in the water. Jess swallowed, pushing down nausea, and turned to Zack. His face was pale, his jaw set. She closed her eyes and took a deep breath. The rain was icy against her cheeks and her body felt constricted by the lifejacket, as if she might suffocate.

Breathe, she told herself. She clenched and unclenched her fists, one at a time. Her hands were shaking.

The light approached and beneath it the outline of a boat.

Much larger than theirs, it looked like a small trawler. Harry gave a grunt of recognition and Jess tapped him on the back. Realising he couldn't feel anything through the lifejacket, she placed a hand on his arm.

"Do you recognise it, Harry?" she shouted.

He nodded. "It's an outrigger. Type of trawler."

This meant nothing to Jess, but his calm was reassuring. The boat didn't look as if it was in trouble; its keel rode high above the waves and it was coping with the rising and falling of the sea better than their own tiny craft was. She wondered why they had sent out a distress signal.

As they neared the trawler, she made out a movement on its deck.

"Ahoy there!" a voice called.

"Hello!" Harry called back. His voice was carried off by the wind. He repeated himself, louder this time.

"We saw your distress signal!" Jess yelled, hoping the silhouetted figure above would hear. Rain was running down her neck now, soaking into her sweater. The nausea was swelling.

She swallowed and wiped the rain from her eyes. "Are you in trouble?" she shouted.

"We're taking on water," the voice called back, the words rising and falling with the waves. "Our engine has flooded and we can't move. We need to abandon ship."

Jess looked at Harry, whose face was impassive. "What do you think?" she shouted into his ear. Opposite her Zack was still and silent. Their boat lurched to the right and she grabbed the hull behind her. He put out a hand to steady her, throwing her a grim smile.

She turned back to Harry.

"Well?" Her throat was sore.

Harry shrugged. "Not sure. Their boat looks OK, but that might be deceptive."

She felt Zack slam into her as their boat tilted again. Water filled her eyes; spray or rain, she couldn't tell. They needed to hurry, or their small boat would come out of this worse than the trawler.

"How many of you are there?" she called.

"Just three!"

Jess looked at Harry and Zack, glad that she'd left the others behind. The dayboat's engine was low now, inaudible against the roar of the sea. The trawler's engine was silent. A wave crashed into them, slamming their boat into the side of the trawler. She yelped.

She nodded to Harry, feeling her stomach protest. "We've got to help them."

"OK!" Harry called. "We're coming up alongside." He adjusted the boat's angle next to the trawler, making it feel even smaller. "We'll throw you a rope."

Zack stood, spreading his legs wide and tossing a rope up towards the darkened figure. Jess had a moment of panic. They knew nothing about this boat and its occupants, yet here they were, offering them the sanctuary of their tiny boat and their village. Maybe Ben – or Harry – had been right.

She pushed her fears down into her churning gut. "Got it?" she called.

"Got it," the voice called back. She felt the boat braking as it came alongside the trawler. It swayed as Zack moved across the deck towards the trawler.

Jess stood up, feeling her legs wobble. She looked up to see the man descending over the side of the trawler. He was placing his feet on footholds on its side. *Hurry*, she thought.

Jess and Zack held their arms out to help him into their boat, but he leapt down nimbly. He turned to face them as his weight made their boat dip further towards the trawler.

"Thanks."

The man was breathing hard. His face was dark, his wild,

ragged hair silhouetted by the bright light that flashed down at them from the trawler. Jess shielded her eyes, trying to make out his face.

"Move to the other side, now!" Harry snapped as the boat dipped threateningly. The man pushed past Jess and slumped down on the bench across from her. Jess felt the boat level itself.

The man stared at her. "Don't look at me, then! Help the others!"

Jess blushed despite her cold cheeks, and turned back to the trawler. Zack was guiding a second man down, his boots nearly at the level of their hull. The boat shifted again as his weight hit the deck and he followed his companion to the far bench, saying nothing. The two of them huddled together, muttering. A cold fist of panic clutched at Jess's stomach.

She looked back to see the final man slip as his foot came into contact with the hull. There was a scraping sound and a splash as he missed his footing and disappeared between the two boats.

"Man overboard!" yelled Harry. Behind her the two strangers went quiet; she felt them lean towards her.

Zack stretched over the side of the boat as he leaned down. Jess grabbed the back of his lifejacket. She could sense his muscles working as he strained to rescue the man.

After what felt like a lifetime Zack straightened up, dragging the third man into the boat. He fell onto the deck, his body slamming into her legs. She stumbled onto the bench opposite the other men.

Harry twisted round to look at them. "He's OK," he gasped. "But we need to get him back to the village, quickly."

She looked down at the man, whose face was blue in the dim light. His eyelashes were tipped with icy water and his lips trembled. She pulled him up onto the bench and sat next to him, taking his weight on her shoulder. To her relief he was slight, his weight against her barely more than that of Ruth's boys combined.

Harry snapped at them again.

"Everybody sit down! Time to go home."

Zack threw Jess a worried look then sat on the other side of the man, sandwiching him between them. Harry turned the boat round in the water, heading for home. They rode the tide, which made progress quicker this time. She watched Zack, who watched the two men opposite, who occasionally whispered into each other's ears. The third man shivered against her. She stared at the dark shape of the trawler as they left it behind; it was still riding high on the waves, with no apparent lean. They'd said it was letting in water. Wouldn't it be starting to sink by now?

Ruth stood at the front of a crowd of villagers. She stared out to sea, and the flashing light. From the voices behind her, she sensed that the crowd was growing; word must have travelled. She glanced back over her shoulder. Some of the villagers were bundled up in coats, hats and sensible shoes against the chilly March night; others had headed out in their night clothes.

Pam came to stand beside her, stamping feet and blowing into her hands.

"How long are they going to be?" she asked.

"No idea," said Ruth, squinting. It was twenty minutes since the darkness had sucked up the small boat. The rain had stopped here but she had no way of knowing what it was like out at sea.

She wished she'd had a chance to dissuade Jess from going out, to let Clyde take her place.

Clyde stood a little way ahead of them, on the beach.

Next to him was a pile of lifejackets and blankets, the lifejackets carried down from the boathouse and the blankets brought by those villagers who could spare them. Blankets were valuable here; with the restrictions on heating and power use, people relied on them as a source of warmth in the evenings and sometimes the daytime too.

A hum was working its way through the crowd: speculations about what had happened to the crew. Ruth kept her gaze trained on the sea, praying for her sister-in-law to reappear.

Clyde let out a shout. "I can see them!" he called, grabbing a couple of lifejackets and hurrying across the sand to the shore. He gasped as the cold waves flowed over his feet. She rushed forwards to join him, holding a pile of blankets high in her arms to keep them dry. She waded into the shallows, calling out to the boat which loomed out of the darkness.

"Jess! Over here! Can you see me?" she called, but the wind whipped away her voice. She clutched the blankets to her. Finally, she heard voices from the boat.

"We're OK! Three extra men aboard!" It was Zack Golder.

Clyde splashed past her, seemingly oblivious to the icy water. The end of a rope curled through the air towards him, its movement like a whip. He grabbed it, trying to pull the boat in towards the beach. He looked back over his shoulder to the crowd on the beach.

"I need help here!"

Samuel Golder came to grasp the rope, soon joined by three other young men. Between them they heaved the boat onto the sand, a job made easier when Jess and Zack jumped out and helped to push. Two men whose faces Ruth couldn't distinguish leaped out after them and added their weight to the effort until the boat was safely on dry land.

Ruth rushed towards them, holding a blanket out towards Jess. Jess took it and let Ruth lean into her, hugging.

"Jess, I'm so glad you're OK," she breathed. Jess felt cold; her skin was like jelly.

Jess pulled back to look at Ruth. "Thanks," she smiled. "Where's Ben?"

"With the boys."

Jess nodded. "Say thanks to him, please. He helped us get out there quickly. He was with me when I – we – spotted the SOS."

Ruth allowed herself to smile. "Will do. I'm sorry, Jess." She hugged her again, feeling Jess's weight pushing down on her.

"You're tired," she said, "We need to get you and the others up to the pharmacy, check you out."

Jess shook her head and looked back at the boat. There was a dark shape next to it, two men standing over a third, who lay on the sand. He was moaning.

"He needs help, Ruth."

Jess looked back at her, her eyes wild. Ruth nodded and put a hand on her sister-in-law's arm. Jess shrugged it off.

"Seriously. He fell in the sea."

Ruth hesitated then approached the man – boy, really. He was convulsing with shivers, his skin pale. She stiffened. *Hypothermia*. No choice, then. She had to help.

She started to move closer but Zack Golder was already beside the boy, lifting him. She threw a blanket over him and ran ahead to the pharmacy, hoping she'd have everything ready before they arrived. Hoping she could save him.

CHAPTER SEVEN

There was a heavy drizzle in the air. Often on days like this, a dark mood would settle over the village, the weather reminding everyone of the days they'd spent walking here, tramping across sodden ground.

But today, despite the damp, everyone Jess met was eager to talk, to ask how she was, to prod her for details of the newcomers. As she passed the allotments where food for the village was grown, people unbent from their work and called questions to her. In the village square, a woman rushed out of the bakery and started asking about the boy, the one who'd fallen overboard. And if they weren't approaching her they were speculating among themselves.

She didn't have any answers. The younger man had been in no fit state for an interrogation and the other two had been allocated a place to stay by Colin before she got a chance to speak to them. When she'd left the pharmacy at 1am the village had been deserted, rain water washing down the Parade, the downpour enveloping the houses in a blanket of silence.

She still didn't know who these men were, or how they

had come to be out at sea late at night. She had no idea whose trawler it was, or what had happened to it. *I don't even know where they are right now*. The thought made the skin on the back of her neck prickle.

As she approached the school she saw that a crowd had gathered in the square. Rain-hooded people formed small groups as they talked, gossip passing through the crowd. Ben was nowhere to be seen, nor were any of the newcomers, but other council members were arriving. As they pushed through the crowds, villagers grabbed at them, eager for news.

She heard footsteps beside her and turned to see Clyde approaching, the doors to the JP banging shut. She smiled at him; he looked tired and his clothes were dishevelled, as if he'd retrieved them from where he'd dropped them on the bedroom floor last night.

"Morning, Clyde. How are you?"

He smiled. "Hey, gorgeous. I'm good, thanks. Glad you stopped me going out in that boat, I have to admit. Bloody freezing out there it was, according to Harry."

Harry. She scanned the crowd but there was no sign of him. His house was towards the beach, hidden from view.

"Do you know where the men are? The ones from the boat?"

He nodded. "Two of them are enjoying the hospitality of the JP," he said, jerking his head towards the pub. "I made a couple of beds up in the lounge bar."

Her surprise clearly registered on her face, because he laughed. "Don't worry," he said. "The stock is all under lock and key. I know we can't spare anything, shipwrecks or not."

"How are they?"

"They're fine. They seem less affected by their ordeal than any of our people who went out there. Unlike their friend though."

She frowned. "Where's he? Is he—?"

"Ruth was worried about him so she moved him into hers and Ben's house. Keep a weather eye on him."

This was a surprise; she couldn't imagine Ben wanting village business intruding on his family right now. "How d'you know that?" she asked.

"Ruth came and told me, when she went back to the pharmacy to get the boy. Man. Not sure how old he is. She left him in there, but then she got worried. She wanted me to tell the other men."

"OK. So where is everyone now?"

"The other two are getting a wash in the JP's gents' toilets, or at least they were a few minutes ago. No idea about Ruth and Ben, and the other one. I thought you'd know?"

She shook her head and started to push through the crowd, anxious to speak to her brother.

She hammered on Ben and Ruth's door.

"Ben! Ruth! It's Jess! Let me in, please."

Ruth appeared, her face pale above her bright pink dressing gown. She looked over Jess's shoulder and shrank back when she glimpsed the crowd.

"Quick, get inside," she hissed, pulling Jess by the arm.

Inside, Ben sat at the kitchen table with a young man who couldn't be more than twenty years old. He had dark hair and skin so pale it was almost translucent. His cheekbones protruded in a way that would be elegant if he had a bit more meat on him. He was wearing Ben's clothes, at least a size too large despite Ben's slender build.

The man glanced up at her, his eyes wide. She tried to give him a reassuring smile.

"Hello, I'm Jess. Ben's sister. You might remember me from the boat. You've had quite an ordeal."

The man nodded. "Martin," he whispered.

Ben looked up at her. He had dark circles under his eyes and his skin had lost some of its colour, but his smile was calm.

"Martin's been filling me in on what happened to their boat."

The man licked his lips nervously, and shifted his grip on the steaming mug that rested on the table before him.

Jess took a seat opposite Ben, next to Martin. Ruth put a chipped teacup in front of her and poured tea from the pot in the middle of the table. Behind her in the living room, Sean and Ollie were playing a noisy game of Snap! Every time one of them shouted their victory with a slap of the cards, Martin flinched.

She let out a long breath. "So?"

Ben scratched his head. "First off, Martin here is OK now. Ruth was worried about him last night—" he glanced up at Ruth, who gave his shoulder a squeeze, "—but he's doing fine. She's been giving him energy drinks. From her rations."

Jess detected a flicker of tension.

"What about the other two?" Jess asked.

Ben shrugged. "I haven't met them yet. They're in the JP, with Clyde."

"Yeah, I know." She looked at Martin. "So what happened? To your boat?"

Martin fidgeted with his mug. "We went out yesterday afternoon. Do some fishing. We got into trouble when it was getting dark. The engine was fine at first, and then it stopped. I think it took on water." His voice was flat and pale.

Jess wondered why this boy who knew nothing about boats had been out there on the North Sea in the first place.

"OK," she said. "I need to go and speak to the other men before the rest of the village does. They're all out there, desperate to know what's going on." She ignored Ben's frown.

"This is better than telly, for them. Especially since they don't have telly."

Ben shrugged, and eased himself up from the chair. Ruth stepped back to let him pass.

"You're right. I'll come with you. Find some council members."

She decided not to worry about asserting her authority and smiled. "Thanks."

They headed for the front door. Outside she could hear the rising chatter of the crowd.

"Take care, both of you," Ruth called after them. Sean leapt up from his game of cards and hurled himself at his dad, who made an 'oof' noise as his son's body hit him in the stomach.

"Where are you going, Daddy?" he asked.

"Just out, Sean. Just like any other day. See you later, big man." He gave Sean's head a rub then turned to the living room. "You too, Ollie. Be good!"

Sean ran back to his brother. As Ben turned the door handle, Jess realised it had gone quiet outside.

The crowd had turned to watch the two men approaching the house. People stepped aside to let them through.

The men's heads were bowed. They didn't have coats and Jess could see the damp settling across the shoulders of the one in front, his T-shirt stained with moisture. She wondered what had happened to their clothes from last night.

As they passed through, the crowd shifted to face Jess. She heard a woman hiss *hush* at a small boy.

The two men ignored the muttering that rose around them. Next to her Ben stood motionless. She steeled herself, ready to do her job.

As the men approached she could make out their hard, angular features and their weather-worn skin. It looked as though they'd had a tough life. One had a single scar snaking from the wrist of his right arm to the elbow. His companion brought up the rear and wore a pristine white shirt, one of Clyde's. He was slimmer than his companion, and shorter.

She heard the door behind her open and then slam shut. She turned to see the boy cowering behind her.

"Robert," he whispered.

The men stopped in front of Jess and Ben. The heavier man at the front stood to one side as his companion pushed past him.

As his eyes met Jess's, she gasped.

Robert, the boy had called him. Martin was so close she could feel his breath on her neck.

She knew this man. Robert Cope.

CHAPTER EIGHT

"I don't like them being here," said Harry, his face dark with anger. "There was nothing wrong with that boat as far as I could tell, and now we've got three strangers pawning off us with no idea where they're from or how long they're going to be here."

Voices rose as council members fought to be heard – to support Harry or shout him down. Ben rubbed his eyes, tired still from last night's broken sleep and troubled by his secret. He'd spoken to nobody about recognising one of the men, not even Jess. But stood on the doorstep, he'd sensed her sharing the same flash of recognition.

By contrast, Robert had shown no sign of remembering them. The four of them had exchanged curt greetings, Ben struggling to find his usual warmth, distracted by memories.

Sanjeev's voice rose above the others. Ben stared at his hands, twisting in his lap. He still couldn't look his friend in the eye.

"Listen, everyone. Jess is right. This village has been offering sanctuary to people in trouble since before even we arrived here. It's right that we've done the same now. But we need to know more about these men. What state is their boat in? Do we need to go out and make repairs? How long are they planning to stay?"

As voices rose again. Ben dug deep inside himself. He had to find the energy to keep up with the tumult of emotions that were playing out around him. He watched Jess lead the meeting, her brow furrowing as she concentrated on giving everyone a chance to speak. He gritted his teeth at the memory of what he'd said to Sanjeev, how he'd gone along with Jess's insistence that they rescue the men. Had it only been last night?

"OK," Jess exhaled. "First things first, I propose that we find them somewhere better to stay, see if there's an empty house somewhere. Colin?"

"Hang on a minute—" Ted interrupted. Jess raised a hand.

"Bear with me, Ted. I'm just trying to get all the facts before we make a decision. Don't worry, you'll all have a say."

Ted grunted and stared at Colin, who was studying a plan of the village, one he'd annotated with the names of the people who lived in each house or flat.

"There's a couple of flats, in the centre of the village," Colin said. "They're designed for two, but one of them could take three."

Jess nodded. Across the table, Toni raised a hand.

"Wouldn't it be better to separate them? Then they can't plot anything."

"What makes you think they would?" asked Sanjeev. Ben felt his stomach tighten and risked a glance at Jess. Her face gave nothing away.

Toni shrugged. "I don't know. But after what Harry said—"

Ben closed his eyes as voices rose around the table. He stood up suddenly, his chair scraping across the faded wooden floor.

"Shut up, everyone! Please. Let Jess speak."

He sat down again, his heart pounding. Jess glared at him. Heat rushed into his face.

Jess sighed. "Look. We can't spare two flats and besides, we don't want to make them too comfortable," she said.

Please Jess, make them very uncomfortable, Ben thought.

"I propose that we put them all in the one flat together," Jess continued. "There are folding beds stored in the back room of the JP, we can move one of them into the flat."

"Jess is right," said Sanjeev. "What do you think, Ben?"

Ben raised his head to see everyone looking at him. Sanjeev offered him a smile and a shrug. Jess was smiling too, but her eyes were hard.

He shrugged. There was silence while they waited to hear what he had to say; he couldn't help feeling gratified, but didn't trust himself to speak.

"Ben?" Jess asked, her voice clipped.

"I guess keeping them together makes sense," he finally muttered.

Jess sighed. "It'll be tight for three grown men but they'll cope," she said. "Until we know how long they're staying, and whether they have people who'll be joining them."

Jess clasped her hands together; her nails were bitten to the quick. "Now, I'll take contributions from Ted, Toni, Sanjeev, then Colin. After that, we'll put it to a vote."

Martin sat on Ruth and Ben's sofa, looking at the same view Ruth had gazed at the night before. It wasn't dark now, not yet, and the grey sea was visible across the grass behind the house.

There were a few shadows on the horizon; the smudged

outlines of distant rainclouds, obscuring any boats that might be out there. That was good.

He ran Robert's plan through his head again, the hurried instructions before setting off in the trawler the previous day. Robert knew about this community north of them along the coast, about the way it still welcomed the occasional refugee from the floods even now, six years after they had ravaged the country. Martin had lived further south back then, near the Norfolk coast. The sea had crashed in on them that night, his grandmother panicking and phoning his mum to babble incoherences about 1953. He knew about 1953 of course, the great storm that had hammered at so much of the east coast, wrecking acres of farmland and altering the coastline forever. 1953 still haunted his village, but they'd learned their lesson and built defences to prevent it recurring.

What they couldn't have known was just how ineffective those defences would prove to be in a modern world that insisted on building houses, factories and power stations on flood plains. The authorities built their coastal defences and erected the Thames Barrier, ploughing in millions as the years passed and the storms worsened. But then when times got hard the defences were neglected, and the influx of Londoners to the vast plains around Peterborough and Norfolk were welcomed as a boost to the local economy.

None of this had concerned him. He had his own life to get on with, earning what little he could from casual farm labour and the occasional job in a holiday village or working security at a festival. Keeping his dad's temper at bay with packets of cash accompanied by bottles of beer in brown paper bags when he had the money to spare. And the weather was a given on this stretch of coast. Harsh winters and wet summers were to be expected, and people barely commented when they found themselves repairing boundary walls and moving livestock further from the sea and the rivers each winter.

When the water had hit his parents' farm they had sat tight, rummaging in the eaves of the barn for sandbags and shoring themselves up, proud of their self-sufficiency. They passed ten days hunkered indoors, peering through the rain at the sandbags outside, dreading the moment when the lapping water would breach them. A couple of times his dad shouted him out of his chair, urging him to venture out and secure their teetering flood wall. When the water finally burst through he was prepared, his valuables packed in a rucksack on a high shelf in his bedroom, wrapped in plastic bags.

His mum panicked, crossing from room to room and staring outside, eyes bloodshot. His dad continued drinking, staring at the TV as the water swirled at the base of his armchair. Martin pulled his mum up the stairs, resisting her efforts to grab the cheap ornaments on the mantelpiece, dragging her heavy frame up to the relative safety of his parents' bedroom.

When the TV exploded in a shower of wet sparks, his dad still stayed put. His back was to the stairs so Martin had no idea if he was awake, asleep, or worse. He knew he should wade through to help the old bastard, find out how he was. Or he could take his chances, abandon this man who'd never shown any care for him, and escape.

"I'll get help, Mum," he promised, after pulling the crumpled dinghy down the ladder from their tiny attic, leaping back when it landed in a cloud of dust. He had no idea if it would hold, but he was prepared to risk it. He entreated his mum to come with him but she refused.

"I'll tell someone you're here. Fire Brigade, Army. Whoever."

The army were out in force, criss-crossing the region with boats and food supplies, pulling people from upstairs windows and ferrying them to safety. But their farm was isolated and so far there was no sign of any rescuers.

He'd folded his mum in a hug, trying not to cry, and lowered the dinghy through the window, inflated with the tiny pump he'd found at the bottom of a trunk full of junk. It had taken what seemed like hours to blow it up but finally it floated on the murky water that was halfway up the kitchen windows by now, its bright yellow sides dazzling against the grey and brown landscape.

He'd straddled the windowsill, throwing a last smile at his mum, who stayed calm as she waved to him. It was as if she was pretending he was heading out for a day's work, not leaving her forever.

And now here he was, the first time in six years he'd slept under clean sheets and rested his tired legs on something as decadent as a sofa. Ruth and Ben were good people, kind to take him in. Ruth had spent the day clucking around him, coming in from the pharmacy every couple of hours to check his temperature and lung capacity. She'd even found him clothes from the back of Ben's cupboard. They hung loose on him but it was good to wear something without holes. In a previous life he would have been irritated but now the ministrations of a woman filled him with gratitude.

Thinking about Ruth, he remembered Robert's plan, the one that he was expected to help carry out. Guilt gnawed at his insides.

Ruth was relieved when Martin went to bed early. He was a nice enough lad, but once Ollie and Sean were in bed, the silence between them was almost chewable. She sat alone for a few moments, listening to him preparing for bed; water running in the bathroom, floorboards creaking overhead. When all she could hear was the whistling of the wind around the kitchen window – she must get Ben to fix that – she lit the gas lamp and placed it on the kitchen table. She turned it down as low as she could while still having enough light to read her book, one she'd picked up from the library shelf in the JP.

Fifty or so pages later, her eyelids felt heavy and her legs itched. She cast around for a bookmark, sandwiching a scrap of paper between the pages, and slid the book onto the shelf above the kettle. Books were scarce now, and precious. She turned the gas off, watching the lamp flicker, and let the shadows guide her towards the stairs.

As her bare toes felt for the bottom step, she heard a key turn in the front door.

"Ben?"

"What!" Ben slammed the door behind him. "Sorry, I thought you'd gone to bed. You made me jump."

She retraced her steps to the table and relit the gas lamp, Ben watching. His chin was dark with stubble. She gave him a sympathetic smile.

"You look terrible, love. Why don't you go to bed?"

He groaned. "In a bit."

He clattered into the living room and slumped onto the sofa, staring out of the darkened back window. She sat next to him.

"Everything OK? How did council go?"

He said nothing.

"Ben?"

She tried to take his hand but he didn't respond. She headed back to the kitchen and started tidying up, washing mugs and plates and sorting through their food rations for tomorrow.

After ten minutes he still hadn't spoken. She moved the kettle and tins of tea and coffee, the battered bread bin and the jug of flowers she'd picked from the dunes, and cleaned under them. When the kitchen was gleaming she heard Ben moving. He stumbled into the kitchen, poured a glass of water and slumped into a chair. She tried not to look at the ring his glass left on the table.

She eased into the chair next to him. "Ben? What happened? Was it the council meeting?"

He frowned. "Hmm? No. We agreed to—" He paused and looked around the room. "Where is he?" he whispered.

"Martin?" She found herself whispering in response. "He's upstairs, in bed. Been up there for a couple of hours."

She glanced towards the stairs. She'd watched Martin through the open door as Ben and Jess met the two other men. He'd cowered behind Jess, as if hiding from his friends. She'd assumed he was embarrassed, but now she wasn't so sure. In fact, she now remembered something in Ben's stance when the men arrived, a stiffening. Why was he so nervous?

Ben nodded. "Has he said anything to you about why they're here? Where they're from?"

"No. Nothing. He hardly speaks. Blushes whenever I go near him. Good manners, though. Please and thank you for everything."

Ben grabbed her hand. "You sure? No clue at all? You haven't heard him talking to the others?"

She could smell coffee on his breath; no beer tonight. She shook her head.

"What's wrong?" she asked. "Why can't you ask them yourself?"

"Oh, nothing. I haven't had the chance, that's all. Thought he might have said something to you."

His voice was too casual.

"Ben, what's wrong? What did they say to you, after you left the house this morning?"

He shook his head.

"You can tell me, love," she said. "Whatever it is. Please."

He shook his head. "I don't know, Ruth."

She tightened her grip on his arm. "What do you mean, you don't know? This kid has been in our house all day and all night and now you're worried about him?"

He looked down at the table, his face under lit by the gas lamp. Her stomach tightened.

"Are we safe? Are the boys safe?"

His head shot up. "Yes. Yes, I'm pretty sure of it."

"*Pretty sure?* Is that the best you can offer me?"

"Sorry. Yes, it's fine. Martin seems OK. You don't need to worry."

"That's Martin. What about the others? What did they tell you?"

He paused, breathing heavily.

"Not much. We took them to the JP to talk, it was amicable enough. They told us they'd come from down the coast, had been moving around since the flooding made them homeless."

"All that time? Six years is a lot of diesel, for a boat that size."

"I don't know. But the council is happy to have them here. The two others are already in the flat the council has allocated them, across from the school. We'll move Martin there tomorrow. Promise."

Behind Ben the clock ticked in the darkness. Above their heads the boys slept, with this stranger in the room next to them. She felt her skin prickling.

"You've got me worried. I'm going to sleep in with the boys tonight, just in case."

Ben didn't argue, but turned out the gas lamp and gave

her a stiff hug. "I'm sorry about all this, Ruth. Sorry about everything."

She let herself relax into him, remembering his promises when he had asked her to flee London with him. Little did she know she'd find herself in a place like this, hundreds of miles from home as the *de facto* doctor to nearly two hundred people. She stroked his cheek then pulled away, anxious to start making herself a temporary bed on the boys' floor.

CHAPTER NINE

As Jess reached the Parade she was approached by a group of men, in hats and heavy jackets. They were little more than boys, lads she'd chaperoned through their teenage years until their makeshift school system spat them out at the other end. No one mentioned that an education was pointless without prospects.

Now, they were heading out of the village – she guessed in search of casual work. Saturday usually meant that the waged men working on the land reclamation around Hull would be at home, so there were more pickings for them. The gangers who ran the work crews didn't stop at the weekend, and nor did the work, which meant that the group leaving today was larger than it was on weekdays.

She had no idea what the salaried men were paid but she knew how little these lads received for their labours. Twelve hours of back-breaking work and no more to show for it than they'd have earned in a couple of hours in the old days. But that cash was a lifeline to the village, letting them buy what they couldn't grow, rear or make themselves. And the men who brought it home received extra rations for their pains.

They muttered greetings as they passed her. She noticed the Golder boys, and thanked them for their help with the boat. Samuel blushed but Zack treated her to a wide grin, showing the gaps in his teeth.

She strolled towards the village centre and past the schoolroom. Voices rang out from inside, the Saturday morning yoga group that some of the women had established. The village was quiet as she made her way up Ben's front path and knocked at his door, before shoving her chilled fingers under her armpits.

There was no answer. She knocked again, puzzled. Ben and Ruth were larks. On a Saturday morning one of them would be out working while the other had long since tidied away breakfast.

She leaned in to the door. "Ben? Ruth? It's Jess!"

She wondered if they were both out, moving their temporary lodger to his new accommodation. As she turned back towards the village centre, the door opened.

She spun round, her smile falling. Ben stood in the doorway, his hair bed-rough and still wearing his pyjamas. Behind him she could hear the screams of a boyhood game or maybe a quarrel.

"Jess. Come in," he breathed. She shrugged past him as he held the door open.

Inside, dirty crockery littered the table and the worktops, there was toast jam-side down on the rug, and a spreading damp patch in front of the back doors.

"You OK?" she asked. "Where's Ruth?"

He plunged a hand into his hair. "That's just it. I don't know. She slept with the boys last night. We— She was—" He swallowed. "She was worried about them. They came down without her this morning and when I went upstairs, there was no sign of her."

"Surely she's at the pharmacy? She gets up early at the

weekend."

Ben was shifting from one foot to the other and scratching his chin. He hadn't shaved since the men had arrived and was showing the beginnings of a beard. He smelt musty.

He shook his head, his eyes bright. "Her clothes are still there. On the floor next to the bed she made up for herself. Neatly folded, just the same as she would have left them last night."

Jess felt a shiver crawl down her arms. "OK," she said, trying to stay calm. "Can I have a look? Please?"

Ben nodded and headed for the stairs. In the living area the boys had stopped fighting and were watching them, their mouths jam-ringed Os. She smiled at them and followed her brother upstairs, the treads creaking beneath their feet. She realised how quiet the house was; Ruth had a radio and allowed herself to use it at breakfast time only, giving the house a bustling, lived-in feel in the mornings.

She hurried up the stairs and followed Ben into the first bedroom. The two beds were unmade, duvets screwed up like soft mountains, and pillows slung on the floor. At the foot of the beds was a heap of blankets and a pillow, also dishevelled. Beyond that was a neat pile of clothes, T-shirt and sweater folded on top of a pair of faded jeans.

"That's what she was wearing, last night," Ben said. Jess turned to him.

"She couldn't have come into your room, got some clothes out?"

He shook his head again. His eyes were red-rimmed. "No. She wasn't here when I woke up. Even if I didn't hear her, I've checked, and there's nothing gone. Her coat's on the hook downstairs. It's cold today."

She took two deep breaths, her mind racing. She walked out of the bedroom and looked around the landing. The door to Ben and Ruth's room was flung open but the other one was closed. She dropped her voice to a whisper.

"What about him? Martin. Has he appeared yet this morning?"

Ben clutched his hair again. "I don't know," he whispered. "I haven't—"

She nodded towards the door. "Why don't you ask him if he heard her go out?" she asked, trying to convince herself as much as Ben that Ruth had left the house as normal.

He bit his lip and knocked quietly on the door. Then more loudly when there was no reply.

"Martin?" he called softly. "Sorry to disturb you, but I was wondering if you'd seen Ruth this morning?"

Still no answer.

"Go in," Jess said.

Ben stared at her. "Should I?"

"Yes. It's your house."

Ben shuddered and grasped the doorknob, knocking quietly as he turned it. His shoulders blocked her view as he eased the door open and peered into the darkened room.

He turned back to her, his face pale.

"He's gone too."

Jess grabbed the stair rail. "Are you sure?" she asked. "Maybe he's gone to the flat, got out from under your feet."

Ben could feel panic rising in his gut. Downstairs he could hear the boys.

Jess's hand was on his arm.

"Look," she said. "You go out and look for her. Check where Martin is. See if he's at the flat. I'll tidy up, keep an eye on the boys."

He nodded. This wasn't like Ruth; she would never go out

without giving the boys a kiss, without telling him where she was. He realised how much more solid than him she was.

He breathed in again and turned away from Jess, closing the bedroom door behind him. He tore open the wardrobe doors and worked his hands through the clothes, his mind numb.

"Jess?" he called, his voice plaintive.

She was still outside the door. "Ben? You OK?"

He plunged his head into his hands. "Can you help me, please? I can't think straight."

She pushed open the door, suddenly brusque, and frowned at him as she shoved a clean shirt, a blue sweater and a pair of trousers into his outstretched arms. He took them from her, letting them hang in his hands.

"Do you need me to help you put them on?" she asked, her voice shifting from annoyance to concern.

He shook his head. "No," he replied. "But stay here for a moment, will you? While I get ready?"

She sat on the bed and bowed her head; it had been nearly twenty years since she'd last seen him dress. He dragged the clothes onto his thin body and laid his pyjamas on the bed.

Jess took his hand. "Come on, bro. She'll turn up, you just wait and see. Do you want me to go and look?"

He shook his head again.

"OK then," she said as she stood up and pulled him towards the door. "Let's get started. You go and check the pharmacy and the men's flat. If she's not there, check the school – I heard voices coming from there on my way over."

He followed her down the stairs.

Jess opened the front door and pushed Ben outside.

"Go on," she whispered. "Be quick, tell me when you've found her."

She watched Ben stumble towards the village square. A few people were out and about now; a couple greeted him and he grunted, alarmed. He picked up his pace and ran towards the schoolroom, disappearing behind the houses that blocked her view. That was good; at last he had some purpose.

Jess closed the door and shot a bright grin at her nephews.

"Now, who wants to help tidy up? There's a lolly in it for you!" she said, hoping Ruth had a stash somewhere.

She threw herself into the task of getting the house back into shape. As she worked she talked with the boys, pushing away any creeping worry.

After twenty minutes by the kitchen clock, the door was thrown open.

"They're gone! The men, all of them!" Ben collapsed into her arms. She shushed him, glancing at the boys. Sean grabbed his brother's hand and was rewarded with a punch. He yelled but Ben didn't react.

"What about Ruth?" she hissed into his ear.

He turned his face to her, eyes wide above blotchy cheeks.

"Nowhere. Not in the pharmacy. Not in the school, or the JP, or at Pam's, or Sanjeev's, or anywhere. The men's flat is empty – no men, no clothes, nothing."

"Oh hell." She'd run out of words to keep his hopes up.

"And Jess?"

"Yes?"

"I saw Toni, in the pharmacy. She told me there are other women gone. Ted's daughter. One of the Murray girls. Sally Angus."

A sob convulsed through him and his body slid down the wall until he collapsed in a heap on the floor.

"Where is she, Jess? What have they done to her?"

CHAPTER TEN

Jess crouched down to give Ben's hand a gentle squeeze. She nodded through the open front door towards the village square.

"I need to go out there, Ben. Talk to people, find out what they know. That's the only way we'll find her."

She was right, of course.

"Can I stay in here?" he whispered.

"Of course you can."

He looked back at the boys, who were arguing over who had helped the most with the tidying up.

"D'you think they heard?"

"I don't know. But they need to be told something. I can do it, if you want."

"Yes, please. No, I should do it." A pause. "Oh, I don't know."

He blinked, his eyes prickling.

"Ben, do you think you can hold it together just for a bit? Until I've spoken to a few people, tried to find out some more."

He made the effort to smile. “I’ll watch from the door,” he croaked.

Ben watched Jess advance on the square. People approached her, calling out questions. She came to a halt and a group huddled round her, anxious voices piercing the air.

“You bloody idiot! What do you think you were doing, letting those men in? My girl has gone!”

The crowd turned; it was Ted Evans, bowling towards them from his house a few doors along from Ben’s. His wife Dawn stood in the doorway, her face grey.

The crowd parted around Jess.

“I’m sorry, Ted.”

“What was that?” Ted demanded. “I didn’t hear you!”

Ben flinched. His sons’ game had got louder. Hopefully they wouldn’t hear.

“I said, I’m sorry,” Jess repeated, raising her face towards Ted.

“Sorry. You’re *sorry*. How the fuck is that going to get my Sarah back?”

On her doorstep, Dawn was wailing, a desperate keening sound. Ted turned back to her.

“Shut up, you bloody woman! Crying ain’t going to get us nowhere, is it?”

Dawn gasped. She seemed to hold her breath, transfixed by this public display of contempt from her husband. Ben had his suspicions about Ted and the way he treated the women in his life; the grey, taciturn Dawn and the quiet, luminous Sarah, both of them cowed in a way that suggested more than just insults were traded behind that front door.

Jess approached Ted and said something Ben couldn’t make out.

“I don’t bloody know, do I?” Ted shouted in response. “I woke up this morning and the girl were gone. These men, the ones you let in here, the ones you insisted on rescuing, they took her. I knew it from the first time we saw that light, from when Harry told me about the state of their boat. They were con artists, you stupid woman, and you were too damn stupid to know it!"

As Jess spoke again, Sanjeev appeared from behind the school building. He picked up speed, heading for the crowd. As he closed on them Ted turned to him, his face contorted with rage.

"And you!" he shouted. The crowd gave a collective intake of breath and drew back. Ben shrank back behind his door.

"Ted," said Sanjeev, louder than Jess. "We know Sarah has gone. She's not the only one. Ben's Ruth has gone too."

Ben swayed and put a hand on his chest.

"We've already started talking to people," Sanjeev continued. "Finding out where the men went, where they came from. We'll find them, Ted. We're just as motivated as you are. We all need to keep calm and work together."

Ted cackled. "Don't give me that, you bloody Paki! You and me ain't gonna *work together*, not in a month of Sundays. My daughter has been taken and I'm gonna bloody well find her."

Sanjeev's mouth was wide and his hands were up at his sides. Jess put a hand on his arm and whispered something that made Sanjeev collapse into himself, all the fight gone. Jess drew herself up and spoke to Ted, just a few words making their way to Ben. *Search – questions – promise*.

"Pah!" Ted thrust his scowling, twisted face into Jess's and then pulled back, spitting on the ground. He turned and strode towards his house, Dawn shifting on her feet as he approached.

"Get inside, woman!" She shrank into the house and he followed her in, slamming the door behind him.

Jess dropped her head in her hands, closing her eyes in concentration.

Four women had gone.

Ruth.

Sarah Evans.

Roisin Murray.

Sally Angus.

Ruth.

She turned back towards the house. Ben was staring at her, his ghostly form silhouetted in the doorway.

She let out a long slow breath. The crowd grew quiet, waiting for her to react to Ted's words.

Sanjeev squinted at her. He looked calmer than she felt.

"What do you want me to do?"

Jess looked at him. The crowd was drawing closer, eager for answers. Beyond it, she spotted Toni running towards them, her face white.

"Jess, have you heard?" she panted, pushing through the crowd. "Roisin Murray and Sally Angus have disappeared."

Gasps rose up from the crowd. Flo Murray ran after Toni, dragging a small child behind her. "My girl, my girl, she's gone!"

Jess turned to Toni. "It's not just them. Sarah Evans and Ruth, too."

Toni's eyes widened. "Shit."

Jess put her hands on her hips. "Everyone, calm down please. There are four women missing. We're going to find them. Start a search of the village. See if anyone heard anything last night."

Jess looked past the crowd. She couldn't see Ben now but she could feel his presence. She couldn't let him down.

Toni turned to Sanjeev. "I'll head back up the Parade, you do the square and the houses by the beach." She ran off.

Sanjeev paused. "You OK?" he asked.

Jess nodded, then caught herself and shook her head. "You won't find anything," she croaked.

Sanjeev gripped her shoulder, as if holding her to the ground. "We might. Don't be so sure. It's worth trying anyway. Someone might have heard something. They might be hiding out in the village."

Jess pushed away a mental image of Robert, staring at her and Ben outside the house. "OK," she said. "You're right. Can you find some people?"

Sanjeev smiled. "No problem. We'll have volunteers coming out of our ears."

He dipped his head to look into Jess's eyes. "You coming?"

Jess nodded. "I need to talk to Ben first," she replied. "But yes, I'll be right with you."

"Yep. Give him my... tell him we're all thinking of him, won't you? That we'll find her for him?"

She nodded again.

Sanjeev headed into the crowd, pointing and pulling people out to help with the search: four council members and six others. The group closed in to hear him better and as they moved away, Jess caught sight of Ben's house.

The front door was closed.

Ruth prised her eyes open. Her head was throbbing in a way that reminded her of student hangovers from a long time ago. In front of her, a flaky patch of damp stained the wall.

She pushed herself onto her back, feeling the mattress bow beneath her. There was a dank, musty smell. She sat up stiffly, her legs curled beneath her and a cold draught at her back.

She touched her face, fingering her jawbone, cheeks and forehead. There was no swelling, and when she dared to prod harder no pain came, no top notes to join the drum beat that hammered at the nape of her neck. She turned her attention to her arms. A band of pain encircled her upper arms. She eased up the sleeves of the T-shirt she'd slept in. Red marks were starting to show signs of blue: fresh bruises. She hadn't been here long, then.

Somewhere outside, a bird was singing. No voices.

She leaned against the wall and released her breath, realising she'd been holding it. She wiped tears away with her sleeve.

The room was small and cell-like. The grey mattress almost filled the entire room. On the floor beneath a bedside table was a tray, embellished with pink flowers and brown stains. It held a metal flask and an unopened packet of oatcakes. Beyond that was a black metal bucket. Next to her on the mattress was a navy blanket pockmarked with loose threads; she imagined it had slipped off her when she sat up, too drowsy to notice.

She grabbed the metal flask and twisted off its lid, its contents swishing. Without pausing to check the contents, she threw her head back and swallowed gratefully. The water was brackish but cold.

When the flask was empty she replaced the lid and pushed it back onto the tray, startled by the clattering noise it made as it slipped from her hands. She looked up at the door and froze, her panicked breathing the only sound. When no one came she reached for the oatcakes and tore open the packet, eating the first of them in one bite.

She eased her feet off the mattress and lifted herself, fighting the cramp that gripped her legs. Finally she was upright, leaning on the table. The table was sticky and its touch made her stomach heave. She stretched her arms above her head, her fingertips nearly touching the sloping ceiling, and looked around again.

Over the table was a window, its faded blue paint peeling and the glass covered in a film of grime. Beyond it was a wire mesh, bolted on from the outside.

Behind her was a wooden door, the kind you'd find on a shed. There was a gap where one of the boards had warped, covered on the other side so she couldn't see out.

She shuffled towards the door, hardly daring to breathe, her bare feet cold on the rough floor. When she reached it she leaned against it. Listening.

All she could hear was her own heartbeat, throbbing in her ears. If there was someone out there, keeping guard, they were silent. She twisted the doorknob and leaned into the door.

Nothing.

She pushed her other hand against the door. It shifted, straining against the lock, but it still wasn't budging.

She let go and stumbled backwards, falling onto the mattress and groaning as her arm hit the table. She pulled her knees up to her chest and folded her arms around them, her lank hair falling into her face.

Finally she let the tears come.

Ben waited for news, stranded on his sofa. Trying his best to answer Sean's questions.

The boys were burrowed in either side of him. He had offered them a story about Mummy going away to get medicine. She would be back soon. *Promise*. Ollie was whimpering into Ben's lap. Jess sat across from them, her face crumpled.

Jess had been a part of their silent vigil for over an hour now. Toni's search along the Parade had proved fruitless and Sanjeev was still out on the beach with his party. Jess had returned after getting the search started. She helped him calm the boys, distracting them with games and stories, and ferried cups of hot tea back and forth from the kitchen. Ben couldn't eat but she'd made the boys sandwiches at teatime. It wouldn't be long before they'd need feeding again, followed by bedtime.

When the door banged open Jess leapt from her seat. Sanjeev stepped into the room. He opened his mouth to speak and then noticed the boys.

Jess bustled past him. "Come on now, boys. Let's see if we can find you both a treat in the kitchen? Come on, both of you up!"

She stood over the sofa, her arms outstretched.

"Go on, now. There's good boys," Ben muttered. They groaned and heaved themselves up, letting him give them a push.

Sanjeev took Ollie's spot next to Ben.

"So?" Ben's skin felt clammy.

"I'm sorry, mate." He sighed, looking up at Ben. "No sign of them. The women or the men. And we can't find anyone who heard anything."

Ben glanced at the kitchen. Jess was opening and closing cabinets, encouraging the boys to pick something nice to eat. A challenge, with their scant supplies. He pictured Ruth, sitting at that table the night before. Questioning him. *Are we safe?*

"You sure you spoke to everyone?" he asked.

"Everyone," Sanjeev replied. "We started out by knocking on doors but then when word started travelling through the village people came out to find out what had happened. We opened up the school room, spoke to each family one by one." He breathed in and out a few times. "Colin found a list, checked everyone was covered. We didn't speak to every individual, but we did get every household—"

"Hang on," muttered Ben. "Who didn't you speak to? Where were they?"

Sanjeev smoothed his palms down his trousers, leaving a faint trail of sweat.

"Some of the young men went out looking for work this morning. Saturday's a good day for—"

"But what if they saw something? They were up early, right? When do they get back?"

Sanjeev looked past Ben at the clock on the kitchen wall.

"Not long I guess."

Ben glared at Sanjeev. "Sanjeev, why are you—?"

"Can you keep your voice down, please?" Jess stood behind him.

"They haven't found her, sis. Haven't found them. But there are men still out there, gone out to work. They might have seen something."

"I know who you mean," she said, frowning. "I saw them, on my way into the village this morning. Not long before I got here."

She turned to Sanjeev.

"There were ten of them," she said. "Including the Golder boys. Zack Golder saw the men, when we rescued them. They were up early, they might have heard something."

She frowned. "Sanjeev, did you think to check the boathouse? They came here in our boat, they might have left that way."

Sanjeev hesitated, not quite managing to make eye contact with either of them. "The boat..." He paused, and finally looked at Jess. "It's gone."

PART TWO

CHAPTER ELEVEN

THE MEN'S FEET AND SHINS FLICKERED IN THE FIRELIGHT, the rest of their bodies receding into the darkness. From time to time the flames caught on the flask that worked its way from hand to hand, glinting amber in the shadows.

They were full of talk tonight. Robert's eyes shone as he surveyed the group, and Bill was pumped up with bravado and tall tales. *Nearly drowned – tiny dinghy rescued us – Martin here had hypothermia – those women didn't know what hit 'em.* There were scraps of truth in his words, coloured by the whisky fumes. Robert let Bill do the talking, content simply to correct him now and then.

The thought of the women in the outhouse nagged at Martin. He pictured the dingy rooms they'd been manhandled into in the early hours of this morning. They would be awake now, staring into the darkness.

He had no idea how Robert and Bill had selected the women. Ruth had always been a target, but the other three appeared out of nowhere. Chosen for their youth, he guessed. He stared into the flames, remembering Ruth's kindness, her friendly goodnight when he'd bumped into her outside her sons' room the night before.

And now here he was, back at the farm with Ruth and her companions shut away behind him. Bill was still bragging.

"The young one, the blonde one, she was easy," he laughed. "I didn't even have to break in. She walked right out of that bloody great house, looking for a cat or something."

Robert smiled. "She'll regret that."

The men laughed, some slapping their knees and one spluttering on the whisky. Martin tried to join in.

"Crept up behind her, I did," Bill continued. "Whipped the rag out of my pocket and bam! Like putty in my hands. So light I carried her onto the boat like she were a bag o' sugar."

"What about the dark one, Robert's woman?" one of the men asked, stifling a belch.

The men stopped laughing and looked at Robert. None of them knew why, but this woman was serious business to him. He frowned.

"We have young Martin to thank for Ruth's presence here," he said. Martin flinched under his glaze.

"Oh yes," laughed Bill. "Did exactly as he were told. Bottle of chloroform, dry rag, put her out of her misery for hours. She's only just woken up, poor bitch."

Robert flashed Bill a look.

Martin wished he had the hip flask so he could swig it and hide the colour in his cheeks. He felt pressure on his arm as someone nudged him with it. He grabbed it and took a swig.

"Would you like to see her again?" asked Robert, leaning over the fire. "Tomorrow?"

Sniggers flowed around the circle.

There was a cough from beyond the fire: Leroy. The man who'd told Robert about the village.

Robert tipped a finger to his forehead in recognition.

"Leroy, you deserve thanks. A happy coincidence that Ben Dyer should be so close to us."

There was muttering: men pretending they knew who Ruth's husband was or why he was important. Martin watched the sparks float up into the sky and tried to forget that he was still wearing Ben's trousers.

"OK," said Jess, her mind ticking over. "So at least that means we have some idea of where they've gone."

"Do we?" Sanjeev looked unsure.

"Yes. Along the coast. In the village boat they won't have made much progress at least."

A keening sound came from Ben. He'd doubled over into himself, his arms folded around his shoulders. Jess glanced at the boys to see Sean watching. She tried to give him a reassuring smile.

"Ben, please hold it together," she hissed. "The boys can hear."

Ben nodded. He gave her a long look. "The men," he whispered.

He mouthed one word. *Robert.*

She sighed. "It's not your fault," she said, not sure if she meant it.

He said nothing, his keening fading to a whimper.

She stood up. "Where do you keep your binoculars?"

Sean was next to Ben now, but Ben hadn't noticed the small hand on his arm. "Top shelf, on the wall," he muttered.

She walked into the kitchen, fumbling on the top shelf. She grabbed the handle of the binoculars case and pulled, bringing it slamming down.

Sanjeev was watching her. "It's been hours, Jess. I don't think we'll—"

"I know that," she snapped. "But I want to check if their trawler is still out there."

Three heavy knocks sounded at the door. Ben didn't move.

Jess went to answer. Zack Golder was outside, panting. He smelt of tar and dirt, and his clothes were stained orange.

"Jess, hi. Mum told me what's happened. I might be able to help."

She threw the door back, letting him push past.

"Ben, San," she called over him. "Zack's here. He says he can help."

Zack headed towards Ben, who raised his head from his hands. His eyes were red and his face stained with tears. Zack hesitated.

"It's OK," Jess said, following him into the kitchen. "He's upset. If you can help us find Ruth that will be a big help."

"Sit down, Zack," Sanjeev said. "Tell us what you know."

Zack dragged a chair over. "I've got an idea where the men came from. Where they took them."

Jess held her breath, leaning in.

"Go on," said Sanjeev. Ben was silent.

"On the flood defence works down by Hull, where me and the other lads go to work?"

"We know it. Go on." Sanjeev's voice was edged with impatience.

Zack shot Jess a nervous look. "Some of the men who work there. They come from a farm past Withernsea. Where the land's nearly blocked off."

Jess nodded. She knew the area. It led down towards Hull, which was a ghost town these days. Since the floods it was connected by just one bridge near the coast at Withernsea. It had been evacuated years ago.

There was another silence.

Zack coughed. "We overheard something today. One of

those men saying something about getting some women, how much they were looking forward to it. Sam asked him what women he meant, assuming it was family coming to join them. But he wouldn't say. Just grinned and said they were women from up the coast."

Jess shivered. Ben was staring at Zack.

Jess pulled her chair closer in. "Did he know where you were from, this man? Could he have made the connection?"

Zack shook his head. "No. Sam knows not to talk about the village, not down there."

"Good. Do you know where their farm is?" she asked, her voice low.

"Not really, no. Somewhere past Withernsea. I thought it was ruined, though. The land. Can't see why anyone'd want a farm there."

"Is it near where you go to work? Can we get there by road?"

Another shake. "Don't think so. Where we go is inland from there, the other side of Hull. They're shifting earth from somewhere, bringing it in on trucks, trying to reclaim some of the city. But it's marshy down there, not safe. That's what the men say."

"Thanks Zack," Sanjeev said. "That's helpful. What do you want us to do, Jess? Ben?"

The three of them turned towards Ben, who had unfurled himself and was staring through the window, towards the sea. He shook his head, squeezing his eyes shut.

Jess scratched her neck, thinking.

"OK," she said. "They either know how to get over that bridge or they've gone in the boat. Unless the bridge is safe now. We can't be sure that what Zack's been told is entirely accurate."

Sanjeev and Zack said nothing.

"So," she continued. "If they've gone by sea, they'll be slow in our boat. Unless..."

"What?" asked Sanjeev.

She remembered the trawler, riding high as they'd left it behind. She stood up. "They've gone back to their trawler. That's how they'll get down the coast."

Sanjeev whistled. "Shit."

She nodded. "We'll have to go after them by land. How far is it, Zack?"

"Um, not sure. It takes about an hour by truck to where we go and the roads are pretty bad, so I guess it's about 30 miles? Withernsea's further down the coast, about 40 miles away?"

Damn. It would take two days to walk that far, longer if the roads were difficult. By then, who knew what might have happened to Ruth? A shadow passed over Ben's face.

"We need to get moving," Jess said. "Head out first thing, as soon as it's light."

Ben shook his head. "We can't do that."

She put her hands on her hips. "Why not?"

"The village has to agree."

"What?"

Sanjeev looked at her. "He's right, Jess. You know how it works. We need to call a meeting."

She stifled a yell of frustration. "OK. Tomorrow morning. We do it then. Ben?"

Ben was staring out of the back window again, ignoring her.

"Ben?" she repeated. "We'll need you there. There could be resistance, you know what people are like about leaving the village."

"OK," he replied, not sounding convinced.

She stared at him, resisting the urge to shake him. "I need to do something," she said. "I'm going to the beach."

CHAPTER TWELVE

THE BEACH WAS DEATHLY QUIET, THE PALE CIRCLE OF THE moon reflected in the ocean waves. Jess shivered and pulled her coat tighter, wishing she'd brought something more substantial out with her. She hadn't set foot inside her own house for more than twelve hours now and was surprised to find herself missing it, or at least missing the connection with Sonia that it gave her. Sonia had loved Ruth, accepted her rushed admission into their little family without comment, and leaned on Ruth's growing medical skills as her illness had progressed.

Jess listened to the swish of the waves pounding on the beach, relieved that the night wasn't as wild as when she had – foolishly – launched the rescue. Would she and Ben have done it without the steady drip of Ruth's strength and decency seeping into them over the past six years? Would that frightened, nervous boy she'd seen grow up into a prickly adult have taken such risks?

She'd come across Toni on her way to the beach, heading home herself, and her friend had joined her. Toni held the binoculars up, scanning the sea for signs of life. This was futile: the binoculars wouldn't make an unlit boat visible, even under this moon. Jess put her hands up to her face, blocking out the moon to see better.

Eventually Toni lowered the binoculars.

"Nothing," she said. "No sign of a boat or a light."

Her voice was flat. She wiped away a tear.

"You OK?" asked Jess.

Toni nodded, pursing her lips. "I'm fine."

"You don't look it."

Toni forced a smile. "It's Roisin."

"Oh. She's your friend. I forgot."

"Not friends. More than friends."

Jess's throat ached. "I'm sorry."

Another nod. "How's Ben holding up?"

"Don't ask."

Toni raised an eyebrow. "That bad?"

Jess shrugged. "He's lost without her. I didn't see it before, but she's the core of our family. The only one of us that's solid."

Toni turned to her and squeezed her arm. "We'll find them."

"I hope so. I really do."

The next morning, Jess woke early and hurried towards the beach. People were already up; it was Monday and the weekday routines were still necessary. No one knew yet that there was going to be a meeting, and Jess would be expected in the schoolroom.

Not many people here had business outside the village. Only the young men went out for work, ferried away on trucks early most mornings in search of cash. But everyone else had tasks. Self-sufficiency, it turned out, made for a lot of work. Jobs had been created that had seemed archaic just a few short years ago; there were people who tended the land, others who reared livestock for milk, eggs and occasional meat. A small, trusted group of people, none from the same family, handled the food, collecting milk and eggs and delivering them to Pam in the store. Toni headed this team and she and Pam held combined but opposed power, each a check on the other.

Then there were those that tended the village itself, keeping the roadways tidy and carrying out repairs to the public buildings in the village centre: the former pizza restaurant that served as school room and community centre, the store and pharmacy and the JP. Then there was the bakery, the old restaurant kitchen where a team of five sweaty women churned out pies and bread with black market flour. It was the kind of heavy bread that would once have been expensive, *artisan*. And for fish there was the smokehouse, sending its fumes inland from along the beach.

She knew the bakers would already be at work, mixing pastry in the cool of the morning. Other workers emerged from their houses, stopping as she passed, their eyes full of questions. She told everyone she met that there would be a meeting at nine. That they had to be there.

As she passed Ben's lifeless house she spotted Dawn Evans shuffling towards her with a lopsided, slippered gait. Jess stopped. She rarely saw Dawn away from her own threshold. She didn't even attend village meetings, represented instead by her sharp-eyed husband. Dawn's front door faced the community centre and Jess did try to greet her from time to time. But she never received more than a tight smile, often followed by a hasty glance back into the house.

Jess smiled, raising her palms upwards in a friendly gesture.

"Woman!"

Dawn froze as if hit by a tranquiliser dart. Ted was behind her in their open doorway. His feet were bare and he wore trousers whose braces hung at his sides topped by a greying T-shirt, his skinny neck protruding over bony shoulders.

Jess looked between the two of them.

"Where do you think you're going?"

Dawn still had her back to her husband. She gave Jess a tiny shake of her head. *Stay out of this.*

"Everything OK?" she asked, her eyes on Dawn's face.

"Is there any news of Sarah?" she whispered back.

Jess cursed herself. She'd forgotten that their daughter had been taken.

"Sorry. We're doing everything we can. To look for them." Jess flushed. "I'm sorry, Dawn. I feel responsible."

Dawn shook her head. "No. It's not your fault." She looked over her shoulder. Ted was still in the doorway, his legs planted wide on the doorstep and his face hard.

"I'll let you know if I hear anything. How can I get news to you?" Jess whispered.

"The bins outside our back door. Leave me a note." Jess looked up to see Ted approaching. "Please."

Dawn turned towards the house. Ted stopped as she passed him, jostling her. She said nothing. Ted didn't follow her but stood glaring at Jess for a few moments. She held her ground but said nothing, knowing that if she angered him it would be Dawn who paid for it. Finally he made a hawking noise and spat on the pavement between them, then turned on his heel and strode back toward his house, slamming the door behind him.

Ben reached out across the mattress, his hand coming to rest on a cold pillow.

He rolled onto his back and blinked up at the ceiling. Last night he had sat up late, staring through the glass pane of the back door in the vain hope he might spot something out there, some sort of clue. Jess had returned from the beach with her eyes lowered and her body drained of the energy from earlier on. By then the boys were in bed, exhausted, and Ben and Jess had sat at the kitchen table together, talking. Or Jess had talked while Ben gazed at his hands, turning his wedding ring round on his finger.

They weren't really married of course, not in the eyes of the law. After their flight north, registrars hadn't been easy to find, and the village council was all that remained of officialdom by the time Ruth had been ready. A simple ceremony on the beach, with Colin officiating. Ruth held flowers that Jess had picked from the scrubland behind the village and wore Sonia's wedding ring – *I don't need it, your dad's long gone*, Sonia had insisted. On his own finger was a ring from a long dead relative of Sanjeev, one of the family heirlooms he'd been trying to rescue when Ben had first met him.

The ceremony had shades of earlier times, when couples would travel thousands of miles to celebrate barefoot on tropical sands. But the rush of the grey waves at their backs and the threatening rain had the guests shivering and stamping their feet on the sand even in July. Colin hurried through proceedings, anxious to seek refuge in the JP. Pickings from the last few weeks' rations had been saved up for a makeshift wedding breakfast.

Of course there was no honeymoon, but they enjoyed a few days together in the house they shared with Jess and Sonia, who made themselves as scarce as possible. That didn't lasted long; Sonia's illness brought her quickly home, and the sound of her coughing in her downstairs room quashed any remaining ardour.

But it wasn't the novelty of marriage he enjoyed about life

with Ruth, or the extra attention they enjoyed as newlyweds, or even the shock when she agreed to come north with him after the floods. The best thing about Ruth was the everyday, the humdrum reality of existence with this woman who became the bright centre of his life, giving him energy and helping him find calm at the same time.

The challenges of life here brought something out in Ruth that he hadn't seen in London. Sure, she'd had a steadiness about her, but it was nothing to write home about. He'd loved her for the sparkle in her eyes, the way she'd tease him for his seriousness, how she'd brush his leg with her foot under the table. But life as a refugee had matured her. It gave her an outlet to become something more, without losing the sense of fun that she directed at the boys these days, sharing private jokes and tickling them until they laughed so hard they couldn't breathe.

He turned now as the boys tumbled into the room. They hurled themselves onto the bed as if nothing was new, as if Mummy had just gone out to work early. Ollie landed on his full bladder and he groaned, then pulled them down onto the bed, kissing each one on the forehead.

Ollie put a hand on Ben's face, *Daddy tickly!* Ben rubbed his stubble: he hadn't shaved yesterday.

Sean pulled back. "Daddy, where's Mummy?"

Ben snuggled in between them, avoiding eye contact. "She's had to go away for a few days, boys. Get some supplies for the pharmacy. Like she did just before your birthday, do you remember?"

Ollie's head moved against his chest as the boy nodded. Sean jumped up to a sitting position, leaning painfully into Ben's chest. He had a birthmark on his chin that Ruth loved to kiss.

"I want her back, Daddy. She hasn't seen my drawing. I want to give her my drawing, today."

Ben ruffled Sean's hair, his throat tight.

"She'll be home soon, Sean. Let's put the drawing somewhere safe in the meantime, eh?"

Sean nodded, his blue eyes huge.

"Why don't you go and get it and I can put it in Mummy's wardrobe? Then when she gets back she'll find it. It will be a lovely surprise for her."

CHAPTER THIRTEEN

Ruth was woken by the sound of a key turning in the lock.

Heaving her body into a sitting position, she remembered where she was. Truth was, she had no idea where she was. Or who was turning that key.

She shrank back against the wall, clutching her knees to her chest. Her heartbeat thudded in her ears.

She watched as the handle turned and the door opened, revealing two men. The first was small and slim, smirking at her. The second was taller and just as thin. His shoulders were stooped and his eyes on the ground.

The one at the back she knew – or thought she had. Martin. And in front, one of his companions, the one who seemed to be in charge.

They shuffled into the room and closed the door. The older man handed the key to Martin and told him to lock it.

"We can't have you running out on us, can we, Mrs Dyer?" he said, turning to her. His voice was gentle, almost melodic.

She shuddered.

"Where am I?" she demanded, climbing stiffly to her feet. "And why have you got me imprisoned in here?"

"Now, now," he said, smiling. "Let's not rush things, shall we?"

"Where are my kids?"

He stepped towards her, ignoring the question. She shrank back. She could smell him: musky aftershave mixed with mint.

He laughed and put his hands on his hips. He was pale, with neat dark hair. His jeans were clean, unlike her own. Just as he had in the village, he was wearing a clean shirt. "I'd say introductions are in order, don't you?"

She met his gaze but said nothing. He looked back at Martin.

"Martin here I believe you've met. Very kind of you to take him in." He turned back to her. "Stupid, but kind." Her jaw clenched with anger: at him, at herself.

"Let me out. Take me back to my family," she hissed.

The man shook his head and put a finger to his lips. "Hush now," he said. "Where was I? Oh yes, introductions. I'm Robert. Your husband may have told you about me."

She scrolled through her memory. Nothing.

"No?" he said. "Hmm. Forgetful of him, considering everything we went through together."

He frowned. "Martin, lock the door please."

Martin hesitated, then Ruth heard the lock snap into place. "This isn't right," he muttered. "We should let her go."

She glared at him. *A bit late for that now.*

Robert swivelled to face him. "Hush. Mrs Dyer is our guest now. You played your part, and you'll get your reward." He looked back at Ruth, eyes narrowing. "We both will."

She felt her fists clench. He was slight, and Martin might not stop her. Maybe if she...

He gave a little laugh. It was high pitched and loose. "I

can see what you're thinking, Mrs Dyer. You want to escape, and you're hatching a plan to take those lovely fists of yours and do me some damage with them." He raised an eyebrow. "Am I right?"

She said nothing, but loosened her fists.

"I wouldn't advise it," he said, reaching into his pocket and bringing out a cylindrical object. A flick-knife.

He brought it between them and applied pressure, flipping the blade up in front of his face. He smiled again, cocking his head to one side. A lock of hair fell over his forehead. He reached up and pushed it away.

"Best not, don't you think?" he said.

She swallowed. The rusty blade was inches away from her face. She thought of Rory in the pharmacy, of his mother's fear of infection. Of Sonia.

He lowered the blade to his side. "It's not in the best condition. I apologise for that. Maybe Martin can clean it up for me later."

Martin's head jolted up. Robert laughed.

"Only joking. This doesn't leave my sight." He flicked the blade shut and pushed it back into his pocket.

"Now, if you'd be so good as to sit down."

She looked around, calculating. The mattress was too low, too vulnerable. She perched on the table, legs swinging.

"Very good," he said. "Move up."

He motioned with his hand and she pushed herself along so that she was almost falling onto the floor. He put a hand out to touch hers on the table. She flinched.

He smiled. "It's alright, Mrs Dyer. I'm not going to hurt you."

He heaved himself up to join her on the table, laying his hand on hers. He stroked her wedding ring. She squeezed her eyes shut.

"Nice," he said.

She nodded, unable to speak. His body was millimetres away from hers, heat emanating from him. Her flesh felt as if hot ants were crawling all over her.

"Take it off."

She felt her body go rigid. "What?"

"Your husband's ring. Take it off."

She looked down at her right hand, at the simple band Ben had placed on her finger, not long after they'd arrived at the village. It had been raining – it was always raining, back then – but they'd darted outside for just long enough to say their vows in front of Colin, who was steward at the time.

He stopped stroking and pushed at the ring with his forefinger. She felt it dig into her knuckle. "Please." His voice was low.

She looked at Martin, who was staring down at his feet. *Coward*, she thought. *Liar*.

Robert moved his forefinger, sliding it around the ring. Her hand was trembling.

"Martin," said Robert. "Help Mrs Dyer with her ring."

Martin shuffled towards her. He was still wearing Ben's trousers, hanging from his hips, too big for him. Ruth drew in a trembling breath.

Martin stared at Ruth. She returned his gaze. Did he know how much she hated him?

"I asked you to help Mrs Dyer with her ring," Robert said. He moved his hand away and put it in his lap. It was smooth and pale, in contrast to Martin's which was bony and calloused.

Martin grabbed Ruth's hand. She pulled it away. "I can do it."

Muttering a silent apology to Ben and Sonia, she pulled the ring off, struggling to get it past the timeworn ridges in her skin. She palmed it, her grip tight.

Robert coughed. "Now, now. Hand it over, please."

Tears were stabbing her eyes. She mustn't cry.

He plucked the ring from her open palm. With effort, she kept her hand still.

Robert gave out a deep sigh and put the ring in the top pocket of his shirt. He patted it.

"There, that wasn't so bad, was it?"

She said nothing. He gave another one of his tight, short laughs and stood up.

"Now, we'll leave you alone. I'll be back later. I'm sure we have lots to catch up on."

"I doubt it," she said, relieved to find her voice.

He placed a hand on her shoulder. She drew herself back, tensing.

"Welcome, Mrs Dyer. We're very pleased to have you here."

"I can't say I'm pleased to be here."

"Well, no. But you'll learn. The truth about your husband. Maybe then you'll be glad we brought you here."

"Never."

He smiled again, his eyes dancing. Martin was fumbling with the door key.

"Adieu, my dear. Until later."

Martin slid out first and then Robert followed him, backing through the door and blowing Ruth a kiss as he did. She grimaced.

The door closed and the air grew still. All she could hear was her own heavy breathing. She slid down from the table, blinking against the daylight that sparked in her eyes.

She was alone.

Jess hurried along the coast path towards the beach. The sky to the north, where the weather came from at this time of year, was dark, ominous clouds reaching down towards the sea. Blurred shadows painted the air immediately above the water: rain. Not the weather for a rescue mission.

She reached the beach and turned to the south where the sky was brighter, the morning's sunshine receding into the past. Near the shore, four figures were moving across the sand, stooped as if looking for something. They were making slow progress, each of them stopping to reach down from time to time.

She ran towards them. As she drew closer, she could make out Colin, Sanjeev, Toni and Harry. They were scouring the sand, sifting through it and pocketing things. As she got closer she spotted flecks of colour scattered around the shoreline. Tiny scraps of red fabric.

She shuddered and picked up her pace. As she approached them, her breath fast and hard, she called out.

"What's that? What have you found?"

"Jess!"

She turned. Ben was sitting alone, huddled on the cold sand. His face was grey and his chin shadowed with stubble. He wore a faded blue T-shirt and a threadbare grey hoody, no coat. He looked like a man who'd seen a ghost.

She changed tack to approach him but stopped when she spotted movement out of the corner of her eye, along the beach.

"What's that?"

Colin straightened, shielding his eyes with his hand. "The little bastards!"

Along the shore, level with the boat house, two figures were wading in the shallows, dragging the village boat between them. They both wore hoodies, raised against the wind.

Colin broke into a run, gesticulating at them and shouting. Jess looked at Ben, then ran after him.

As they got closer, one of the boys looked up and spotted them. He grabbed his friend's arm, shaking it violently. The other one fell backwards, splashing in the waves. Then they started to run.

By the time Jess and Colin made it to the boat, the boys were too far away. They ground to a halt at the water's edge, panting.

"When I get hold of them!" Colin grunted.

Jess bent over, pressing her hands into her thighs for support. "That was them, wasn't it? The ones from the playground."

Colin looked after them, his face scarlet. "None other."

She looked at the boat. "How the hell did they get hold of the boat?"

"No idea." He looked out to sea. "One thing's for sure, though."

"What?"

"If those men left the village boat behind, then they're definitely using their trawler. No point looking for it."

Harry ran up to join them. "Did those kids have the boat?"

Jess nodded. "It must have washed back in. How come you didn't see it?"

Harry shrugged.

"It wasn't there when I got here," said Colin.

Jess stared at it, puzzled. Were the boys connected to Robert and his men, somehow? She doubted it. It must have just washed up and they thought they'd try their luck.

"Does it look damaged to you?" she asked Harry.

He heaved it further onto the sand. "Looks OK."

Jess allowed herself a moment's relief. This would make going after Ruth easier. She looked over Colin's shoulder. Sanjeev and Toni were still moving around the beach, picking things up.

"What's all that, on the beach?"

Colin followed her gaze. "We're not sure. Looks like clothing, but we don't know where it came from. We've been going through it, trying to find some clues."

"Is it all the same?" she asked. All she'd seen was red. She and Colin started walking back to the others, leaving Harry to secure the boat.

Colin shook his head. "No. The red scraps are the most obvious, but there are others. The red fabric is thick, seems to be part of a sweater. Then there are thin scraps of yellow; maybe a T-shirt. And we've found a couple of white socks."

Jess felt her stomach churn. "How clean is it?"

"Clean? What does that have to do with anything? It's all clean, I suppose. But if it came out of the sea..."

Jess shrugged; she could be wrong. But it felt as if clothes that had been out there for longer than a day would be dirty, maybe stiffened by salt.

They reached Ben. Jess squatted next to him on the sand and he leaned against her.

"Ben?" she asked softly. "What was Ruth wearing, when she went to bed on Friday night?"

He closed his eyes. "Grey T-shirt. Old. Black jogging bottoms. At least, that's what she'd laid out on the bed, earlier on. I didn't see her get ready, because I – she—"

He collapsed into her, sobs shuddering through her body.

"She slept with the boys," Jess said, remembering what he'd told her. "That night."

He wailed, the sound echoing across the sand.

"Jess, why did I let her? Why did I let that bastard in? I told her I'd keep her safe, Jess! *I told her I'd keep her safe!*"

CHAPTER FOURTEEN

Ben sat in the front row with his boys, the hum of gossip rising behind him. Jess and Colin sat at the top table, waiting for everyone to arrive.

Once they'd got back from the beach, Colin had joined Toni, already out speaking to the families of the missing women, asking if they recognised those clothes. First the Murrays, then Ted Evans, with Dawn nowhere to be seen during the brief moments Colin had spent at the doorstep. And finally Mark Palfrey, Sally Angus's boyfriend. Mark said that Sally had some white T-shirts, but normally wore one under a shirt and he couldn't be sure if she had that night. There was no owner for the red sweater.

And now, two hours later, they were waiting for Jess, the new Steward, to reassure her community.

Ben was glad it wasn't him.

As the voices died down and Pam shut the doors at the back of the room, Ben checked the clock above Jess's head. 9.05am and the space was full, with people standing at the back. Tables had been cleared to one side and some people sat on those, legs swinging. Every household seemed to be here, including children.

Jess leaned towards Colin and muttered to him. "All these children."

Colin nodded and beckoned to Sheila, two seats up from Ben, her hand clutching Ollie's. She approached them and bowed her head towards Colin's. She nodded and stood back, surveying the crowd.

Jess looked at Sean and Ollie before lifting her eyes up to the rest of the room.

"Can I have your attention, everybody," she said in her best teacher's voice. "I know that everyone wants to be here today, which means you've had to bring your children. But we think the children would be happier doing something else. If all the children can go with Sheila, she'll take care of them in the JP. There are some games in there."

Mutters rippled through the room, accompanied by the scraping of chairs as people ushered their children towards the back doors. Sheila helped, gathering the children up. Eventually the younger children were gone, including Sean and Ollie, the doors clattering behind them and the high sound of their voices receding as they headed for the JP.

People shifted along the rows to fill the vacated seats. Ben stared at his hands, clasped together in his lap. In front of him Colin scanned the room, waiting for quiet.

Eventually Colin leaned towards Jess and muttered something. Jess cleared her throat, pausing to sip from a mug of water.

Ben's vision swam as he tried to focus on his sister and not on the empty seat beside him. The room was so quiet he could hear the clock ticking high on the wall, almost muffled by the sound of his own breathing in his ears. He waited for Jess to speak.

"Hello, everyone."

Ben felt himself overcome by coughing, bringing his hand up and wiping spittle on his trousers. He thought of the clothes that Ruth had been wearing two nights ago, and nearly slid off his chair.

Jess glanced at him. He sent her a nod, moving his gaze up to the clock to avoid eye contact.

"Thank you for coming," Jess said, her voice carrying over their heads. Behind him, a chair scraped on the parquet floor as someone shifted in their seat.

"We wanted to bring everyone together to update you on what we know about the kidnappings."

The silence broke at the use of the word, whispers stuttering through the room. Colin raised his hands.

"Please," said Colin. "Let the Steward speak."

Jess frowned at him. Village meetings weren't usually that formal.

"As I'm sure you all know, four women disappeared on Friday night, or in the early hours of Saturday morning. Also the three men that we rescued from their trawler on Thursday. We believe that the women were taken by these men."

Silence. Jess looked down at her notes. Ben knew that Jess had three lists: the men's names, the women's names and the clothes they'd found. He steeled himself for the sound of Ruth's name.

"The three men we rescued were Robert, Bill and Martin, or those are the names they gave us."

He watched Jess, thinking of Robert's full name. Did Jess remember him? Did she remember what happened between them?

"We believe they came from a farm on the land south of here near Hull," she continued. "A piece of land that's almost waterlocked, south of Withernsea."

Along from him in the front row Zack Golder was nodding furiously, and a few people leaned towards him and his brother for confirmation of what Jess had said. More muttering.

"The women—" Jess swallowed. "The women were Sarah Evans, Sally Angus, Roisin Murray and Ruth Dyer." She looked at Ben.

He willed himself to breathe. *How would Ruth be behaving now, if it was he who had disappeared?*

"We believe they were taken in the early hours of Saturday morning," said Jess, her eyes scanning the crowd. "We think the men stole our boat and used it to sail out to their trawler, which it turns out wasn't damaged."

"What are you doing to get them back?"

A man was standing, immediately behind Ben. Around him people turned to see who had spoken. Ben hunched low in his seat.

"We've been scouring the beach for clues. This morning," Jess checked her third list, "we found the boat – our boat – washed up on the beach."

Colin cleared his throat. Ben looked at him. Was she going to say anything about those boys?

"And we found the remains of some clothes," Jess continued. *So she wasn't, then.* "Something red, a sweater. And what we think was a white T-shirt."

Above the hum of the crowd he heard a loud sob: Mark Palfrey, sitting in the second row with his hands over his face. There was a ripple of voices and movement as people craned their necks to see. A woman placed a comforting hand on his arm. Mark was only twenty-two and this wouldn't be easy for him.

Colin was speaking now, letting Jess gather her breath.

"Please, we know this is hard for everyone to take in. But please show some respect for the families affected. We all want to know what's happened, to find the women, but they have a greater need than the rest of us."

"Why aren't you idiots doing anything? Why hasn't anyone gone to go and get my girl?"

Ted Evans was standing up in the front row, jabbing a finger at Colin.

"Ted," Jess said. "I'm very sorry about Sarah being taken. We all are. I assure you that the council is doing its best—"

"Doing its best? *Doing its best?* You fuckers wouldn't know what doing your best was if it hit you with a ten pound sledgehammer!"

"Ted, you're a member of this council too, please can you—"

Shouts came from the back of the room. *Yeah, what are you doing? Be quiet, sit down! Listen to Jess! Get a bloody move on!*

Ted paced the short distance across the floor to Jess and Colin's table. He leaned over Jess, ignoring Colin's protests. Behind him, Harry had stood up and was calling to him, trying to calm his friend. Dawn was nowhere to be seen.

"Look at me, you stupid woman." His voice was low and menacing. Jess turned to Ted and returned his gaze. Their faces were inches apart.

"Know this," he hissed. "If my girl dies or never comes back, it'll be your fault. If your brother never sees his wife again, it'll be your fault."

"Ted, please." Colin's hand was on Ted's shoulder, trying to ease him away from Jess. Harry was behind Ted now, shaking his arm and pleading with him to sit down. Ted pushed Harry's hand away. He stormed through the crowd, shouting expletives at anyone who got in his way. The doors at the back of the room clattered open and Ted turned round to send one last threat across the hall.

"If you won't sort this out, I will. You're a godawful steward," he said, before shoving his way out of the building.

Jess felt her muscles tighten. "I'll go after him."

"No," said Harry. "I'll go. Trust me, it's better coming from me."

"Thanks," said Colin. "Everyone!" He called over the heads of the people who were moving around the room now. "Please sit down. The meeting isn't over yet."

Jess stared towards the back wall, watching the doors. They swung open as Harry chased Ted outside.

"Sorry about that," Colin, said to her. Jess nodded and took a few shallow breaths. Had he been right? Was she a godawful steward?

"It's OK, Colin," she said, pushing her doubts away. "He's angry. I'm not surprised." She looked at Ben. "We need to get those women back."

She turned to the room.

"We came together tonight to talk about how we're going to respond to this as a community, and that's what we're going to do. We've got an idea where the men have gone and now our boat's back, we can go looking for them. The council is proposing we put together a group of people who'll leave as soon as possible, head down the coast and look for signs of this trawler. If no one's on it, they'll put ashore and look for the women."

Jess paused to glance at Colin who nodded, giving her a smile.

"But we need to get the village's agreement," she continued. "So I'll take your questions first."

Hands shot up, and Jess steeled herself to give what answers she could.

After the meeting ended, with the villagers agreeing to the council's plans, Jess went straight to Ben. His skin was sallow and his clothes dirty from the beach earlier, and he looked ready to collapse.

"Let's take you home."

Ben sighed. "Thanks, sis." He extricated himself from a conversation with Sanjeev and followed her out.

Outside the square was empty, the only sound a bird calling from beyond the flats where they'd billeted the men. She left Ben at home with the boys then hurried back towards the village hall, casting a wary eye at Dawn and Ted's as she passed. The bedroom curtains were drawn and no sound came from inside. Jess shuddered as she imagined Dawn in there, hostage to Ted's anger after the meeting. She stopped at the end of their path and wondered if she should knock on the door, offer help. She shook her head and looked away.

Then she remembered her promise to Dawn. She delved into her coat pockets and found a scrap of paper and a pencil; *ever the teacher*. She pulled them out, picking off the accumulated lint. She squatted on the path to write, the tip of the pencil pressing into her thigh. The paper was crumpled and coffee stained but it would do.

Village boat washed up on beach. No one aboard, she wrote. *We found the remains of clothes. A red sweater or hoody and a white T-shirt. Please leave note if these sound familiar. Sorry.*

She resisted an impulse to write Dawn's or her own name and folded the paper up, slipping it into her pocket as she made her way around the house.

She took a circuitous route, passing Sanjeev's next door to reach the back of the row of houses.

She peered around the wall, hoping no one was watching. The Evans's house wall stared back at her, its bulk looming in the mist rising from the sea. There was no window on this side and the bins, thankfully, were at the corner closest to her.

She hurried across the damp grass and reached into her pocket for the note. She slid it beneath the bin closest to her. She would have to hope that Dawn would check soon.

Once the paper was safely concealed she backed away, keeping her eyes on Dawn's wall. Reaching the shelter of Sanjeev's house, she turned and dashed back to the village hall. They needed to move fast.

As she reached the square, she was stopped by Clyde coming the other way. Sanjeev was with him.

"Clyde!" she panted. "Just the person. We need to get the boat ready as quickly as possible."

Clyde shook his head. Sanjeev let out a low-pitched moan.

"What?" asked Jess. "What is it?"

"It's gone, Jess," replied Sanjeev. "The boat's gone."

CHAPTER FIFTEEN

Sleep was impossible. Every time Ruth closed her eyes, she could feel the empty space on her ring finger, cold and empty. She thought about the band of gold in Robert's pocket, wondered if it was still there now.

She lay still for a while, staring at the blank wall, willing her mind clear. She tried to think about Ben and the boys, but the rough ache that left in her stomach just made things worse.

Eventually she gave up and propped herself against the wall, eyes scanning the room. Perhaps they'd been forgetful. Perhaps there was something in here she could use.

The room was gloomy, with no light showing under the door. Moonlight filtered through the window's film of green. It felt like being underwater. The smell of mildew mixed with the heaviness of her own unwashed body.

She moved to the farthest wall, examining the plasterwork. There were cracks, scuffs and red patches, eczema attacking the walls. She reached the corner next to the window and turned to face the outside wall, bringing her ear to the side wall.

A faint whimper, beyond the wall.

She froze, her breathing as low as she could make it. She listened. There it was again.

There was a person beyond that wall, crying.

She narrowed her eyes, squinting at the fogged-over window, and sent her mind back to the night she'd been taken.

She remembered Martin going to bed early. Ben had come home and they'd argued about the men, about how safe it was to let them stay in the village. *Amicable*, he'd said. *Happy to have them here.* Martin had been coming out of the bathroom when she went to bed, prompting an awkward moment as they said goodnight. He'd watched as she slipped into the boys' room.

If she'd slept in her own bed, with her husband, could he – or they – have taken her? Would Ben have woken? Or would the boys, alone in their room at the top of the stairs, have been the ones at risk?

She shivered. She had no reason to believe they were here too, not from anything that had been said. But then, she couldn't be sure they weren't.

She leaned into the wall, numb. There it was again, the crying. *Who is it?*

Jess felt herself crumple. *Was it never going to stop?* One thing after another.

"No. You've got it wrong. It came back. Harry said it was OK to use. We need to get it ready, go after—"

Clyde blushed. "No. It's gone again." He bit his thumbnail. "I'm sorry. But the boat house has been opened. And it's gone."

"Are you sure?" she asked Clyde, her voice dull. Finding Ruth and the other women felt impossible now.

He nodded. Next to him, Sanjeev pulled at the skin on his face. This wasn't easy for any of them.

She felt tears rise in her throat as she thought of Ruth tending to Sonia on their journey, of the awful decision they'd taken to walk here from Leeds. She couldn't know if the effort had killed her. But she did know that she could have tried harder to convince Sonia to stay behind, with her sister Val.

Val's face swam in front of her vision now, announcing what she'd heard about the village. *Just opened – accepting refugees – jobs – food supplies – only option.* She was right, they knew. Val and Liz's flat was cramped and they couldn't stay there and eat all their rations. Sonia had insisted, despite Jess and Ruth's protests. The coughing was persistent by then and they knew it was a risk.

But Sonia was her mother, and she couldn't defy her. Now it was Ruth who was going to be sacrificed to this village, to the desperation they'd all felt since leaving London.

No. It won't happen, she thought.

"When did this happen?"

"During the meeting. Or maybe just after."

Jess pulled herself in and tried to picture the community hall during the village meeting, the sea of expectant faces that had faced her. But she hadn't been able to see everyone, couldn't know who might have been missing.

"Right," she whispered. "Ben's too much of a mess to do anything." *And I'm not risking him too*, she thought. "We need to let him be with his boys and get on with doing what we can to find the boat, find the women."

Clyde nodded, buttoning up his coat. "Let's go."

Jess sent Clyde to the village shop, to start gathering provisions for their rescue mission. She needed to speak to the council members, to tell them what had happened. As far as she knew they were all still in the village hall.

The mist was settling into a thick fog now that shrouded the houses and plunged the village into silence. There was no sign of the birds she'd heard earlier. As she and Sanjeev passed the row of council members' houses, she spotted a light at a front door: Ted's. She grimaced. Was he waiting for her?

She tapped Sanjeev on the arm and gestured towards the light. The faint glow of a gas lamp flickered in front of a shadowed human figure. Sanjeev winced.

"Ted?" he suggested.

"Let's ignore him," she replied, and picked up her pace.

But as they neared the house she heard a female voice.

"Jess?" Dawn stood in front of her front door, holding that flickering light. Her hair was stuck to her face, her grey cardigan darkened by the damp.

Jess walked hesitantly up Dawn's path.

"Dawn? Are you OK?" She lowered her voice to a whisper. "Did you get my note?"

Dawn nodded, her eyes huge above cheeks so translucent it was as if Jess could see the blood flowing beneath.

"The red sweater. It's hers," she sniffed.

"Oh Dawn," Jess gasped, not knowing what else to say.

Dawn drew into herself.

"Are you OK?" asked Jess, cursing herself. Of course she wasn't.

"Have you seen Ted?" she muttered.

Jess frowned. "Ted? Didn't he come home after the meeting?"

"No."

Jess wouldn't have thought it possible, but Dawn paled even more. Her skin was grey now, with veins showing on her forehead. She sensed Sanjeev waiting behind her, soundless in the darkness.

"Dawn, does that mean you don't know what happened at the meeting?"

Dawn shook her head. Jess felt a lump form in the pit of her stomach.

"He stormed out. He was angry with us, for not doing enough." She paused, wondering how much Ted might have told Dawn. The woman was probably as much in the dark as Jess was. "Apparently, he was intent on taking matters into his own hands."

Dawn nodded. "What was he like? His mood?"

"Angry."

Dawn glanced over her shoulder, towards Harry's house.

"Dawn? Is there anything I should know? Something Ted might have told you?"

Dawn pulled at the rough wool of her cardigan.

"Dawn? You can trust me, I promise. I won't tell anyone it was you who told me."

Dawn looked up at Jess, searching her face. "I don't know, Jess. I'm not sure what I heard, but—"

"Yes?"

"I... I overheard something between Ted and Harry. They were whispering. Ted didn't want me to hear. He doesn't like me knowing about his council business, normally sends me upstairs when Harry comes round."

Jess waited.

"Ted said he was going to get a boat, head down the coast and get Sarah himself. Harry tried to talk him out of it, at least I think he did, I could only hear Ted. He was quite angry."

Jess wondered what *quite angry* meant, for Ted. "Please Dawn, what did you hear? Which boat?"

Dawn looked up at her, puzzled. "The village boat, of course. What other boat is there?"

CHAPTER SIXTEEN

GREY LIGHT FILTERED THROUGH THE THIN CURTAINS OF the room Martin shared with two other men. He yawned and stretched his arms, curling his lip at a twinge in his back.

This room was at the back of the farmhouse, one of the few rooms not ruined by damp. The wallpaper that peeled off the walls next to Martin's mattress carried images of Buzz Lightyear. He often wondered about the child who'd slept in this room when that paper was hung. They would be a teenager now. Where could they be? Did they wonder about to the house they used to live in, dream of returning?

The blue curtains were threadbare and rough to the touch, sunlight glinting through holes. Curtain hooks were missing and the fabric slumped on its rail, leaving looping gaps that let the light – and the cold – in. Martin turned onto his back, hands entwined behind his head, and watched as the light got brighter. Any time now the peace would be shattered by the morning wake up call. He readied himself to move as soon as the door opened, knowing that if he didn't, two things would happen. The door would hit his head as it swung open, and he would feel a sharp kick as Bill woke him for the day's tasks.

Next to him, Leroy snored gently beneath his mop of curly black hair. Beyond him, Dave was quiet. He might be asleep still, or waiting for the day to begin, like Martin. The three old mattresses they slept on almost filled the floor and the only other piece of furniture was a battered chest of drawers under the window that hit their feet if it was opened while they slept. The chest was made from a flimsy particle-board, covered in white laminate except for the places where it had peeled off.

He sat up, just as the door swung open, sending a draught of air rushing through the room.

"Wake up!" yelled Bill, just like every other day.

Martin wondered what Bill did before he woke them, whether he had just woken himself or if he had his own responsibilities earlier in the morning. By the time they were dressed – a brief process that consisted of nothing more than grabbing yesterday's grubby jeans from where he'd dropped them at the foot of his mattress and pulling them back on – the kitchen would be warming up. The aroma of cheap coffee would be curling up the stairs and, if they were lucky, the accompanying smell of bread being toasted or maybe some sort of meat being grilled. If one of their raiding parties had got lucky yesterday.

He knew there wasn't much hope of this today. Efforts were focused on their new arrivals and no one had left the farm since he, Bill and Robert had come back with the women, bundling them into outhouses at the back of the farm. It would be a breakfast of weak coffee, eked out for as long as possible. For some of them, accompanying slugs of vodka would soften the edges.

Leroy grunted and muttered something under his breath. He sat up in a sweeping arc and lifted his legs to pull his trousers on, all without opening his eyes. Dave was standing and dressed; he'd already been awake. Martin quickly followed suit, pulling on jeans and socks that he preferred not to sniff or even handle that much, and staggering down the narrow stairs.

He was last into the kitchen. Four men were huddled over the coffee pot, helping themselves to the morning pick-me-up. Robert sat at the table, reading a book.

"Good morning, young man!" he smiled at Martin.

Martin knew to be wary of Robert's good moods just as much as the bad ones.

"Morning," he mumbled.

"Oh, that's not the spirit. We've got a treat in store for you this morning."

The men at the table turned towards them. Bill knelt on the floor, rummaging in a cupboard under the sink. Martin shivered. Being involved in the raid on the village had been a 'treat'. He thought of Ruth in the pharmacy, the calm way in which she'd checked him over and treated his hypothermia. He reddened.

"That's good. I can see you're keen." Robert leaned back, bestowing a broad smile on his audience. Bill raised his head and barked out a laugh before his head disappearing back into the under-sink cupboard. Maybe he was repairing the plumbing again.

"And well you should be," Robert continued, fixing him with his dark eyes. "You're going to be meeting someone new. Not Ruth today, I'll be visiting her alone."

Martin breathed again, guilty at his relief.

"The young one, the girl," said Robert. "She's timid, hasn't said a word since she arrived. Maybe you can bring her out of her shell."

Martin felt cold. This younger woman – Sarah – was the last to be loaded onto the boat, lifeless over Bill's shoulder as he carried her down to the beach from the village. Martin had noticed her long white-blonde hair and her smooth complexion. She had looked calm and unsullied, hanging in Bill's arms.

Robert stood up, sending his chair toppling back. "Come on. Let's pay her a visit. Come on, what are you waiting for? We don't have all day, you know."

He followed Robert out and eased the back door shut behind him, knowing it hung loosely on its hinges. A few metres from the back of the farmhouse was a row of outbuildings, probably used as storage back when this had been a working farm. Robert strode on ahead of him, pulling a fistful of keys from his pocket. He picked out a large, old-fashioned key and turned it in the lock of the door ahead of them. The door swung open and Robert motioned for Martin to go on ahead.

Martin ducked his head to pass through the doorway and stood inside the narrow corridor that ran across the front of the building. The room closest – Ruth's room – he had already been in. He listened, trying to make out signs of movement in there, but there was nothing. She was either asleep, or trying not to attract attention.

He felt Robert's hand on his back pushing him down the corridor, locking the outside door behind them.

"Second door," he said, his voice firm. Martin stopped to face it. He tried to imagine what the girl was doing inside, whether she had heard them.

Robert frowned. "You really don't need to look so miserable. I'll give you twenty minutes with her. Get her to talk, please, I don't like silent women. Up to you how you do it. I have things to do."

Robert cast a sideways glance towards Ruth's cell and Martin shivered, imagining his 'things to do'. Robert took another key and unlocked Sarah's cell, heaving the door open and pushing Martin in. He didn't follow but pulled the door shut again and locked it.

"Get on with it," he hissed.

Jess heard footsteps at her back and turned round: it was Toni.

"Everything OK?" she asked.

"It's Ted," said Jess. "He's taken the boat."

"*Shit.*"

"Mm-hmm."

Jess looked back at Dawn. "Dawn, are you sure about what you heard? Sure Harry didn't manage to talk him out of it?"

Dawn shook her head.

"Harry?" said Toni. "What's he got to do with it?"

Jess turned to her. "We need to speak to him. Now."

They crossed to Harry's house. Toni started hammering on the door.

"Harry! We need to speak to you, now!" Jess called.

No answer. The house was in darkness, but that was nothing unusual.

"Let's look round the back," suggested Toni.

Jess sped round the side of the house. Her earlier mission at the back of Dawn's house felt like a lifetime ago.

Harry's curtains were open but the room was dark. Jess cupped her hands to the glass, forming a seal between them and her face. She peered through the gloom. There were discarded clothes on the sofa. No sign of any light or movement.

"Harry!" she called again. "Are you in there?"

Nothing.

Sanjeev and Toni were skidding to a halt next to her on the wet grass.

"Maybe he went with Ted," Toni suggested.

Jess shrugged. "I guess that would be a good thing. Ted's likely to sink that boat if he's on his own."

"S'pose so."

Sanjeev leaned into the glass, making it vibrate. "We need to talk to Clyde, find out how long the boat's been gone, if anything else was taken. We need to let Ben know, too."

Jess pulled at the back of her neck. Beyond the dark hedge opposite she could hear the sea pounding against the shoreline. She didn't have the stomach for Ben again. She knew he was struggling but irritation with his apathy was starting to overtake sibling sympathy.

"No, San," she said. "We need to stop talking and bloody well do something."

Toni smiled. "Attagirl."

Sanjeev didn't look impressed. "You can't do that. Ben needs to know what's going on. And besides, if you're planning on heading off to find Ruth and the others, you'll get nowhere in this fog."

Damn. He was right. About the fog, if nothing else. And he did owe Ben a huge debt.

"OK. We spend the rest of the day getting ready. Let's gather a search party, dig out some tents – I know there are some that people brought with them when they first got here – and then we'll head out at first light tomorrow. The fog'll have lifted by then, I'm sure it will."

Toni smiled. "Count me in."

The glass pane shuddered as someone pounded the door

Ben heaved himself off his chair. *Why couldn't Jess use the front door, for Christ's sake?* He unhitched the latch and slid the door open, surprised to see Sanjeev. His damp hair stood up and his face was red.

"Ben, it's Ted!" He half walked, half fell into the room. Ben slipped behind him to latch the door again, checking for Jess first.

"Where's Jess?" he asked.

Sanjeev ignored the question. "Ben, it's Ted. He took the boat. Harry's gone with him. They must have stolen it after the meeting, when Harry went after Ted."

"Harry?" Ben was confused. Harry had been helping out all day, joining in with the search on the beach, checking the boat. *Could he have known all along?*

Sanjeev nodded. "He tried to talk Ted out of it. But he's not at home, so he must have gone with him. Keep him from killing himself, I suppose. Keep him from wrecking the boat."

Ben's mind raced. Ted and Harry were out there in the fog, trying to make their way south along the coast. They had no chance. But then... Harry was a good sailor, experienced. He knew what he was doing. And the tide was with them.

He froze. They could be there by morning. Ted and Harry, the world's worst rescue party. What on earth would happen to Ruth, if Ted was introduced to the mix?

How would Robert and Ted react to each other?

He blushed, remembering that Sanjeev knew nothing about Robert. Only he knew what Robert could be like. But they all knew what Ted could be like. Two fireworks, ready to go off. Getting closer to each other.

He grabbed Sanjeev's arm, his fingernails digging in. Sanjeev shook him off.

"We have to do something."

"I know." It was Jess, coming through the front door. *Had he left it open?*

Sanjeev looked from Ben to Jess, rubbing his arm.

"Like what?" Sanjeev asked. "We can't go after them in this weather."

Jess shook her head. "We follow them. At first light. Gather together a group."

Sanjeev's eyes flashed. "Yes. If we set out tomorrow morning we might beat Ted, if we're lucky. If he gets lost on the way, maybe. Or if Harry slows him down." He hesitated. "If we can find transport and work out exactly where we're going." Another pause. "It's worth a try, surely?"

"I want to go," Ben interrupted. Jess and Sanjeev stared at him.

"I don't think..." said Jess. He shook his head.

"She's my wife, and I want to go get her."

Sanjeev looked at Jess. Jess ran her fingers through her hair.

"Ben," she said slowly. "I'm not sure it would help you. I know how hard you've found Ruth's disappearance. And I'm not sure that going off on a search is the best thing for you right now."

"But I need to get her back." *Who was she, to tell him what to do?*

She took a deep breath. "The boys, Ben. They need you here. They can't be without their dad as well as their mum."

He felt his frame sagging. "You're right, I suppose." He pulled himself up. "But you could look after them for me, couldn't you?"

She frowned and shook her head. "No, Ben. I love those boys but I'm not their mum. They need a parent right now. And I need to be in the search party."

She put out a hand but he jerked out of her reach. "Are you telling me you won't help me?"

"No, Ben. That's the exact opposite of what I'm saying."

Sanjeev put a hand on his shoulder. "I know it's hard,

mate," he said. "But you need to trust Jess. She knows what she's doing."

Ben clenched his fists, frustrated.

"Ben?" Sanjeev was looking into his eyes. "We'll get her back. Promise."

Ben nodded, then marched into the living area, where he sank onto the sofa.

"Thanks Ben," Jess called over. "This is for the best, I promise."

CHAPTER SEVENTEEN

Robert's smile made Ruth shiver. She'd overheard his conversation with Martin in the corridor and was torn between relief that it wasn't her boys next door, and fear. How exactly was Martin expected to make the other woman talk?

"Good morning, Mrs Dyer. How are you today?"

She held his gaze and focused on her breathing, keeping it as steady as she could. She glanced at the bucket under the table. It stank.

Robert followed her gaze.

"I must apologise. It's not exactly the Ritz."

She exhaled. "Where am I? Why have you brought me here?"

He watched her for a moment, as if coming to a decision. She fidgeted, her fingers going to her ring finger.

He smiled and patted the pocket of his shirt. "You'll get it back eventually. When you're ready."

She glared at him, wondering what *ready* meant.

"But we won't worry about that for now," he said. "You

need to earn your keep. This place stinks. You can start by cleaning out that bucket."

She looked at it and resisted an urge to retch. "Where?" she asked.

"There's an old privy, outside this building," he said. "Then there's work for you in the main house."

Her eyes widened. She wondered what the 'main house' was, whether it might afford a means of escape.

He gave one of those tight laughs. "And don't go getting any ideas, my dear." He approached, making her flinch. "Young Sammy will be watching you. He doesn't like women very much, not really *his type*. So watch out for him. No escape back to your doting husband."

She nodded. A lie.

"Nothing to say to me, Mrs Dyer?"

"Yes," she said. "What do I have to do?"

"Get that bucket sorted first, I can't bear it. And then you can clean the bathrooms in the house. The men don't like doing it themselves, don't make as good a job of it as I'm sure you will."

He motioned towards the bucket and she dragged it out, aware of his breathing behind her as she turned away. She heaved it up and headed out of her cell behind him, her eyes scouring the walls of the corridor, scanning for an escape route.

The girl stood opposite him near the window, her back so firmly against the wall that he thought it might swallow her up. She stared at him, pale grey-blue eyes in a white face stained with dirt and tears.

As the key turned in the lock behind him she pulled into

herself, cowering. He offered his most reassuring smile. "Hello. I'm Martin."

She said nothing, just carried on staring at him and trembling. He tried taking a step forward. She let out a sound, something between a sob and a wail.

He raised a hand in reassurance, but she wrapped her arms around herself and turned her body sideways, her eyes still trained on him. The spotlight of her terrified stare didn't dim for a moment. He stepped back towards the door and placing his hands against it. They were as far away from each other as they could get.

She dared to take her eyes off his face and quickly look him up and down. Assessing his strength, he imagined. He wondered who had been in here already, if Robert had paid a similar visit to all of the women as the one he'd invited Martin to yesterday. Had Robert brought other men here? Despite her grubbiness and fear, the girl had an ethereal beauty. It would have an effect on men who'd been starved of female presence for so long.

He turned his head to place an ear at the door, listening for Robert. A door closed along the corridor, the bolt clattering. Robert was in with Ruth.

They were alone.

"I'm not going to hurt you," he whispered, his voice echoing. She continued staring at him. He wondered if she could speak. He tried stepping forwards again. She made no sound this time, but her body stiffened.

He stuffed his hands inside his pockets and pulled at the fabric, turning them inside out.

"I've nothing on me. No weapons. I'm not going to hurt you," he said, wondering if the repetition made his words more or less convincing.

"I'm Martin," he said, blushing. "I live here." More blushing: *Stop stating the bleeding obvious.*

He hunched up his shoulders in an attempt to release the tension he'd felt since leaving the kitchen. Maybe if he made himself smaller...

He slid down to the floor, his back rubbing against the rough slats of the door. Finally he was on the floor, his legs splayed out across the concrete. He took care to avoid touching her mattress with his shoe.

He threw her another smile and motioned with his head for her to slide down too, to come down to his level. She shook her head, the first sign of communication. He put his arms out to his sides, placing his palms where she could see them on the floor. He straightened his back against the door, feeling it shift beneath his weight.

"I was in your village," he said. "Ruth and Ben were very kind to me, they let me stay in their house."

Her eyelids relaxed a little and some colour returned to her face.

He decided to continue. Robert expected him to fill twenty minutes, after all. Maybe talking would help her fear.

"I'm sorry for what's happened to you. Do you know where you are?"

She shook her head slowly, as if expecting some sort of trick.

"You're in an outbuilding at the back of a farmhouse. I've been living here for about two years with a group of men. There are thirteen of us here, all men."

Her eyes widened.

"We're about thirty miles down the coast from your village, on a piece of land that's almost water locked. It was abandoned after the flooding but Robert brought us back here to find a patch of land we could make our own." He lowered his eyes. "It's not much of a patch, though. The crops here were ruined by the floods, and what wasn't washed away or waterlogged rotted in the end."

He looked up to see her wiping her eyes with her sleeve. He carried on talking to cover his unease. His mum hadn't been one for displaying emotion, and it was nearly five years since he'd been in the company of a girl his own age.

"So, we've made a sort of home here. More of a camp, really. Some of us – the ones who got here first – sleep in those rooms in the farmhouse that are still OK. Others sleep in the barns. There were men in this building until last week, but Robert told them to clear out before we left for your village."

She watched him steadily, possibly convinced that he meant her no harm. He tried gesturing downwards with his head again and she eased herself to the mattress, not taking her eyes off him for a heartbeat. He smiled but stayed absolutely still.

"What about your village?" he asked. "How long have you been there?"

She shook her head. His openness wasn't about to be reciprocated. They sat for a few moments, staring at each other in silence. From outside he heard birdsong. She cast a brief glance up at the window.

The silence was making him uneasy and his legs were cramping. He stood up, keeping his back against the door. She flinched as he moved. When he was upright he stood still, his arms at his sides, the flapping pockets of his jeans brushing against his palms.

"I don't know what I'm expected to be doing here with you," he said. He paused.

He thought of Ruth the previous morning, of the look on her face when Robert had opened up the knife. Of the tension that had overwhelmed her body when he'd sat next to her.

"All I want to do is talk to you," he said. "I'll try to keep Robert, keep the others from hurting you, if I can."

At Robert's name her eyes flicked off him to the door. So Robert had been here.

He felt the door vibrate behind him.

"Finished?" It was Robert's voice. Sarah bolted upwards, standing against the wall. Trying to let it suck her in again.

He smiled, and was rewarded with the same silent stare.

"Sorry," he whispered, turning to the door.

"Finished!" he called, standing back as the door opened. Robert pushed it open and put his head round, looking between his captives.

"Very good," he said, smiling, and opened the door further so that Martin could follow him out.

Jess was up early again the next morning, striding along the Parade before the village came to life. Her only company was the wildlife that reclaimed these dark streets during their power-free nights. In the trees that sheltered her house from the main road, blackbirds heralded the morning with throaty cries. They flitted between nests high up in the reddening branches, gathering building materials and feeding their young.

As she walked towards the village centre she spotted a fox trying to get inside the large bins outside the JP. Those bins had heavy lids, she knew, and not much waste was in them compared to what there would have been in the past. She thought back to the profligacy of their earlier lives, the amount of perfectly usable food and more that had been thrown away. Now there were no waste collections, no bottle banks. Bottles and boxes were reused as much as possible and any waste that couldn't be composted or repurposed had to be dug into the small rubbish pit at the southern edge of the village.

She stopped in her tracks, waiting for the fox to notice her. It stood on the bin's metal lid, its paws scrabbling at one edge in a vain attempt to get inside.

Finally she tired of watching it and carried on walking. The fox looked up, scrutinising her. It was more interested than scared; surprising, considering how many wild animals were hunted for meat these days.

As she got closer it stilled, sniffing at the still morning air. It gave her a final stare and then slid off the bin, slipping round the side of the JP. She heard movement, some other animal it had disturbed maybe.

As she reached the row of houses that included Ben's she paused, looking from it to Sanjeev's next door. Facing Ben wasn't her preferred choice of activity this morning, but she knew it was unfair to up and leave without speaking to him.

She dragged her feet up his path and knocked on the door. She blew into her hands while she waited: it was cold today, but at least the fog had cleared.

When no answer came, she tried again. She knocked on the door three times but he didn't answer it. *Where is he?*

Ruth could feel her guard's eyes boring into her as she scrubbed at the kitchen floor with a grubby rag. There was no sign of any cleaning products here – something she was used to –but nor were there any of the makeshift concoctions from salt, baking powder and vinegar that she used back at the village to keep the pharmacy and her own house clean.

Bent to her task, she felt vulnerable, as if he might grab her from behind at any moment. But she felt safer here in the farmhouse than in the confines of her cell. This man was younger than Robert or Bill, and had watched her in silence since Bill had left her with him.

This was her second time out. Yesterday she had been made to clean the toilets, scrubbing at the tidemarked bowls with a balding toilet brush. The floors around the toilets had an ammoniac smell that reminded her of potty training, but was made worse by its stale heaviness.

As she'd been ushered around the house the previous morning she'd sharpened her senses, watching and listening. Trying to ascertain how many men there were, what the pecking order was and what she might expect from them. Once Robert had deposited her in the farmhouse kitchen she'd not seen him again, and there'd been no sign of Martin. She caught glimpses of small groups of men, passed open doorways to rooms whose occupants had fallen quiet when they spotted her. She saw – or heard – nine men in total, mostly young – early to late twenties – with just Robert, Bill and one other older man. This man seemed to hold a place in the hierarchy similar to Bill's, below Robert but above the others. She heard him and Bill planning an excursion to gather supplies. To steal them. He was resentful that Robert wasn't going, wanting to know why he rarely left the farm.

"He can't," Bill hissed. "You know that."

Bill lowered his voice but Ruth's ears were good.

"He's scared of the authorities, isn't he? That's all I'm saying."

She wondered what Bill knew that the others didn't. Robert didn't strike her as the wary kind.

Robert had visited her cell again last night, alone this time. As he had shut the door behind him, smiling at her in the dusky gloom, she caught a gust of alcohol on his breath. She backed into the wall as he approached, flinging out a protective hand as he almost tripped on the edge of the mattress on the floor.

He stopped in front of her, not touching but close enough

that she could feel his breath in her face. She resisted the urge to close her eyes, wanting to see him. To be ready.

He reached out a hand and she shrank back, leaning back over the table. Then his face flickered and he dropped his arm.

He frowned, looking her up and down. Her T-shirt was grubby and she probably smelled. He, on the other hand, smelled fresh, soap overlaying his aftershave which was less heavy today.

"You need a shower," he said. He stared at her for a few moments. In the light, his eyes were like slate.

"Very well. You should use the bathroom tomorrow morning."

"Thank you," she muttered, hating herself.

"You'll have to clean it afterwards," he told her. "Of course."

She resisted an impulse to nod, staring him down instead. His hand skimmed her cheek as he pushed a lock of hair behind her ear. She stiffened.

"I'll see you tomorrow then, Mrs Dyer," he said. "When you're nice and clean."

He'd turned and left the room, muttering *Mrs Ben Dyer* under his breath. When the door had finally banged shut she'd slumped back onto the table. The room was dark now, only the faintest light coming through the window.

Remembering this now, her insides crawled. She was clean now, had been led to the bathroom this morning and cleaned it before and after washing, Sammy standing outside the whole time. But now she wished she hadn't, wished she'd left herself dirty. She focused on the floor below her knees, on getting it as clean as she could and on trying not to think about Robert's repeat visit tonight.

CHAPTER EIGHTEEN

THEY HAD ALREADY STARTED GATHERING IN THE JP WHEN Ben arrived with his boys. Sanjeev was with Colin, checking the food and equipment they'd need for the journey. Toni was talking to Clyde, debating how far they could walk each day. No sign of Jess yet.

He started helping Colin, sorting through food and identifying what was suitable to take. They needed things that were light and non-perishable. It felt like packing for a scout trip. Not that he'd know, of course. His hadn't been that kind of childhood.

The boys were restless, flitting between adults and getting in the way. More than once he had to remind them to keep quiet. But it felt good to be involved, even if Jess had stopped him from going with them. Thank God Sanjeev would be with her.

Jess clattered in half an hour after him, laden with rucksacks. She paused when she spotted him.

"Oh. You're here."

He gave her an insincere smile. "Where else am I going to be?"

She shrugged. "I knocked on your door."

"Look, sis. You may have banned me from going with you, but you can't stop me helping."

She looked at him for a moment, then smiled. "Thanks. We need all the help we can get."

Sam and Zack appeared and she turned to them, talking over plans. How dare she treat him like just another helper? He clenched his fists but then spotted Colin giving him a look that said *calm down*. He gritted his teeth and returned to his task.

He watched Jess with the Golder boys out of the corner of his eye, envying their ease with her. Zack was flirting, he was sure. He snorted. *Fat chance, mate.*

In the centre of the floor were two small tents from the storage rooms at the back of the community hall, tents that had arrived with villagers who'd used them on their journey here.

Ben watched them packing, and thought back to the last time he'd carried a rucksack, to the journey they'd made here. To the day he'd met Sanjeev. *I owe you my life*, Sanjeev had said, after Ben rescued him from his blazing house. A gas explosion, one of plenty that they saw on their way here.

Now it was time for Sanjeev to repay that debt.

"All ready," said Jess, bringing Ben back to the present. Ben shrank into the pub's shadows as the others pushed outside into the bright morning. He was relieved when Sanjeev stopped to give him a tight hug.

"We'll get her for you," he said.

Clyde was first out of the JP, slapping his hands together to brush off dust as the doors swung behind him. Jess thought about the equipment they'd gathered together, equipment that had been in storage for years. Dust would be the least of their troubles.

A crowd was gathering: gawkers and well wishers wanting to see them off as well as those who knew the future of their community was at stake. In the five years since the authorities had left they'd been entirely self-managed. Electing their own council, growing their own food, carrying out repairs and pooling their scarce resources.

Jess emerged behind him and stopped to look around, raising a hand to shield her eyes from the glare. Clyde shuffled into place next to her with his customary grin.

"Hello, gorgeous," he said. As always, she ignored the flirtation but offered a friendly smile in response.

"Have we got everything we need?" she muttered.

"Seems so," he replied. "Two tents between you, sleeping bags, as much dry food as you can carry, a couple of flasks of water each." He fell quiet. "I don't know about you, but that's a lot more than I had when I came here."

She nodded. Everyone here had experience of difficult journeys, some harder than others. The Evans family, she knew, had walked all the way from Somerset, with no guaranteed shelter on the way and no tent or sleeping bags. Ted's sheer force of will must have got them the three hundred miles. Either that or dishonesty and intimidation.

A hush descended over the crowd as Colin emerged from the JP, followed by the others who'd volunteered for this mission. There was Toni, who she knew now was doing this for Roisin; Ben's ambassador Sanjeev, and finally Zack Golder. He and Sam had decided between them that one should stay behind and the other should come along. The low sun illuminated them as if they were coming out on stage, the world's most unlikely rock band. Each of them squinted and raised a hand against the light as it hit them.

Jess looked around the crowd and then cleared her throat.

"Good morning, everyone," she said, taking one pace forward. The crowd quietened, letting her voice catch on the buildings opposite.

"Thanks for coming to see us off. We know you're all concerned about Ruth, Sarah, Sally and Roisin." She paused, scanning the crowd for the families of the missing women. "Some of you more than others. And I know you're concerned about Ted and Harry too. We all want to know that they're safe, and we want to bring them home."

The silence was broken by a hum of assent, pierced by the sobbing of Flo Murray, face buried in her husband's chest. Around them, the three younger girls clung to each other, a forlorn huddle in the centre of the crowd. Jess searched for Dawn Evans, but there was no sign of her. Sally's fiancé Mark was at the front, arms folded across his chest. He'd tried to talk them into letting him come along but she'd said no. He was highly strung and she didn't need him slowing them down.

"As soon as we've found them," Jess continued, "we'll send back word. One or two of us will come back as quickly as possible to let you all know that our family members and friends are safe."

She swallowed, aware that the news might not be so positive.

"And while that happens," she continued, "we'll be working on bringing everyone home as quickly as we can. We don't know why the men have taken them; we don't know for sure they have done so. But whatever we need to do to reunite us all and bring everyone home, we'll do it. I promise you that."

She bent to her rucksack, gathering things together and conferring with Colin and Toni.

"Who'll be in charge while you're gone?" a voice called

from the crowd. At the end of the front row, Ben straightened, his eyes not leaving her face.

She shielded her eyes with a hand and peered into the crowd.

"Ben. If you've got questions or concerns while we're gone, talk to Ben."

She looked at her brother. She smiled at him but he didn't smile back.

"I assume that's OK?" He nodded. A murmur ran through the crowd as people turned to look at him.

"What if you don't find them?" The same voice.

"We will," called Jess. "Zack and Sam have given us good information on the men and we think we know where they are."

"What about Ted?" called someone else.

"We intend to find Ted and Harry as well as the women. Hopefully they can help us make sure everyone gets home safely." Colin placed a hand on her shoulder. "Now if you don't mind, we need to get started."

Sanjeev and Toni moved into the crowd, clearing a path for them to pass. Sanjeev gave Ben's shoulder a squeeze as he passed him, and they exchanged some words. The crowd turned inwards, watching them make their way through.

As they proceeded along the Parade to the village's edge, people followed as if participating in a marriage or a wake. Others stood at their open doors, clutching their children. Some waved and wished them luck, but most were quiet. As they reached the low wall bordering the western edge of the village Flo Murray ran forward and grabbed Jess by the arm.

"Get my girl back home safe, please," she whispered, tears rolling down her face.

Jess nodded, and gave her a hug.

"We will," Toni assured her. Flo looked up, her face clouded. "I promise."

Flo trembled, her weight dragging on Jess. She nodded at Toni then lowered her eyes.

Jess pulled back and held Flo at arm's length, exploring her face, memorising her features in anticipation of seeing them in her daughter's face very soon. "You'll hear from us soon."

Flo gulped in a shuddering breath and fell back into her husband's arms. Her children gathered in a tight circle around them. Jess swallowed the lump in her throat.

Ben had moved to the front of the crowd. She gave him a feeble wave. He came over and took her hand.

"Good luck, sis," he said, his eyes bloodshot. "Take care." He paused. "Watch out for Robert."

She smiled and stretched up to kiss his forehead. It was cold and damp. As she pulled back, a look of understanding flashed between them.

After one last wave she turned and walked out of the village, leading the group with Toni next to her. She glanced back for a final time to see Ben stood with Colin and Clyde at the head of the villagers, watching them leave. As they reached the main road and turned left, the village disappeared out of sight.

There was nowhere to go but south.

Robert visited Ruth again the next night as promised.

Despite her newfound cleanliness, he didn't touch her. Instead, he insisted that she sit on the mattress while he perched on the table and told her stories about Ben. School stories, of Ben as a rebellious teenager. There was a wistfulness in Robert's eyes as he did this, and for the first time she felt his guard slipping. Despite a desperate need to understand what had happened between the two men, of how all this could possibly lead to where she was now, she pulled her attention away to the door. The keys were in his pocket. But he wasn't large and maybe she could wrestle them off him.

As always he was a step ahead of her.

"Stop looking at that door, my dear," he snapped, interrupting a tale of Ben disrupting a chemistry lesson. She flinched and looked at him.

He cocked his head. "You won't be in here forever, you know."

"What do you mean?"

He smiled. "When you're ready you can join me in the house."

A shiver ran through her. "I don't think so," she replied.

He snorted. "We'll see. When you've heard all I have to tell you about your husband, you'll thank me."

"Never."

He gave one of his tight laughs and moved towards the door. "Stand up," he said.

She stayed where she was on the mattress.

"Oh, heaven save us from disobedient women," he sighed, rolling his eyes.

She scowled.

"Please," he said. "Stand up."

Reluctantly she pushed herself up. He reached out a hand and she pulled back, almost stumbling onto the mattress.

He shook his head. "Dear, dear," he said. "I only want to hold your hand."

She stood still. He sighed and reached into his pocket, drawing out the knife he'd shown her on his first visit. He didn't open it but instead turned it over in his hands, admiring the floral pattern on the hilt.

He smiled and plunged the knife back into his pocket. "Well?"

She took a deep breath and held out her hand, her arm quivering.

"Thank you," he said. He took her hand and raised it to his face. She stared, horrified, as he brushed it with his lips.

"Delighted, Mrs Dyer," he said, letting go. Her arm fell limp at her side.

He laughed again, his eyes creasing, and turned to the door.

After she had heard him lock both doors she turned to the table. Her heart was pounding. She grabbed the oatcakes and devoured the last of them, suddenly starving. When the packet was empty and her breathing had slowed, she turned to the window, thinking.

A new moon gleamed from a still, cloudless sky. If she stood at an angle to the window she could see it through the green haze, along with the shadow of another building behind her own, further from the farmhouse. She wondered if some of the men slept in there, or if it was used for storage. She hadn't seen any men going in. Sometimes she heard voices from the other direction, behind the wall her mattress was against. She knew now this was the building's end wall.

Returning with Bill from today's cleaning duty, she'd taken a moment to scan the corridor outside her room. There were four doors spaced along the corridor, and only one door to the outside, near hers. At the other end, symmetrical to the outer door, was a window.

She knew there was at least one other woman here. But she had no way of knowing if the other rooms were inhabited.

She held herself as still as she could, calming her breathing, and listened to the sounds of the night. An owl – maybe two, conversing – was hooting intermittently outside, which meant there had to be trees or some kind of cover. No sound from next door.

Her stomach clenched. The longest she'd been away from the village was just one night, on her trip to Scarborough for medical supplies. What would Ben have told the villagers about her absence? Would he try to find her? Would the village council send out a search party? She had no idea where she was. When she crossed from this building to the farmhouse the air felt familiar, with the background hum of the sea telling her she was still near the coast. The sun set behind her cell, glowing orange through the window on the first night. So the farm was to the east, and the sea beyond. She wondered how far away it was, whether she was north or south of home.

She sighed, closing her eyes and wiping away tears. She needed to find out more about this building and about any other prisoners. Then, maybe, she could devise some sort of escape.

CHAPTER NINETEEN

THE FOUR OF THEM MADE QUICK PROGRESS AT FIRST. THE road passing the village was still used by trucks carrying earth down to Hull for the land reclamation, along with a team of labourers, and the road surface was maintained as well as could be expected. There were potholes, but plenty had been patched up. They walked in silence, each of them deep in memories and fears.

Jess thought about the walk from Leeds, and to Leeds from London. Watching Ben with Ruth, the way that she had changed him. Jess hoped he could keep it together while she was gone. With herself, Sanjeev and Toni in this party, plus Harry and Ted ahead of them, not much more than half of the village council was left, and that half had a community of frightened people to watch over. Even with Colin there, they would be looking to Ben.

Sonia's memory haunted her as she walked too, the vision of her slight form struggling to reach the village. Her face had been tight as they walked but she didn't complain. Instead she accepted the help she was offered and walked as fast as she was able, apologising repeatedly for holding them up.

And finally Ruth. Ruth, so steadfast and calm. So full of goodness. Where was she and what were they doing to her?

After six or seven miles and a couple of hours, their progress slowed. The main road continued to the south west, to the ghost town of Hull. They took a left hand fork to follow what remained of the old coast road. The road was torn up in places, ravaged by misuse and the tide. From time to time they left it to find a smoother way across fields. Leaving the road was risky: the ground was marshy here and would only get wetter, and a misstep might mean a sprained ankle or a tumble into the sodden ground with the heavy rucksack pinning you down once you were there.

After an hour or so they stopped to reconsider their route and share a loaf of bread. Toni had an old Ordnance Survey map in her rucksack. The changing shape of the coast meant it couldn't be relied upon, but at least it showed them where the roads had been.

The map told them that their road followed the coastline a mile or so inland. As they approached Withernsea it would hug the coast and the fields inland would become impassable. Given this, and the difficulty of identifying which fields were safe to cross and which weren't, Toni suggested that they walk along the beach.

"But walking on sand will slow us down," complained Zack. "And get sand or water in our shoes. I don't know about anyone else, but I haven't brought a spare pair."

Jess squinted at the map and looked across the dunes.

"We could take our shoes and socks off," she suggested. "Tie the laces and drape them around our necks, keep our hands free."

Toni nodded. "That could work. I just think the beach is more predictable."

Jess looked at Sanjeev. "What do you think?"

"Beach makes sense," he replied. "We can see anyone who might be coming. Keeps us clear of any critters too."

"No. That means anyone can see us," added Zack. "Makes us vulnerable. And walking on sand is no fun."

Zack had a point. Making quick progress was important, but so was stealth, or what they could approximate of it in a group of four bickering people. She didn't want to give Robert any more notice of their arrival than absolutely necessary.

"Zack's right," she said, consulting the map again. "We don't want them to know we're coming. We have no idea how many of them there are or if they've got weapons. Our only advantage is surprise. We have to hang on to that. We stick to the road. Where we can, we move through the trees and vegetation, places we're less obvious."

She scanned the landscape: first the occasional patch of trees and some scrubby grass leading down to the beach. Cover wouldn't be easy to come by. Still, they had to do what they could.

Toni nodded and traced a line on the map. "Right you are. We follow this route. There's a green patch five or six miles ahead. When we get there, we can rest. Hopefully there are still trees there."

They continued along the disused road, taking detours around collapsed sections, and taking care to avoid the wettest ground. They learned the tell-tale signs of boggy ground: dark green, jagged spikes above brown, matted grass that sometimes glistened in the low sun. After about three hours it was starting to get dark and the promised patch of trees was getting nearer. They reached its shelter gratefully and struck camp in a silence broken by groans as their unaccustomed limbs complained at the walking. Only Zack was unaffected. No stranger to physical labour, he erected his and Sanjeev's tent with deft movements, and then helped Jess and Toni with theirs. The four of them sat in a tight group between the tents as they ate some more of the bread and cheese they'd brought and took swigs from a flask of water they passed between them.

While they ate, the woods descended into darkness. The air seemed to be closing in on them, damp smells of night rising with the sound of the distant sea.

"We don't know who could be out here," said Sanjeev. "Or if the men are looking for us. I think we should keep a lookout all night, take it in turns."

"OK," sighed Jess, longing for sleep. "I'll take the first watch. I'll wake Toni after a couple of hours, then Sanjeev and Zack can take the second half of the night. That gives us six hours sleep each before it gets light. OK with everyone?"

She was answered with low murmurs as they prepared themselves for the night, Sanjeev brewing coffee over the camping stove and the others half crawling, half falling into their tents.

Martin saw nothing of the women the next day. He was put to work away from the house, clearing land for cultivation. He and Leroy had already spent long hours on this patch of earth, ferrying barrow-loads of sand from the beach a mile away to lighten the damp soil, make it possible for crops to take root. He thought of what Ruth had told him about the allotments back at the village, the fruit and vegetables they'd cultivated with nearly five years of trial and error. Robert had only recently agreed to start growing food here. For years he'd been satisfied with stealing it: sending raiding parties to Filey, Scarborough or what remained of Hull each month. Scavenging from allotments, looting empty warehouses, or using stolen cash to buy black market alcohol. But now those supplies were running out.

Today he and Leroy had been digging a trench two spades deep, then filling it in again as they passed the same spot on the next row. They paused only once, to return to the farmhouse for lunch. When they arrived the men were sitting around the kitchen table. An uneasy silence thickened the air. A loaf of bread and a hunk of cheese were in the middle of the table: goat's cheese, stolen by Martin from Ben and Ruth's kitchen. He blushed to see it but devoured it nonetheless, feeling hollow from his morning's hard work. But he hadn't stayed for long, uncomfortable with the tension. Besides, the longer he rested his limbs, the harder it would be to start work again.

Now the work was finished and he'd had a makeshift wash in the tin bath full of salty water that sat at the back door of the farmhouse, his senses alert for voices or movement coming from the outhouse where the women were kept. He hadn't seen Ruth, Sarah or either of the other captives, but their presence was unmistakeable. Dinner tonight had been different from the usual plain fare: a fish stew cooked with tomatoes and wild garlic.

As he ate it he listened to the men's conversations, wondering which of them had had contact with the women today and hoping they hadn't been hurt. The kitchen was cleaner than usual: Ruth's handiwork.

When the meal was over, plates wiped clean, chairs pushed back and appreciative belches echoing around the room, the hip flask had emerged, passing from hand to hand. Robert was the first to drink and when it came back to him he took another swig and raised it in front of him.

"Here's to the women," he said, smiling. Martin shuddered. "Damn good cooks and cleaners."

"The women," came the chorus of voices.

"Not bad looking either," added Robert.

Martin clenched his fists, digging his fingernails into his palms and struggling to breathe. He forced a smile with the others.

"Will they be staying in the outhouses, Robert, or will you be moving them in here with us?" asked Dave, to Martin's left.

Robert frowned at him. "That's none of your business."

There was a hush, broken by nervous coughs and the scrape of Dave's chair on the floor as he shrank into it.

Robert laughed. "Oh, don't worry. I won't bite. They'll be staying where they are for now."

Dave blushed and pursed his lips. Bill was silent next to Robert, watching Dave.

"But I might consider moving the lovely Ruth in with me when she's ready," Robert continued, knocking back another tot of brandy. The men said nothing. Martin wondered if they were jealous.

"I expect you all to take good care of them though. There are just four of them – well, three – to go around and we need them fit and healthy for work."

The men watched Robert. Martin wondered how many of them had encountered the women, if more of them had been allowed in the cells.

"They're our guests, aren't they? We have to make them feel welcome," Robert said. "Show them some love." He winked. Some of the men laughed, but others looked sheepish, their smiles forced. Martin thought of Sarah, of her delicate features so incongruous in the cramped cell, and made a private vow to get her away from here.

CHAPTER TWENTY

Martin stared across the room at Sarah. She sat on the floor, her arms around her knees and her eyes lowered. Behind him, he heard the key turn in the lock: Bill this time, not Robert. He hadn't seen Robert yet this morning.

"Hello again," he said, running a hand through his hair. She looked up at him through narrowed eyes, saying nothing.

"Look," he whispered. He crouched down to her level then pulled back as she flinched. "I don't know what's happened to you in the two days since I was here last. I dunno if you've been allowed out at all." He swallowed. "Or if anyone else has been in here. Any of the other men."

He felt his cheeks flush. She looked down, her gaze on his chest, and nodded. He didn't know which of his questions she was answering.

He lowered himself to the floor. Her eyes tracked his movements. He looked at the door and listened for a moment. Not a sound from the corridor or the neighbouring rooms.

"Look, I know I've said this before," he continued, still

whispering, "but I'm sorry about what's happened to you. I want to help make it better."

Her eyes darted up to his. He couldn't tell if it was a question he could see in them, or fear.

"I want to get you out of here. To help you escape."

She nodded, more vehemently this time.

"But I need your help," he said, "I need to know if they let you out of here, and when. I know that some of the women—"

"Women?" He started at the sound of her voice: it was gentle, like silk. He nodded.

"There are other women here. Four of you. All from your village. Ruth is in the room through that wall."

He gestured. She reached out and held her palm against the brickwork, spreading her fingers wide.

"And two other women on the other side, each in their own rooms. I don't know their names. Sorry."

"How did I get here?" she asked. He closed his eyes, ashamed.

"We took you. In a boat. You were drugged and carried to your village's boat. We stole it. Then we took you to our trawler. Brought you here."

He wondered how much she'd taken in the last time he was here. "Do you remember what I told you about where you are?" he asked. "About this farm? The men?"

She nodded and looked down again, her pale cheeks darkening. He risked another question. "Who else has been in here? Apart from me?"

Her nails dug into the pads of her fingers, making the flesh white. "Just one," she muttered. "Leroy."

Martin shuddered. Suddenly the man he'd been working so easily alongside became a different person.

"Did he – did he hurt you?" he asked.

She nodded, averting her eyes. His stomach clenched.

"We've got to get you out," he whispered. "Soon as possible. I know. Have they let you out to work? Housework, cooking, anything like that?"

She looked at him again. "Yes. An older man came yesterday afternoon. At first I thought—" She shuddered. "He took me to the house. Made me scrub floors."

"Did he say what else they want you to do? Anything that gets you outside?"

"There was something about bins. Pig food, scraps. I don't know. He didn't say it to me, but I overheard."

He grinned. The pigs were kept around the back of this outhouse, out of sight of the farmhouse. Within reach of the woods that flanked the farm's boundary, about 200 yards away. Running distance.

"Brilliant. That's perfect."

She was watching him, her face creased. She probably thought he was mad.

"OK. One last thing. D'you know what time they normally let you out?"

Her face fell. "Sorry."

"No worry. We can get round that. The pigs are fed late afternoon before we eat. They get peelings and rind. Anything they'll eat, which is pretty much anything."

He'd grown quite attached to the pigs, but she didn't need to know that.

"I'll get you out of here," he whispered, daring to move closer. "This afternoon. I'll make sure you're sent out to feed the pigs and I'll come for you. Wait for me."

She blinked at him. Her eyes were rimmed with red, her hair wild around her face and her skin streaked with dirt. But her smile was beautiful.

Their second day was slow going. Jess was tired from the previous day, as were most of the others. Only Zack was unaffected.

The road was almost non-existent now, with the route blocked by marshy patches and dense vegetation. The boggy ground was worst: they had no means of getting dry and if they stepped into a deep patch, the least they could hope for was a damp night shivering in thin sleeping bags. But that was the least of it. Zack had heard stories of ground around here that could swallow a person up to their waist. No one relished the idea of pulling someone out, let alone being the one pulled.

Sanjeev and Toni talked between themselves as they walked, but she and Zack stayed silent. As they stumbled onwards Jess listened to the hum of the sea to the east and the birdsong.

Toni would call out the occasional warning of rough ground and give instructions to help them get round a marshy patch. Zack took charge on these occasions, helping to haul everyone onto dry ground. Jess smiled at him as he pulled her to safety, glad he'd agreed to come. She couldn't believe this was the boy she'd taught for the last two years of his school career. He was a man now, nearly twice her size.

As the day progressed, Sanjeev sank into silence, no longer responding to Toni's attempts to make conversation.

"You OK, San?" Jess asked after passing a ruined tractor rusting at one edge of a field.

He grimaced. "Fine."

"It's not easy, this ground," she continued.

"It's not that."

She tensed. "Oh?"

His brow was furrowed. "I'm worried about Ben. And Ajit."

"He'll be OK. How old is he now – eighteen?"

He shook his head. "Twenty. It's not that. I'm worried he'll do something daft. Try to get involved."

"Oh." She'd never really thought much about Sanjeev's little brother, just saw him as one of the band of young men who worked on the allotment. He was quiet but cheerful, always quick with a joke at Sanjeev's expense.

"He doesn't know how much we owe Ben," Sanjeev continued. "What life would be like for him if he hadn't—" He paused. "Maybe I should have stayed back there, with them both."

He went quiet as they reached a low clump of bushes, heaving their way through it. As he put out an arm for balance she grabbed it.

"Ben will be OK," she said. "We'll find Ruth. That's the best thing you can do for him. Really."

He drew to a halt. "I'm here for Ben, you know. I betrayed him, and I have to put it right."

She sighed. "You didn't betray him. If you hadn't voted for me, it might have been Ted. Can you imagine what that would be like? With everything he's done?"

He shrugged and pulled ahead.

After two more hours they'd not made more than a few miles' progress and stopped again to assess their route. The land bore little resemblance to the map now, with areas marked as fields just as likely to be marshland, and streams far wider and trickier to pass than the thin blue lines suggested.

Toni squatted on a dry patch of earth and unfolded the map in her lap, tracing the route she thought they were following with a finger. Her hands were swollen with the cold and damp.

"I reckon the beach is less than two miles away from here, just over that rise." She raised a finger eastwards then placed it back on the map. "I think we should leave the road and take the most direct route. I know there's the risk of being seen from along the coast, but if we carry on like this it'll take us days to get there."

"And we need to catch up with Ted and Harry," Sanjeev said. "I don't like thinking about what Ted could do when he gets there."

Jess gave him a tight smile, wondering what he'd been thinking since they spoke.

"There's another thing," said Toni. "If we're on the beach we'll see if their boat has come ashore anywhere."

"Our boat," corrected Jess. "It belongs to the village."

Toni shrugged. Jess looked between the group for signs of objection, but today there were none.

"OK," she said. "The beach it is. Toni, lead the way."

CHAPTER TWENTY-ONE

Bill opened Ruth's cell door and motioned her out, grunting. She followed him, carrying the bucket – she knew the routine by now – and headed towards the farmhouse to empty it and then continue with her cleaning jobs. She hoped he'd take her to the rooms at the front of the house. There she could get her bearings, work out how far from the sea she was.

But today was different.

"Leave it there," said Bill, pointing. "By the door. One of the others will clean it."

One of the others. So there were at least two more. She assumed they were all in the same outbuilding: the four doors off the corridor made four of them.

She placed her bucket next to the door, taking a moment to look inside and note that the kitchen was empty. Silently she apologised to the nameless person who would have to clean out her mess.

"Follow me," snapped Bill, heading around the side of the outbuilding.

She trailed a few paces behind. Bill looked to be in his late forties and was developing a bald patch on the back of his head, whirls of black and grey hair surrounding sun-darkened skin. The skin on his arms and face was leathery, almost obscuring the tattoo that snaked upwards from his right wrist. The men here were weathered by the outdoors, not unlike many of them back at the village. What was it that separated the kind of men who ended up here from the people at the village, she wondered. Did the two groups attract different personality types or was it blind luck? She considered Martin, and his behaviour. She shivered.

They rounded the outhouse, picking their way through muddy patches, and came out onto an area which stretched out for about three hundred yards. To the right was a pigsty. She could smell their muck and make out pink flesh moving between the two pig houses, upside down U-shapes of corrugated iron. That would explain the pork she'd cooked for the men's dinner last night. Next time she'd steal some.

Beyond the pigsties, and some scrubby, nettle-infested ground, was an expanse of ground. Bill pointed to the bare earth.

"You're working here today. Sowing potatoes."

"On my own?"

He squinted at her. "Yes. On your own. Got any complaints, Lady Muck?"

She shook her head. He headed towards the outhouses and grabbed a hessian sack, one of three propped against its back wall.

"Know how to sow potatoes?"

She nodded again. If it meant a few hours outdoors, then she knew how to do anything.

"Good. Three sacks. Sow them all. Young Martin will be keeping an eye on you."

She bristled and looked around, but Martin was nowhere

to be seen. Bill walked to the side of the outhouse and cupped his hands to his mouth.

"Martin! Back field!" he hollered.

Back field. So the farm had more than one of them. She wondered if the others were already cultivated, or if she would be required to do those as well.

Bill had dropped the bulging sack again and some of its contents spilled on the floor: chitted potatoes. "Well, go on then. We don't have all day."

She walked to the sack of potatoes and tried to lift it. She recognised the markings on the hessian: stolen from her village.

"Let me help you with that."

She looked up to see Martin standing a few paces behind her. Bill had gone. She drew away.

He lifted the sack, scooping up the potatoes that had fallen out. Not looking at her, he carried it to the first trench.

"There you go," he muttered. "I've been told to watch you. I'm not supposed to help."

He withdrew to perch on the upended crate between her and the pigsty.

She gathered up a handful of potatoes, holding out the hem of her T-shirt to use it as a makeshift carrier. She made her way along the trench, placing potatoes at an interval of a foot or so. She'd never planted potatoes before, but she'd seen it done on TV and she remembered them being pushed into the soil so that they weren't completely covered. The spacing was pure guesswork.

After five minutes or so she'd done the first row and trudged back to the sack to pick up more. After half a dozen rows the sack became lighter and she was able to drag it along the edge of the field. Martin stayed where he was, drawing in the packed earth with a stick and occasionally looking back towards the farm.

The constant bending and lifting made her shoulders ache and she knew her back would complain later. But it was good to be outdoors. She sucked in the heavy scent of the earth each time she bent to it, followed by the sharpness of the salty air when she stood up again. It felt like she was cleaning the fetid stink of her cell out of her lungs.

Each time she returned to the sack she would take a moment to survey the edges of the field, pretending to stretch her back or her arms. On two sides it was flanked by trees. At the end where Martin sat, there was a wire fence. Some of the wires were barbed and others were straight, making her wonder if it was electrified. Maybe they had a generator.

It wasn't long before she'd emptied the first sack. She approached Martin, pointing to the second one.

"Can you bring that one over for me, please?"

It felt wrong being polite to him, still behaving as though he was the well-mannered young man that she'd invited to sleep in her spare room.

He stood up, clicking his fingers behind his back, and lifted the sack. He placed it a couple of rows along, further up than she'd asked him to. He was being helpful.

"Thanks," she said. He smiled and nodded.

She continued with her task. When she had reached the point where she could lift the sack she looked back towards the farmhouse, to see what Martin was doing. She was nearly halfway along the field now, and he would need to move if he was going to keep a close eye on her.

The crate where he had been sitting was empty. She scanned the field, her heart racing. Maybe he was in the pigsty, or nearer the outhouse. But he was nowhere to be seen.

She dropped the sack, wincing as it fell on her foot. She

looked over to the woods at the field's far end, considering how long it would take for her to reach them.

Deciding on stealth, she picked up a handful of potatoes and turned along the next row, placing them haphazardly without pushing them into the soil. She kept her eyes on the trees she was approaching, scanning for a fence. Then she saw it: a barbed wire fence, not at the edge of the trees but set back, snaking its way through thick bushes. It wasn't high. As long as it wasn't electrified, she could climb over, or even leap it.

She was disturbed by voices behind her: two men, distant. *Damn.* She turned to see Martin and Bill again, near the back of the outhouse. But they weren't looking at her, and they weren't alone: there was a slight, blonde woman standing between them, her hair in messy tangles.

Sarah Evans.

She crouched down, pretending to be placing the last potato in the row, and watched them. Bill was speaking: she could distinguish the rough tones of his voice but couldn't hear what he was saying. He was pointing at Sarah, then at the pigsty. Sarah held a bucket in front of her, gripping it in both hands.

Ruth stood and made her way back to the beginning of the row and the sack of potatoes, throwing furtive glances in the others' direction. Bill walked back around the outhouse, leaving Martin to guard both women. Martin stayed close to Sarah but kept looking over at Ruth, and back at the outhouses.

When she reached the sack she stopped to watch them. Sarah was in the pigsty now, emptying the contents of her bucket. Martin stood behind her, watching. He was ignoring Ruth. She turned back to look up the field, at the woods. She was closer to them now than she was to the outhouse. She might reach them before anyone reached her.

She glanced back to check where Martin was, fighting her guilt at taking flight without Sarah. She could come back for the girl, get help, she told herself.

But there was no one in the pigsty and no one watching. Martin and Sarah had disappeared.

CHAPTER TWENTY-TWO

In her bedside drawer Jess had kept an old sweet tin. Now, it was in her rucksack, plunged deep into an inside pocket. Bringing the tin gave her courage.

When they stopped for lunch in the shelter of some trees, she found a spot away from the others and delved into her rucksack for it, her fingers pushing clothes and rations aside. Pulling it out, she slowly twisted the lid, revealing her mother's rings, given to her when they became too loose for the dying woman's fingers.

Nestled in cotton wool that still smelt of Sonia, they taunted her. Her mother had wanted her to wear them.

"Take these, Jess. Wear them. They should be seen, shown off on your lovely young hand." But once Sonia's body had been returned to the earth Jess had put them away, unable to stomach the pain of looking at them.

Until now.

She raised the tin to her face and breathed in its heady scent; her mother's perfume,. Then she snapped it shut. The scent of the trees hit her nostrils again, undercut by the salt of the sea. She pushed the tin back into its hiding place and heaved herself to her feet, remembering how Ben had refused to let Sonia meet Robert when they were young. She shuddered.

"Now, run!" Martin hissed at Sarah's back. "Straight in front of you, there's a hole in the fence behind the pigsty."

She stared back at him, wide-eyed, still clutching the bucket.

"Now! Go! I'm right behind you!"

He knew that Bill might be back at any moment, that they had to take their chance. He also knew that Ruth was in sight across the field.

Sarah dropped the bucket, stumbling over it and nearly falling into the pigs' muck. She ran across the pigsty and vaulted the low wall, landing with a thud. He ran around the sty: it was firmer ground and he was with her before she reached the fence. She looked at him as he drew level with her. Her face was flushed and she was panting. He smiled.

"Here, quick." He pulled the wire to make the hole bigger. She shrugged her way through and he followed.

On the other side, he grabbed her hand and she pulled it quickly away.

"Sorry," he panted. "But we need to stick together. I know the best way."

She stared at him. Her hair had been made even wilder by being dragged through the fence. He looked back at the fence and saw a clump of hair caught in a twist of wire. *That must have hurt.*

"Please," he said.

She nodded and he took her hand again, pulling her into the woods and taking a diagonal course away from the farm. The going wasn't easy: low branches snapped at his face and the undergrowth threatened to trip him with every step. Having only one free hand didn't help but if he let go he might lose her. He thought of Ruth, working her way through those potatoes. What would she do when she saw them gone? He pushed his guilt to the back of his mind.

After a few minutes he heard a whistle from behind them. He froze and stared at her then back towards the farm. But the foliage completely obscured them now. Surely, no one had spotted them? Still, there was no point in hanging around.

"Hurry," he whispered.

They ran. At last they came to the other edge of the woods. Empty land opened out in front of them. They would be vulnerable out there.

"This way," he urged, and pulled her sideways, following the edge of the wood. He could hear noises behind, distant shouting and the crashing of large men struggling through the thick vegetation. The sound made him go cold.

They reached the point where this wood met another one at the far end of the field they had skirted. He knew this wood was flanked by a ditch. He led her into the dense woods, dry leaves rustling beneath their feet. They were soon at the ditch. He let go of her hand and jumped in, turning back and motioning for her to follow. She leapt down into his outstretched arms.

They collapsed onto the ground, breathing heavily. She pushed her hair out of her face and, for the first time, he saw that she was laughing.

A stillness descended over the village after Jess and the others left. People retreated to their homes. Clyde closed the JP after the first day and when only Sean and Ollie turned up at school on the morning of the departure, Sheila decided to close that too. Instead she took over Ruth's responsibilities in the pharmacy, sending Ben's boys home with him.

It wasn't easy to keep the boys amused at home so Ben crept into the school room on the first afternoon, using the Steward's key he still had. He borrowed books and writing materials, and set the boys up on the kitchen table. Anything to keep them from asking when Jess would come back with Ruth.

Every morning he walked to the outskirts of the village and stayed there for as long as he could, scanning the horizon. But all he ever saw were trucks taking men and supplies south to Hull, and the occasional individual or group walking towards Filey. He ducked behind a hedge when people passed close by, wary of being seen.

On the second night he made his way down to the beach while the boys were playing at a friend's house, thinking of all the times he had come here with Jess. It was one of those rare clear evenings when the vast sky made him think of a Van Gogh painting. Ben gazed out to sea. His wife was out there, somewhere.

The image of Ruth invaded his thoughts day and night, sending a shooting hollowness through him that would settle in his stomach and make him want to cry out. Ruth knew nothing about Robert, about their past, and had no idea that Robert might want revenge. He wondered what Robert had told her. There was a version of their story that would horrify Ruth, could even make her refuse to come back. She had to know the whole truth, to understand how much he'd changed.

Tonight the breaking waves hummed under a sky full of stars. He turned his torch off, not spotting the silent figure that crept up behind him.

"Ben."

He started and turned to see Dawn silhouetted against

the starlit sky. She sat next to him with a stillness Ben hadn't noticed before. She gazed out to sea.

"I need to speak to you about Sarah and Ted." Her voice rang out in the cold air.

Ben turned to her. "Go on." Dawn shifted her hands in her lap. "I won't tell him anything that you tell me, if that makes it easier," he reassured her. He knew enough about the Evans family to understand that Dawn had secrets.

A smile flickered across Dawn's face. "Thank you," she said, the words catching in her throat. "There are some things I don't like to talk about. But I'm worried about them both. If there's any way of getting a message to your sister, of contacting her."

Ben shook his head. "I'm sorry," he sighed. "We don't have any way of communicating until one or more of them comes back. They said they'd send a messenger back, let us know what's happening. Once they find them."

Dawn said nothing, continuing to look out to sea. She brushed a stray wisp of grey-brown hair away from her face.

"I'm sorry, Ben," she said. "You've got enough to worry about, with Ruth."

Ben pushed down the knot that rose from his stomach. "Yes. But please, that doesn't mean you can't talk to me."

Dawn took a deep breath and put both hands up to her hair, gripping it at the sides and pulling it behind her neck and down her back. She still didn't look at Ben.

"Thank you." She paused. "Ted isn't a happy man. He finds life in this community challenging." Another pause. "I try to make it easier for him. To smooth the way, as you might say. Sarah does her best too. But it isn't easy. He – he gets angry. Sometimes."

Ben resisted the urge to tell her he already knew this. Everyone knew that Ted had a temper.

"I don't worry for myself," she continued. "Ted and I have

been together for thirty-two years. A wife comes to know her husband, to anticipate his needs. I know how to manage things, to help him find calm. I get help. I pray every day and God shows me how to be a good wife, how to stay constant."

Ben blinked, surprised. To him the floods had proved there was no benevolent god, but he knew there were others for whom religion was a source of support. That it gave them hope, helped them believe there was a purpose to all they'd suffered, that they would be rewarded at some point.

"But I worry for Sarah."

He nodded again, less surprised. Sarah was nineteen now, with none of the independence of the other village girls her age. She should be a productive member of the community, allocated some useful role. She should have friends, a boyfriend maybe. But instead she stayed at home with her parents.

"Any mother would worry for her daughter," said Ben, feeling inadequate.

Dawn's sigh was edged with a high note. "Yes. But Sarah's different. She's vulnerable. She's lived her whole life in Ted's shadow. I don't imagine I've been the best role model. She's got no fight in her, Ben. If those men threaten her she won't know how to resist them."

She sobbed, her body convulsing, and raised her hands to her face. "I'm so scared of what they might do to her."

Ben put a tentative hand on Dawn's back, patting it. He was scared too.

Dawn turned to him.

"I don't understand," she muttered.

He frowned. "Sorry?"

"Jess left you in charge here. I see that. But why aren't you going after her?"

He stiffened. "Sorry?"

"I'm surprised you're still here."

The cold damp of the rock suddenly made him shiver.

"I don't think—"

"Sorry," she said, her voice low. "I shouldn't have."

No, I—"

But she was on her feet, making her way across the sand and back towards the village.

As Ruth scanned the field for Martin and Sarah, she heard the shriek of a whistle behind her.

"You! Stay right where you are!"

She turned to see Bill running from the outhouse with three other men. She hesitated, wondering whether she had time to run too, but then Bill stopped and stared at her. She felt her muscles slump.

There was a commotion near the pigsty; the men were shouting at each other. Bill pointed to the trees beyond and the others headed in that direction. They ducked one by one through the fence, and Ruth cursed herself for not noticing a hole there earlier.

Bill ran to her, grabbing her arm.

"Ouch!" she shouted. "There's no need for that. I'm not going anywhere."

At least, not yet.

"Shut up," he barked. "What did you see? Where did they go?"

She shrugged. "I don't know. I was sowing potatoes." She gestured along the row she was working on. "And I heard shouting. I looked up and you were there."

His eyes narrowed and his grip tightened.

"Are you sure?"

She nodded. He yanked at her arm, pulling her back towards the farm.

"Robert won't be happy if you're lying," he said, panting with the effort of dragging her across the rough soil. She stumbled after him, kicking potatoes out of place.

"Stop!" she cried. "What about the potatoes?"

"Forget the fucking potatoes. You've got far more to worry about."

She matched his pace. "Where are you taking me?"

He said nothing.

When they were near the outbuildings she looked sideways at the spot where she had last seen Sarah. Sure enough, there was a hole in the fence. Beyond it she could hear the men crashing through the undergrowth, cursing at each other. Bill tugged on her arm again and led her round to the front of the outhouses. The sounds of voices died away behind them.

Bill unlocked the door and shoved her inside, marching her back to her cell. She looked at the farmhouse: there were men in the kitchen now, shadowy figures whose conversation stopped when they spotted her. Her bucket was still at the back door.

As she stumbled inside, Bill gave her a look of contempt.

"Wait there," he said. As if she could do any different.

"What about my bucket?" she asked. "What if I need to go?"

"Forget about that. You just focus on telling Robert the truth when he gets here."

Then he slammed the door, leaving her crouching on her mattress, heart pounding.

CHAPTER TWENTY-THREE

Jess's group reached Withernsea at dusk. It was a bottleneck: the River Humber had flooded inland, making the land between here and the estuary all but an island.

Jess had no idea if the town was inhabited or if that bridge was guarded, but she wanted to be careful.

They found some trees within sight of the bridge and took cover. They settled in to wait. Sanjeev fished in his rucksack for a bag of apples. Jess drew Ben's binoculars from her own rucksack, kneeling to get a better view of the deserted bridge. No vehicles, no sign of recent habitation, nothing.

She handed the binoculars to Sanjeev, trading them for an apple.

"You're right," he said. "There's no one here."

Jess nodded. "It worries me."

Sanjeev raised an eyebrow.

"Well," said Jess, "It's hard to believe a place this big hasn't got anyone living here. Not even somewhere this badly affected by the floods. Somebody always comes back."

She crouched down to get closer to Zack. "What have you heard about this place? From the earth works?"

He shrugged. "I've heard talk of the men camped out in a farmhouse past here. The ones we're looking for. But nobody really says anything 'bout Withernsea."

"You sure?" asked Toni. "I'd imagine if there were people here, they'd be working with you. Some of them, anyway. You've never seen vehicles heading this way? With groups of men? Or even just one person."

"Nothing."

Jess frowned. "Still. Best to be safe."

Zack nodded and smiled at her. His eyes were dark, boring into her.

They sat in silence, watching the bridge as if it would give up its secrets to them in the blue dusk.

"Must be a ghost town," said Toni, letting out a thin whistling breath. She stood to get a better look.

"Get down!" hissed Sanjeev. "Just because we can't see anyone doesn't mean they're not here."

"You're right," said Jess. "We wait here till dark."

Toni slumped down, giving Sanjeev a pained look and hunting through the rucksacks for a flask of water.

An hour later they were cold and stiff, and itched to get moving. The sun had set and a nearly full moon was illuminating the waterlogged fields around them, making the ground glisten.

Jess eased herself to standing, stretching her stiff limbs while scrutinising the bridge. There was still no sign of life, even through the binoculars.

She looked down at the three expectant faces in the moonlight.

"OK," she whispered. "Time to go. I'll go first with Sanjeev. Then Toni and Zack. We'll walk in pairs. Leave a gap just in case. Follow me and no talking till we're over the bridge and we've found shelter on the other side."

The others nodded and joined her on their feet, groaning

as the blood rushed back to their legs. They took a few moments to stretch, then Jess put a finger to her lips and gestured towards the bridge. The group stilled, waiting for her move.

She turned and picked her way through the undergrowth. She kept low and moved as fluidly as possible, aware of the rucksack rustling on her back. She watched the bridge, and the town on the other side.

She could hear movement behind: the others were following. She turned to see them hunched, focusing on the dark ground. Only Zack was looking up at her. He gave her a thumbs up. Nobody spoke.

Soon she was out in the open, where the ground rose up to the road. She quickened her pace, leading the group as they flowed up the muddy bank and onto the bridge. As she stepped onto tarmac, the bridge was lit up by the moon, its low stone walls casting shadows. She could hear the lapping of the water beneath her feet and smell the saltiness of the sea which the river met to her left, mixed with the sulphuric smell of drains somewhere. Her senses pricked at the smell, wondering if drains meant current human activity. But there was no sound except the eddying water, and the quiet slap of footsteps behind her.

Halfway across she heard a clattering sound ahead, and froze. Sanjeev stumbled into her.

"Sorry," he whispered. "What's up?"

Jess pointed towards the sound. It came again, a metallic bang echoing off the buildings ahead. Beyond the bridge was a crossroads and at the far side was a row of houses, with dustbins outside. One of them had fallen over in the wind. Or that's what she thought... She brought the binoculars up to her eyes and peered at the bins. Another clatter. A bin tottered and fell onto its side.

Sanjeev gasped. She could feel a stillness behind her, as if everyone was holding their breath. She pulled the binoculars away from her face. Suddenly there was a flash of movement as someone darted out from behind the bin, streaming across the road and disappearing behind a building.

"What was that?" whispered Sanjeev in her ear, his voice tight.

Jess heard laughter at the back of the group and spun round, glaring. Zack was laughing hoarsely, his hands on his thighs.

"Sshh!" she hissed. "What the hell—?"

Zack raised a hand, shaking his head between gasps.

"Oh dear god," he laughed. "We were all so scared. Look at us!"

Jess raised an arm. Sanjeev placed a hand on it.

"Shh," whispered Sanjeev. "Zack, what are you on about?"

"It was a fox!" gasped Zack. "Just a stupid, bloody fox!"

Toni started laughing with him. Jess felt stupid. Sanjeev was looking at her, a question on his face.

Jess nodded, remembering the flash of movement, the colours illuminated in the moonlight. Orange and white. Small, quick.

She looked back at the group, irritated.

"OK," she said. "So it was a fox. But that doesn't mean we shouldn't be careful. Let's get a bloody move on."

Toni and Zack fell into step at the back. Jess started moving again, trying to regain the fluidity of movement she had been striving for. They were soon across the bridge and standing next to the bins; one upright, the other overturned. Its lid lay on the floor, still rattling.

They scanned the surrounding buildings. Still no sign of activity. What rubbish was in those bins was old and long since rotted.

"OK everyone. Let's get through here as quickly as we can

and find somewhere to set up camp. Those men could be anywhere," she said.

Ruth couldn't stop thinking about Sarah and Martin, wondering if they'd got away or if the men had caught them. From her cell she couldn't hear much: occasional footsteps and voices passing outside her window. She went to stand at the window, sliding in behind the table and getting as close as she could to the glass. She tried wiping the film of dirt from the pane of glass with her sleeve but it was no use: the fabric came away with black marks but the green remained, coating the outside of the window.

After a while the noises increased. There was a sudden crashing sound, followed by raw shouting.

"What the fuck!" came a voice. There was a splintering sound and a crash, followed by muttered curses.

She retreated from the window and slid the table back into place. She slumped onto the mattress, leaning against the wall in the hope of hearing something. She was rewarded with the clatter of the outside door being opened, followed by footsteps in the corridor. No voices, though.

She watched the lock turn, the handle being pushed up, hoping it wouldn't be Robert.

It was.

His face was dark with anger and his blue eyes flashed. "Where are they?"

She drew back, protecting her chest with her knees. He advanced, leaning over her.

"Get up," he ordered. She staggered to her feet, sliding her back up against the rough wall and feeling her T-shirt catch on a worn patch.

"Speak to me, Ruth. You were out there. What aren't you telling me?"

He grabbed her wrist and she yelped, pulling away. But he was stronger and she found herself toe to toe with him, trying not to stumble forwards into his grip. He smelt of smoke and sulphur: it made her gag.

She drew her head back. He had her by both wrists now. If he let go she would fall backwards and hit her head on the wall. But the alternative was pulling closer to him.

"Tell me," he hissed into her face. "What did you see? Where did they go?"

She shook her head, staring him down. "No idea," she said, her voice level. He let go, sending her off balance.

She managed to stay upright, throwing an arm out. He was scowling. He eyed her for a few moments as if weighing up what to do next. She made herself meet his gaze.

Finally he smiled. "I really hope you're not lying to me."

She said nothing. Her eyes stung from the effort of not blinking.

"Don't worry, my darling." She felt bile rise in her stomach and swallowed heavily. He continued talking. "It won't be long before you choose to talk. I'll find out where they went, and whether you had a hand in it." He paused, leaning in. She shuddered. "You'll be singing like that kid who informed on me, back when your beloved husband was my so-called friend."

She felt her breathing shorten.

"So he hasn't told you, has he? Of course not. Purer than snow, your husband."

He threw back his head and laughed again. Ruth pulled herself in to the wall, her muscles tight.

He looked back at her, his face hard. "What did you do, Ruth? Did you help them escape?"

She shook her head. "I didn't, you bastard."

His eyes sparkled. "Talking now, are we?" He cocked his head to one side. "I believe you, thousands wouldn't." He reached his hand out and placed it on her cheek. "Hmmm. I wonder if it's time." He raised an eyebrow. "Not going to ask me what it's time for?"

She clenched her teeth. He moved his hand down to her neck.

His hand was inside her T-shirt now, stroking the skin below the neckline. Her body filled with hot anger and she pushed down the urge to hit him.

He smiled. "Yes, I believe it is time. Tonight." He cocked his head. "No, tomorrow. We'll need to get things ready. Your new home, Mrs Dyer."

She clenched her toes, willing herself to stay upright. She knew what he meant. Her face was hot.

He smiled. "I know you're looking forward to it too. You'll be very happy with me in the farmhouse. You'll find me much more attentive than your husband."

"Never," she said.

He laughed. "Well that's not really up to you, is it?"

"I won't let you touch me."

His eyes flashed and he grabbed her wrist, locking it in his hand.

"You damn well will." He pulled her towards him. His breath was heavy on her cheek. "And you'll enjoy it."

He let go, sending her tumbling back to the mattress. He laughed.

"Well, get up then. There's work to do."

She pushed herself up while he waited, his nostrils flaring. She slid past him to the door, desperate not to make contact. His breathing was heavy and she could sense his arousal. She swallowed, nauseous.

When she was out of the cell she paused, wondering if the outside door was open. If she too could make a run for it.

There were voices outside. But if Martin and Sarah could do it, then so could she.

His finger jabbed her shoulder. "And no thinking of escaping," he whispered in her ear. "We'll be watching you."

The next morning was cold and musty. Jess poked her head outside to find the tents blanketed in a shroud of grey. The air was still. In the distance the sea hissed and thrummed, salt infusing her nostrils and making her skin feel dry.

Toni stirred behind her, shrugging off her sleeping bag.

"What's the plan?" she asked, covering a yawn with her hand.

Jess zipped the tent shut and shivered.

"It's foggy. Gives us cover to find them by. Good news."

Toni nodded. "Like Zack said, pea-soupers coming in off the estuary. How far can you see?"

"I can barely see the other tent. It's thick, but it won't last once the sun gets up."

"Let's get moving then."

Ben shivered as he watched the fog roll in from the sea, looming over Ollie and Sean as they played on the beach. They were bright flashes of colour, bundled up in coats and scarves. He had on his warmest jacket, but still the damp penetrated his bones.

In his head he was calculating walking speeds and distances, and had decided that the group had to be past Withernsea by now. If they'd got past the town safely, then they might reach the farm today. Ruth could be within his grasp. He tried not to imagine her with Robert.

Ben had known Robert at school, as a lonely, troubled figure who generally sat apart from the other kids and seemed to have no friends. He'd watched him from afar, wondering about the acts of petty rebellion he staged against the teachers, acts that seemed to result in more trouble for him than they could possibly be worth. Until the day when Ben had been sent to detention, and had caught Robert's eye.

Ben shuddered and pushed himself upwards, turning to look down the coast, where the sand disappeared into the mist. Jess, Sanjeev and the others were along there somewhere.

The sooner they reached Ruth, the better.

CHAPTER TWENTY-FOUR

SARAH CROUCHED IN FRONT OF HIM, HER BACK RISING AND falling with each breath. Her head was cocked and she had her eyes softly closed. Concentrating.

"Sarah? What is it?" he whispered.

"Ssh." She raised a finger to quiet him then placed her hand back down to the earth: fingertips, not palms.

Martin shuffled towards her, taking care to keep his body low in the ditch. He stopped just short of touching her. She was calming her breathing, her nostrils flaring with each carefully drawn breath.

After a few moments, she opened her eyes. The proximity startled him: those clear, milky-blue eyes, just centimetres from his own.

"Can you hear it?" she murmured.

He shook his head.

He tried to still his body, slow his breath, quieten his heart, but it was impossible with her so close.

The fingers to her lips again. Eyes wider now.

"There it is again," she said, her eyes scanning his face.

Martin shrugged, raising his eyebrows. Worried.

"Footsteps," she whispered. "It's like drumming, coming through the soil."

He tensed himself to listen, lowering his ear to the ground, feeling foolish. Nothing.

"How on earth can you hear anything?"

With anyone else, he'd assume they were imagining things. But there was something about Sarah that made him believe every word she said.

"On the journey north. To the village," she murmured. "I picked up some skills. Survival skills."

Her face clouded. "And at home..." She dropped her gaze to the ground. "I learned to listen for trouble."

He could hear it now. Not footsteps, but voices. And breathing.

They stared at each other, wide-eyed.

"Run?" he suggested.

She inched towards him. "Where's the sea?"

"Up ahead. That way."

She craned her neck to look round, but at this angle there was nothing to see. She'd have to trust him. She started to shuffle along the ditch and he followed. He could hear those voices again, off to the left.

He followed, hands and knees pushing forwards through the dirt as quietly as possible. Hoping he was right about the ditch. That it led to the sea.

The farm felt different. It was as if someone had draped an invisible blanket over it, smothering sound but lending a thickness to the air.

Ruth crept from her cell to the farmhouse, Robert storming along in front of her. He was muttering under his breath. She scanned the back yard for signs of what was happening, and strained to hear voices. But there was nothing. In a scraggy tree, a robin sang in defiance of the tension. The sun sloped into the yard, illuminating long-disused fragments of farm machinery. The sharp smell of the pigs crept around the outhouse behind her, overlaid with the cloying stench of a toilet bucket that had been deposited at the back door. It wasn't hers, and it hadn't been there earlier so it wasn't Sarah's. Once again she wondered how many prisoners there were here.

Robert stopped at the back door, toeing the bucket with a sneer of distaste.

"First thing, sort that out," he snapped. She nodded. "Then there's a meal to cook. Food's in the kitchen."

Cooking was easier than cleaning, and with luck she could steal some food, quieten the roaring emptiness in her stomach. Her mouth felt dry from the oatcakes that were still being left under her table. A packet a day was nothing to survive on.

She heard movement in the kitchen. A young man emerged, no more than twenty-five. She'd spotted him before, perched on a bed with two others, playing cards. When she'd passed he'd stopped, card frozen in his hand. He and his companions had stared at her, open-mouthed. It was a stare that told her just how long it was since these men had encountered women, or strangers of any kind.

The man's gaze travelled slowly up and down her body, alighting on her hot face. Then he gave a low grunt. Robert glared at him.

"No nonsense from you, Dave. You keep an eye on her. She needs to empty her mess out first." He paused, eyes narrowed. "But don't touch her."

The man's gaze dropped to his hands, which were large and rough, with blurred letters tattooed onto the knuckles.

The grey ink was mixed with dirt and crossed by deep-set scars.

"No, boss," he muttered.

"Hmphf," said Robert. "I mean it, Dave. You cause me problems again, you'll be out of here."

Dave said nothing. He cocked his head, defiant. Ruth wondered if Robert's authority was often challenged, and if she could use it to her advantage.

Robert pushed past him and disappeared into the darkness of the farmhouse. Dave looked at the bucket and then at Ruth.

"Where d'you empty this?"

She shrugged. If he didn't know, she wasn't about to tell him. If he took her somewhere else, it might give her an opportunity.

His face darkened. She shuddered but held her ground. There was a sound behind her, past the outhouses. She glanced back before turning back to Dave, reluctant to take her eyes off him. The yard was as still as it had ever been. Even the robin was quiet now.

"In there, huh?" His voice was sharp now Robert had gone, and he had a strong London accent.

Her eyes widened. *Was there a toilet in the outbuilding?* If there was, why was she using that damn bucket? She nodded, her mouth clamped shut against the stench of the bucket that stood between them.

"OK," he grunted.

She picked up the bucket and its contents shifted. She closed her eyes and turned her face away for a couple of gasping breaths.

He was watching her, waiting for her to move. She set off in the direction of the outhouse but had no idea where to go. He sat down on the step, pushing his large feet out in front of him and clicking his fingers. He was wearing battered adidas trainers, one with a hole so large she could see his naked big toe.

"Aren't you supposed to come with me?" she asked.

"What?" He grunted, then heaved himself upright. "Fuck this." He headed for the side of the outhouse, the opposite end from the door. She followed, the bucket banging against her thigh as she walked.

When he reached the side wall he stopped and faced her. "Go on, then." There was another door at the end of the building. Like the door to her cell it was made from wooden slats. Shavings of paint indicated that it had once been blue, but now it was faded and warped. One of the slats was torn at eye level, leaving a large gap. The smell from behind it was thick and ripe.

She grabbed the latch and pulled. It didn't budge. She pulled again. Nothing

"I can't open it," she said. "It's locked."

Dave pushed her aside, making the bucket jerk ominously. He tugged at it but it held firm. "Right," he huffed. "Leave that and come wi' me."

She placed the bucket on the ground, glad to be rid of it, and followed as he ambled back to the farmhouse. He had a slow, lopsided gait. He stepped inside the back door and reached around it, half closing it. His hand emerged with a rattling set of keys.

Her heart was racing. *Was it really as simple as this? A simple hook, hidden behind the open back door to the farmhouse?* The keys looked familiar: a bundle of different types, some rusted but others worn from repeated use. They were clustered on a pair of key rings joined by a fob in the shape of a London bus. A relic.

He passed her again and strolled back to the outhouse, still in no rush. She followed. He fumbled with four keys before finding the right one and yanking the door open.

The stench gusted out and he ducked away from it.

"Get a bloody move on, then," he urged.

She put one hand up to her face and picked up the bucket with the other. Ahead of her was the foulest toilet she'd ever seen. It had no lid or seat and its sides were smeared in black. Holding her breath, she hurled the contents of the bucket into it, then took a lurching step backwards and dropped the bucket. She sucked in a deep breath then tiptoed back to the toilet, grabbing the chain between thumb and forefinger and pulling it to flush. She jumped back as the toilet gurgled. She leaned on the door to close it, preferring not to check if it had flushed successfully.

As her hip met the wood, she felt cold metal dig into her. The key was still in the lock.

She glanced at Dave then down at the keys, mind racing. If she took them now, even he would spot what she'd done and take them straight back. And next time – if there was a next time – his guard would be up.

No. It was enough to know where the keys were kept, and that they weren't careful with them. She was bound to find a better opportunity. All she needed to do was wait, and watch. Closely.

CHAPTER TWENTY-FIVE

MARTIN RECOILED AS HIS HAND SANK ONTO THE MUD AT the bottom of the ditch. They'd been shuffling along on hands and knees for about ten minutes now, Sarah casting glances at him over her shoulder but saying nothing. The sound of their pursuers had grown fainter now, despite a moment's panic five minutes earlier when they had heard a close rustling sound accompanied by short, panting breaths. Martin and Sarah had frozen in their tracks, too scared to look at each other or barely to breathe, only to collapse in relief when a fox had picked its way across the ditch just feet ahead. Startled by their reaction, the animal had stared at them with unblinking, beady eyes, before leaping out of the ditch and slipping away under a low hedge.

But now it was quiet, the only sounds accompanying their progress the warbling of a chiffchaff in the trees and the dim, distant sound of the sea.

Martin could almost taste it now, a salty heaviness on the air that promised an eventual end to this ditch, and some respite for his tired limbs.

"Mud," she whispered, looking back at him with a smile. Her cheeks were red. "You were right."

She put up a hand for him to stop and eased herself around to face him. She grabbed a fistful of mud and daubed herself with it, motioning for him to copy. He squeezed a lump of mud between his thumb and forefinger. It was cold and gritty. Feeling foolish, he reached in for a handful and started plastering it onto his skin: face, hands, hair, anywhere that was exposed. Once he'd done that he followed her lead and started to smear it onto his clothes too, wondering if his threadbare jeans would survive the ordeal.

She smiled at him, her eyes even more wide and blue in her muddy face.

"What now?" he whispered. "Make a run for it?"

He looked up at the darkening sky. If they stayed out here till nightfall, they would freeze.

"No," she breathed. "Is there any shelter around here? Anywhere we can spend the night?"

He shook his head.

"Not here," he replied. "But there's huts up by the beach. Falling apart, but they'll do."

"OK. Let's wait till it's nearly dark. Can you find your way?"

He nodded. He'd been roaming this barren patch of land for the last four years, conducting ever widening sorties for Robert in search of food, building materials, livestock, anything they could use at the farm. He'd been organised about it, using a spiralling route to enlarge his search area each time. His forays had taken him as far as Withernsea to the north and almost to Hull in the west. Both were desolate, abandoned by humanity but not by the wildlife that was slowly feasting on what the people had left behind.

Here, not more than two miles from the farm, was part of

his territory, land that he had mapped in his head with a detail worthy of any cartographer. This ditch ran alongside a set of fields belonging to a farm long since abandoned, flooded as badly as his own home had been. On the other side was thin, scrubby woodland only a couple of trees deep in places but enough to shield them from the men. He was confident now that they hadn't been followed, but there was always the chance that they lurked there, on the far side of the trees...

"It'll be dark in an hour," she whispered. "Let's rest, get our breath back?"

He nodded and slumped onto the ground, flattening himself in the bottom of the ditch and trying to ignore the stench of decaying vegetation mixed with fox dung. He rubbed his aching calves then rolled onto his back and watched the sky dim.

Ruth was woken by thumps and voices in the corridor outside. She blinked herself awake, waiting for the key to turn in the lock.

The cell was only starting to lighten. As her eyes adjusted to the gloom, charcoal gave way to silver. She sat up, not wanting to be laid out on the mattress when Robert came in.

Fatigue weighed down on her limbs. She'd lain awake in the dark after Robert had left her last night, trying to piece together the jigsaw of his past with Ben. He'd taken to visiting her each night, trying to engage her in conversation. At first he had threatened her when she remained silent, pulling that knife from his pocket. But then he had given up, preferring to talk himself. She was bored with hearing about his past, his excuses for what he had become. And so far he'd revealed little about what had happened between him and Ben, other than the fact that they were friends at school.

She stood, stretching her arms. She had started exercising, trying to remember the yoga routines the village women moved through on Saturday mornings. Wishing she'd joined them more than three times in the last two years.

The cell door next to hers was opened and a clattering sound echoed along the corridor, accompanied by an angry male voice.

"Get your hands off me, you fucking idiot! You can't do this!"

She knew that voice.

Ruth stilled her breathing. Surely she was wrong. It could be any one of the men. Anger and foul language were commonplace here.

"Calm down, please." Robert's voice was unmistakeable.

"No, I will not bloody calm down! Get your hands off me, right now!"

She heard scuffling and muffled thuds followed by the sound of a door rattling on its hinges.

"Come on mate, get a grip. We're only leaving you here for a short time. Then we want to talk to you." Bill's voice, lower than Robert's.

"Talk to me! More like keep me bloody prisoner, you mean! Nobody locks me up against my will. What have you done with my daughter, you bastard?"

Ruth gasped. She was right; it *was* Ted. Being thrown into the cell that Sarah had vacated just yesterday.

There were more shouts and bangs, followed by the rasp of tape being torn from a roll. More thuds and voices, lower now and coming through the wall between her cell and the next.

"Now stay there and don't move!" Robert snapped, his anger making the hairs on her arms bristle.

"Here's your friend," he continued, his voice level now. She could hear a smile in it. "You'll be sharing."

She heard another slam and felt a draught billow under her door. More scuffling sounds in the corridor outside and another voice.

"Ted, I think we need to calm down a—"

The voice was interrupted. A blow, more tape being applied over its owner's mouth or the shock of being thrown into a stinking cell: Ruth couldn't be sure. But she could be sure of one thing.

Ted Evans and Harry Mills were in the cell next to hers. Her skin prickled.

She threw herself at the door and pounded on it with her fists, her voice wild.

"Ted! Harry! Ted! It's me, Ruth! Ruth Dyer! Is Ben with you? Have you come to rescue—"

She fell back as her door was flung open.

"Be quiet! Nobody told you to speak."

Robert loomed over her, framed by the doorway, fingering his jeans pocket. She shrank back and drew in her breath. She staggered upright, meeting his eye.

"Who's that next door, Robert? Who else is with them? Ben?"

"Shut up about your precious husband!" he screamed, slapping her across the face. She cried out and a hand flew up to her cheek; she could feel it throbbing.

"Damn it, Ruth," he snapped, lowering his hands. His cheeks inflamed. "If you knew half the truth about your husband you wouldn't be holding out for any kind of rescue."

He spat out a laugh. A drop of spit hit her hand and she flung it out to shake it clean. He flinched.

Her mind racing, she glanced at the open doorway then barrelled into him. He was taller than her but slim, and she was surprised to find her weight knocked him into the door. She brought her knee up and he crashed to the floor, clutching his groin.

She leapt over his prone body. He made a lunge for her, howling in pain. She was too quick for him, and threw herself through the doorway into the corridor outside.

Panting, she looked from side to side. At the far end, Bill was coming out of the furthest of the four doors. *Who was in there?*

She snatched a wide-eyed glance at Sarah's cell – now Ted and Harry's. Should she try to rescue them? A moment's hesitation, then she threw herself in the opposite direction – towards the door to the outside world.

It was unlocked.

CHAPTER TWENTY-SIX

MARTIN WAS WOKEN BY SUNLIGHT SLANTING THROUGH THE window onto his face. He raised a hand, cursing his hard mattress. His room-mate's breathing was lighter than usual, less laboured.

His eyes shot open.

Above him wasn't the patchy, damp-infested ceiling of his bedroom in the farmhouse, but instead the pitched roof of the hut he and Sarah had hidden in last night, curls of brittle paint floating down over them like flakes of snow.

He pushed up on his elbows, feeling the floorboards shift.

He looked up at the bench above him, more of a glorified shelf really, where he had persuaded Sarah to sleep.

She was lying quietly, staring down at him.

"Morning," she smiled, making his heart lurch. "It's a lovely day out there." She paused. "Good escaping weather."

He drew his feet up, scraping his heels along the floor, then stretched as he hauled himself upright. He clicked his knuckles behind his back to wake them. She grimaced. He resolved to break the habit.

The floor shuddered as he moved towards the window, imagining someone out there watching.

"Are you OK?" he whispered, sitting beside her on the bench as she swept her feet round and onto the floor.

"I'm fine." She brushed a wisp of hair away from her eyes. It caught the sunlight, glistening. "Better than I have been for days."

There was a moment's stillness between them. His heart was pounding, sending blood rushing to his face.

"Thank you," she whispered. His heart lurched. He wondered what had happened to her back in that cell. Which of his companions had paid visits during the night.

He shook his head and looked out to the beach. The waves sparkled for once, brightening the loneliness of this stretch of coast. In the shallows seagulls paddled, dipping their beaks into the water. Patches of seaweed littered the sand, ribbons of kelp interspersed with green clumps that took him back to swimming in the sea as a boy, his father mocking his yelps when his legs had been tickled by the fronds.

He scanned the coastline, pondering their next move. Should they head up the coast, follow the beach? Or should they go inland, take cover where they could?

Further up the beach, surrounded by a group of gulls, was a low shape, silhouetted by the reflections off the sea. It was squat and hunched, like a mound of earth or a small boat.

A boat! He turned to Sarah. "Can you see that?"

She turned to follow his gaze. "What?" she muttered. "The birds?"

"No, not the birds," he replied, impatience making him sound shrill. "That shape, halfway up the beach. Looks like a boat."

She leaned on the glass, her hands smearing the condensation.

"Where?" she asked.

"Right there!" He grabbed her hand and pulled her off the bench. "Come outside and look."

He bounded out of the door, his feet suddenly light. She dragged on his arm.

"Martin, slow down. We don't know what – or who's – out there."

"Shit," he breathed, throwing himself against the wall of the hut. "You're right."

He peered up and down the beach but it was deserted, their only companions the wading birds.

"It's OK," he said. "No one's here. Come out, please. Look."

She emerged from the hut, squinting up and down the beach and keeping her movements small. After a few moments, she relaxed and put her hand on his. It was cool and smooth.

"Up there," he said, pulling himself in behind her so they had the same view. He bent to bring his eyes to her level and pointed up the beach, his arm reaching over her shoulder.

She gasped. "The boat," she whispered.

"The boat?" He dug his fingernails into his palm. "What do you mean, *the* boat?"

She span towards him. Her eyes danced. "The village boat," she said. "It has to be – they've sent someone to get us!"

"Us?"

She blushed. "Me and Ruth," she said, lowering her gaze. "Not you."

He thought about Ben and Jess, about the kindness the villagers had shown him. Ruth's gentle touch in the pharmacy. The warmth of her spare room duvet. *What would Ben do, if he found him here?*

He cleared his throat. "Sarah, there's something I need to tell you."

"Yes?" Her hands rested on his arms. Her face was flushed and pupils dilated.

He shook his head. "Nothing," he said. "I'll tell you later. Let's investigate that boat."

She frowned. "Are you sure?"

He nodded. She started towards the boat, pulling him along, her hand still clasped in his.

Ruth paused in the yard, panting. Outside, a low morning sun was emerging over the hedge Sarah and Martin had escaped through yesterday.

She tossed options around in her head. She could follow Sarah's escape route, run round the side of the outhouse and squeeze through the hedge. But there was a good chance Robert and his men had blocked off that escape route now.

She could run across the fields. But she'd be more vulnerable on open ground. Maybe she could skirt the farmhouse; head for the coast that way. If Ted and Harry had made it this far, they must have brought a boat. And there would be others with them. Maybe Ben. They would be near the beach, hiding or guarding the boat. She looked back at the outhouse and sighed. *Ted and Harry*. She couldn't leave without them. And three of them stood a better chance in a fight.

Which left only one course of action.

She darted across the farmyard, keeping watch for any sign of the men. The yard was quiet. A magpie was clattering its morning call somewhere in the hedge and she could hear the pigs snuffling in their sty. Beyond the stench of the toilet, the warm aroma of coffee floated from the kitchen door. The doorway itself was dark, with no movement or sounds.

She slowed as she reached the door and shot a quick glance inside, pulling her head back quickly. Empty. A rough pile of dirty dishes was piled up in the sink.

She risked taking a step inside and reached an arm around the back of the door, groping for the keys. Hoping that this was a spare set, as well as the one that hung from Robert's belt.

Cold metal brushed her fingers and she closed her eyes in relief. She eased the keys off the hook, palming them so they wouldn't jangle.

"Get back here, you bitch!"

She looked round to see Robert stumbling from the outhouse, his face red. She'd done him more damage than she thought.

Good.

The only way was forwards. She stepped into the kitchen, scanning for a hiding place. Nothing.

The door on the other side of the room was closed but wouldn't be locked. She thundered towards it and threw it open, hoping there was no one on the other side.

There wasn't.

She took a deep, whistling breath, her senses sharp. Behind her, in the yard, she could hear Robert calling for help. She had to hope that all of the men were out working, or that anyone still inside wouldn't hear his strangled cries.

In front of her was a dingy hallway, brown patches seeping up the walls. And a door. The house's front door, which led to the beach. To safety. To Ben...

She carried on running and slammed into the door, yanking its handle. It was locked.

She leaned back and tugged, muttering under her breath. Behind her, Robert's voice was joined by the shouts of other men.

She opened her hand and studied the keys. The skin of

her palm was patterned with the white imprints of the sharp metal.

Six keys. Which one matched this door? She grabbed one at random and fumbled it into the lock, her fingers shaking. It didn't budge.

She glanced round to see that the kitchen had darkened. The silhouetted figure of a man was in the doorway, blocking the light.

There wasn't time to try them all.

She threw herself at the staircase behind her, grabbing the balustrade and swinging herself round. The stairs were uncarpeted and her clattering steps reverberated around the house, but that was the least of her worries now.

At the top of the stairs she paused, glad that she'd paid attention last time she was here. Ahead of her were bedrooms, inhabited by some of the men. At the far end of the hallway, overlooking that hedge, was a stinking bathroom and a separate toilet, both of which she'd had the pleasure of cleaning yesterday. Behind her was another hallway and more bedrooms, unused rooms that still smelt of damp. Through one of those was a small doorway leading to more stairs and an attic room.

She had two options. The furthest from her pursuers was that attic room, full of junk she could hide behind. She squeezed her eyes shut, trying to remember if there was a lock on that door. Nothing came to her.

The other option was the toilet. It did have a lock, a flimsy thing high up on the doorframe, easily broken. But it would give her time.

The toilet it was. She slowed her pace and crept along the hallway, hoping the men downstairs wouldn't hear. Below her, doors were being thrown open and the men were calling to each other between rooms.

Then she heard it: the creak of a foot on the bottom stair.

She forced herself to stay quiet and not break into a run. The beating of her heart, loud in her ears, was accompanied by the wooden creak of weight on the staircase behind her.

When she reached the toilet, she shut the door behind her and slid the bolt, then slumped down on the toilet lid to catch her breath. As the air hit her lungs the room blurred and swayed. Sparkling lights danced like dust captured in sunlight.

She blinked three times and bowed her head, her hands on her knees. She didn't have time for this. Pushing away the dizziness, she stood and turned to kneel on the toilet lid, exploring the window frame with her hands.

"What are you doing?"

She froze, then relaxed as she realised the voice was muffled by the locked door.

"Shut up! I don't want her hearing us."

Too late, she thought, as she returned to the window. One pane of glass was cracked but even if she broke it, she couldn't squeeze through. She had to open it.

She pushed at the wood. The frame was warped and reluctant to move, but she managed to shift it a little, jolting the bottom part of the sash window upwards. The gap was big enough to reach through and get purchase against the bottom of the frame. The air outside warmed her fingertips and made her heart race.

The door behind her rattled as it caught on the lock. There was a pause then a thud as her pursuer leaned into it.

She turned and stared, watching the flimsy lock rattling. She tensed.

Robert's voice came through the door, making her turn cold.

"I know you're in there, my dear."

CHAPTER TWENTY-SEVEN

MARTIN STUMBLED AFTER SARAH, WATCHING HER RACE across the sand towards the silhouetted boat. Her hair flew out behind her .

The first time Sarah had seen him had been in that cell, he was sure. No flicker of recognition had passed over her face when he'd entered, no clue that she might have seen him before.

In the boat – that boat she was running towards right now – she had been unconscious. And he had been gripped by horror at what he'd done.

He paused for breath, scanning the beach for people. If that was the villagers' boat, it meant they had retrieved it somehow, or it had washed back to shore. That it had still been seaworthy. And that they'd sent out a rescue party. At least one of Jess and Ben would be in that party. Possibly both of them. Possibly Colin and Sanjeev too.

He dropped to the ground, ignoring Sarah's cries to keep up, scrutinising the beach and dunes behind. The sand itself was deserted, but there were patches of rough vegetation inland behind which a person could hide, as well as mounds of sand, sculpted by the tides. And the boat. Who could say they wouldn't be behind that, poised for an ambush?

Sarah was on the edge of the shallows now, her shoes dangling from her fingertips. A braver man, a more honest man, would be out there with her, prepared to face whatever was coming for him.

Could he be that man?

At the sound of Robert's voice, Ruth felt her heart squeeze. No longer needing to be quiet, she heaved at the window frame with all her weight, grimacing as the strain shuddered through her wrists and elbows.

On the first heave it budged an inch or so, dislodging a few dry flakes that sprinkled the black toilet lid. She pushed again and almost fell out as the window shuddered upwards, the sound reverberating in the tight space.

"What are you doing in there? Get out here, right now!"

She ignored him and leaned forward to push the window up as far as it would go. The frame shook and splinters of glass broke free, plummeting to the ground below.

The top pane held a single jagged shard of glass, piercing the space she needed to push herself through.

"There's nowhere for you to go, you know."

There was a splintering sound behind her as the door was pushed against the lock. She glanced back to see the wood around the handle crack but not give way. Yet.

She yanked off her grimy t-shirt and wrapped her hand in it. She pulled the tightest fist she could and punched the remaining glass, close to the frame. It came away whole, sailing down to shatter on the pockmarked tarmac below.

She stuck her head out to check her landing site. Below her, shards of glass were strewn across a rough path that bordered the side of the house. Beyond that, about four feet away, was the hedge. It was tall here, almost at the level of the window.

"Now!" There was a cry behind her as the door shook once again. The lock was almost gone: two of the screws holding it in place had flown off and it would only need one more heave.

Biting her tongue, she pulled herself onto the top of the cistern and pushed her legs through the window frame. She hunched her shoulders and squeezed her upper body through, hooking her arms around the frame at the sides, her palms flat on the wall.

She looked down but instantly regretted it. Her head swimming, she looked back up towards the horizon. Beyond the hedge were fields and ditches, interspersed with patches of water that sparkled in the sunlight. To her right, past the front of the house, was a neglected road, the remains of a stile, and a ridged field, maybe one that the men cultivated.

And beyond that were the low hummocks of sand dunes, the flat, dark beach and the shimmering beauty of the sea.

Moving across the field were dark human shapes.

Four men, about to thwart her attempt at escape.

A crash echoed behind her as the door finally gave way, followed by breathless shouting and recriminations.

"Get down, now!" Robert screamed.

She took a deep breath and found a target in the hedge, about two thirds of the way up. As she steeled herself to jump she took one last look at the figures in the field.

One of them was watching her, hand lifted to shield their eyes. There was something about the silhouette... *Was that a woman?*

Ben was woken by insistent knocking on his front door. He fumbled for the T-shirt he'd dropped on the floor the previous night.

Yanking it over his head and glancing at the boys' closed door, he shuffled downstairs.

"Alright, it's alright," he muttered, yanking his keys off the hook next to the door. "I'm coming."

He opened the door to a bright, sunlit morning, and threw an arm to his face to ward off the glare. In front of him was Colin. His face was red and glistening.

Ben took a deep breath. *News of Ruth?*

"Colin. What is it?"

Colin spotted the hope in Ben's eyes. He shook his head.

"Not what you think, Ben. Sorry."

Ben's shoulders slumped.

Colin looked at his watch. "Sorry to wake you. You're normally up by now."

Ben shrugged, aware of the mist of sleep and despair that had settled over him. Last night he had sat up late poring through the few photos of Ruth that he owned, gorging himself on her image. Before that he'd taken the boys out to the beach for a dusk game of rounders, then treated them to chocolate from the village shop on the way home, Ruth's keys heavy in his pocket.

"Sorry," he sighed. "There doesn't seem much point. But what's with the pounding on my door?"

Colin's face dropped. "We've had another visit."

Ben felt a chill wash over him.

"What do you mean? Is it the men? Who's—?"

He looked past Colin into the square, expecting to see agitated villagers. But there was nothing. Every house had their door closed despite the brightness of the day and there was a heavy silence.

Colin shook his head. "No, not that." He coughed. "Come with me."

Martin shook himself out and pushed up to his feet, sprinting after Sarah. He had to face whatever was coming to him.

As he reached the boat, panting, she was already exploring it. There was nobody hidden in or behind it, no assailants waiting to spring on him.

She was inside the boat now, opening hatches and looking for clues.

"This is the village boat alright," she said, her eyes shining. "But there's nothing to show who brought it here."

She continued rummaging through coiled ropes and neat boxes of supplies, before giving up and slumping onto the bench seat at the boat's rear. He climbed on board and sat down too, looking around the empty boat. Remembering the last time he'd been in it.

He took a deep breath.

"There is a chance it wasn't brought here by the village," he muttered.

"What d'you mean? How can anyone else have—" Her hand shot up to her cheek. "Oh." She looked at him. "Do you think the men brought it? That they stole it?" Her face was creasing now, a dimple forming in her chin.

He took a shaky breath. "How much do you remember of when you were brought here?" he asked, trying to keep his voice steady. "Of when... they took you?"

She stared at him. "Nothing," she replied. "I was out looking for Benjy – my cat – and then suddenly I felt hands on me from behind, then... nothing. The next thing I knew I was in that stinking cell." Her voice went quiet. "With Robert."

He shivered. She was twisting her hands together on her lap, staring at her fingers.

She looked up at him.

"Martin, is there anything you're not telling me? Do you know what happened?"

He held her gaze, resisting the urge to leap out of the boat and run.

She narrowed her eyes. "*Were you there?*"

Ben followed Colin to the boathouse, growing more and more puzzled. As they neared it he had a moment of panic.

"The boys! I left them in bed. On their own, in the house."

Colin looked at Ben, sighing with exasperation.

"Oh, Christ." He licked his cracked lips. "Right, let's make this quick."

Ben stopped in his tracks. "But what if they—?"

Colin sighed again. Then he looked towards the boathouse and his face darkened.

"OK," he said. "You're right. I'll run back and get Sheila. Stay here."

Ben's objections hung in the air as Colin ran off. He watched him head back to the houses, puzzled. He'd never seen Colin run before. And he'd certainly never seen him behave so oddly.

As Colin disappeared between the houses, Ben shook the sand off his shoes and turned to the boathouse. The sun might be out but there was still a chill in the air. He shuffled towards the shelter of the building, feeling last night's bottle of whisky pulling at his limbs.

As he approached the building the rear door opened and he froze. Colin hadn't told him to expect anyone.

He darted to the side of the path, trying to flatten himself against the hedge. But at six foot four he couldn't use a low gorse hedge to conceal himself.

A man backed out of the door, locking it behind him.

He breathed a sigh of relief. It was Clyde, probably checking on the supplies inside.

He peeled himself away from the hedge, relieved Clyde hadn't witnessed his foolishness, and strode towards him, raising a hand.

"Clyde," he said, "Hi there. What's going on with Colin?"

Clyde stiffened, the key still in the lock, then turned. His face was thunder.

"Ben," he said. "What the hell is going on?"

Ruth ran across the road, picking bits of greenery out of her hair and straightening the T-shirt she'd thrown back on as soon as she'd regained her balance. Her arms and chest were covered in scratches. It would smart later but there were no serious injuries.

The road was empty and there was no sign of the people from the field; maybe they'd headed into the house. But that woman watching her so intently, surely she'd have worked out where Ruth was going, known where to look for her?

She crashed into the wall separating the road from the field, wincing as her knee dragged on the rough brickwork. She crouched on the grass, poking a finger through the tear that had formed in her jeans, then regretting it as a jolt of pain shot through her knee. She was overwhelmed by a desire to stop , to give up – to lie down on this grass verge and let the day wash over her.

She looked back at the farmhouse, its windows dark against the glare of the sun, and imagined Robert's reaction as he saw her disappear out of the window. She smiled. But she had to keep moving.

A short distance away, there was a gate leading onto the field. It was either that or chance her luck on the road. If the men had transport, they would easily catch her that way. Across the fields, it would be more difficult – for her, but for them, too. And beyond the fields, lay the sea.

She paused, listening. The air was still, only the distant hum of the sea for company. She shook her head and heaved herself up to standing.

Cautiously, she peered over the wall. A pair of eyes gazed back at her. A face split into a smile.

This wasn't one of her captors.

PART THREE

CHAPTER TWENTY-EIGHT

MARTIN STARED AT SARAH, UNABLE TO REPLY.

"Were you? Did you come to our village?" Her eyes narrowed. "Tell me, Martin."

He opened his mouth to speak but nothing came out. She threw a glance over his shoulder, scanning the beach.

"Is this a set up? Are they following us now?"

"No. I—" he stammered.

"Why did you kidnap me, only to rescue me again?"

She pushed past him and scanned the beach. He put a hand on her shoulder.

"Leave me alone!" she hissed. "You're leading them here, aren't you? Lulling me into a false sense of security then springing me just as I thought I was safe."

"No. That's not it at all." He licked his lips.

She pulled back, her face twisted in horror.

"What were you going to do to me, in that hut?"

He stepped forward. She flinched and threw a punch at him, hitting him on the jaw. He gasped but did nothing to retaliate. He spread out his hands, desperate for her to listen to him.

"Leave me alone, you lying – you lying – you liar!" She ran past him down the beach, towards the hut. He watched as she sped along the sand, trying not to trip on her full skirt each time she threw a terrified look over her shoulder. He could hear the thwack of her bare feet on the sand and the whimpering of her voice, rising and falling each time she looked back.

He stood helpless for a few moments, torn between letting her go and running to catch up, to explain himself. Dragging in a trembling breath, he raced towards her across the sand, calling her name.

"Sarah, please! I can explain!"

But it was useless. His words were whipped away by the wind.

She continued running, her skirt gathered in one hand now and her bare legs pumping across the beach. When she reached the dunes she stopped, looking between the fields beyond and the two huts – three if you counted the far one with no roof and a missing wall. He didn't break stride, thundering across the sand towards her, muttering under his breath, rehearsing what he would say when he caught up with her. He wasn't sure the words existed that would convince her to forgive him.

Spotting him, she headed onto the scrubby grass behind her. His laboured breath and pounding heart rushed through his head. He willed himself to keep going, to speed up.

Running like this was something he had only needed to do a few times since leaving his first pursuer, his father, in their flooded house.

A few steps into the dunes she paused and bent to grab her foot. He remembered her shoes, placed together on the damp sand next to the boat. She looked back at him and put her foot down, stumbling. She pulled herself up and started moving through the dunes again, her earlier sprint reduced to a hobble.

He slowed a little. Catching up with her was a certainty now. The huts were little more than a few strides away and she wasn't far past them. But he couldn't hurl himself at her like this.

When he reached the huts he paused, jogging on the spot. "Please! I can explain, I promise!"

She turned and cried out as she lost her footing and stumbled to the ground. He resisted the urge to run after her, to help her up. Instead he sat on the ground, close enough for her to hear him but not so close that he could rush her.

"I'm sorry. I really am. Yes, I was at your village. I was involved in taking you, but it was someone else who grabbed you." He took a deep breath, placing a hand to his pounding chest. "But I regret it. I wish I'd never gone along with it."

She sat cross-legged, cradling her foot in her hand.

"I want to make it right," he called across the dunes. "I want to help you get back to your village. You, and Ruth, and the others."

"Others?" Her eyes were wide; she stopped massaging her foot. "What others?"

Clyde stood with his back to the boathouse, staring at Ben. Damp patches of sweat soaked his T-shirt. Tight-lipped, he opened his eyes wide, daring Ben to reply.

Ben shrugged. "Clyde. I've got no idea what you're on about. Colin told me to come here—"

"Colin?" Clyde placed his fists on his hips. Behind him, a mountain bike lay next to the boathouse, its back wheel spinning in the breeze. *Whose?*

"Clyde! I didn't know you were here." Colin ran up behind Ben, panting. He put a hand on Ben's shoulder. "The boys are fine, Ben. Still asleep. Sheila's at your house."

Clyde didn't move. "Colin. Does this have anything to do

with you?" he asked. His voice was rough and he was clearly trying not to shout.

Colin took his hand off Ben's shoulder and pushed past him. "What? Does what have to do with me?"

Clyde waved a hand back at the building. "The boy, Colin. The boy in the boat house."

Ben frowned. "What boy?"

He weighed the possibilities. *Martin?*

Colin took a deep breath. "He's one of the yobs that were here the other day. The ones in the playground. The ones that tried to take the boat."

Ben stepped forward. "So it's not Martin?" he asked.

Colin turned back to him, sighing. "No, Ben. Not Martin. The boys that hurt young Rory Stewart. Remember them?"

Ben nodded, irritated at Colin's tone. "But what's he doing in the boat house?"

Clyde stepped forward. "He's imprisoned in there. Tied up."

Ben felt lightheaded. "What?"

Colin turned to him, his voice calm. "We found him. Attacking a girl. Roisin Murray's little sister, to be precise. He needs to be punished."

"Hang on a minute," Ben said, raising a hand to his forehead. "You found this kid attacking a girl so you brought him in here and locked him up? Just you, Colin?"

Colin shook his head. "I had help."

"Who?" Ben asked. Since when did individual council members take the law into their own hands? Since when did Colin, of all people, ignore the law?

Colin shook his head again. "No one you need trouble yourself with. We've had enough trouble from outsiders these past days. It's time we fought back."

"Fought back?" Clyde stepped towards Colin, his nostrils flaring. "And what d'you think's gonna happen to us if we do that, eh? If the people up the coast get wind that we're imprisoning their kids? If they tell the police?" He jabbed at Colin's shoulder. "You think we'll be allowed to stay here with this sort of thing going on?"

Colin shrugged, blushing. "I don't know. I guess I – I just snapped."

Ben tried to compose himself, looking between the other two men. A muffled shout came from the boat house. He shuddered, glancing at Clyde.

"OK, Colin," Ben said. "I know this sort of thing's hard for you, after what happened to your brother." Colin had started his journey to the village with his younger brother. But after a confrontation with some pumped up kids – kids just like this one – the brother had been left behind. Ben didn't know why, but he had his theories.

Colin glared at him. He raised a hand. "Sorry. But look, tell us what happened. Where did you find this kid?"

Colin relaxed a little, smoothing his hands down his trousers. He let out a long, rattling breath; Ben hadn't noticed that before. "Behind the boat house here. He was with Sinead. He'd grabbed her, I think. If I hadn't got here when I did, I don't know what would have happened..." He tailed off, casting his eyes down at the ground.

"So where's she now? Sinead?" asked Ben.

"She ran off. She's with her family, I hope."

"So do I," said Ben. "Look, Colin, I think you should be away from this boy before you do any more harm. Why don't you go back to the village and check that she got home safely? Give her parents some sort of explanation?"

"But—"

He raised a hand. "No. I don't think you're in a position to argue right now. Don't tell them we've got the boy. We can think of what we're going to tell the village later. Just reassure them, see if she'll tell you what happened."

Colin sighed and nodded, shuffling towards the village. He glared at Clyde as he passed. "He should be punished."

Ben closed his eyes and prayed for strength. They watched Colin retreat in silence. Ben knew his cheeks were flushed. But it felt good to take charge again.

When Colin's footsteps had been swallowed up by the wind, Ben turned to Clyde.

"Well?" said Clyde.

"Well, what?"

"What are we going to do about him?"

Ben drew in a long breath, thinking of Robert and what he might be doing to Ruth. Of this boy, a younger version of Robert. *What would I have done, if I'd had the chance to change his ways years ago?*

The walk from Withernsea hadn't been an easy one. Wary of the open shoreline, they'd picked their way through a maze of narrow lanes alongside waterlogged, impregnable hedgerows. By the time they came upon the farmhouse and the cultivated field in front of it, Jess's feet had been aching and her calves tight.

They crouched in the tangled hedge separating the field from the dunes, hissing plans and questions to each other. Jess longed to look over the hedge but couldn't shake off a nagging dread that someone would be on the other side, listening. The sea was calm now and she could hear birds singing further along the hedgerow.

They decided to risk crossing the field, keeping low and making fast, quiet progress. When she was near to the wall on the far side she spotted movement in a side window of the house.

She waved at Sanjeev and Toni behind her.

"Look up there," she hissed, raising a finger. They stopped moving.

A rattling sound came from a small window at the side of the house, following by scrapes and squeaks as it grated its way open, a slender arm – a woman's? – pushing it up. Jess watched, open-mouthed.

First one leg and then another emerged, as the figure started to climb out. Jess's heart picked up its pace. That was an adult up there. And someone heaving themselves feet first out of an upstairs window could only be attempting one thing. Escape.

When a head appeared she gasped and shot a hand out to grasp Toni's shoulder.

Ruth. It was Ruth.

She watched as Ruth cast her eyes about the landscape; waited for her to jump. When the figure finally threw herself into the air, Jess held her breath. There were muffled shouts as Ruth hit the hedge and tumbled down it, the sound of her body dragging against the branches unmistakeable.

Then there was silence. Jess ducked down next to the wall and the others followed suit. She paused to catch her breath then raised her head to see over the wall. There was shouting coming from inside the house but the windows were dark and the door closed.

Then as if from nowhere, Ruth's face appeared right in front of her. It was all she could do to keep herself from crying out with joy.

Ruth was less guarded. "Jess!" she cried, and burst into noisy tears.

Jess looked past her at the farmhouse: more shouts, and banging from behind that door. She beamed at Ruth.

"Oh my god! Am I glad to see you! Get over here, quick."

Ruth nodded and heaved herself over the wall, Jess dragging her body across the rough brickwork. The two of them tumbled onto the ground, clasping each other. Ruth was shaking, tears shuddering through her body. She pulled back and covered Jess's face in kisses.

"Thank you, thank you!" she cried. "I knew you'd come for me."

Toni and were at Jess's back now, Sanjeev patting Ruth's arm over Jess's shoulder. Zack stood behind, half crouching, eyes roaming over their surroundings.

Ruth leaned back, grasping Jess's arms and shaking her. Smiling. She looked around the group and was rewarded with smiles and whispered greetings. Then she paused, her face pale.

"Where's Ben?" she asked.

Jess felt her stomach tighten. There wasn't time to explain. "He's at home, with the boys."

Ruth frowned. "No," she muttered. "Why didn't he come? Why didn't he come for me?"

Jess tightened her grip but Ruth pulled away. "I want Ben," she snapped.

Jess sighed. "I'm sorry. The boys needed him. We came for you." She smiled at Ruth, confused. Expecting more gratitude.

Tears brimmed in Ruth's eyes. "Sean and Ollie! Oh thank god! Are they missing me?"

Jess nodded vigorously. "They can't wait to see you," she replied, blinking back her own tears.

Ruth wiped the back of her hand across her face. She was covered in scratches, and bits of hedge littered her hair. She smelt of greenery mixed with the mustiness of the unwashed.

"Is Ben OK?" she asked.

Jess nodded. "Yes," she lied. "He's fine."

"Did they—?"

"Who?" Jess looked back at the farmhouse. "Oh. No. The

men didn't do anything to Ben. Or to the boys. They're OK, Ruth."

Another nod. Jess licked her lips.

"I'm so sorry."

Ruth took a deep breath. Behind her, Jess could feel the group's tension.

"It's not your fault," Ruth said.

A lump rose in Jess's throat, thinking of the night they'd rescued the men. Her second night as steward. She shook her head.

Ruth cleared her throat. "Have you seen Sarah?" she asked.

Jess frowned. "Sarah?"

Another nod. "She escaped. Yesterday." A pause. "With Martin."

"Martin?" Jess frowned, puzzled. Worried. Ruth nodded again.

"Yes. They went through a gap in the hedge, the other side of the farm." She pointed back in the direction of the farm building. "They must have gone another way."

"What about Sally and Roisin?" Jess asked, hearing Mark cough behind her. "Did you see them? Are they still in there?"

Ruth looked surprised. "Sally and Roisin? Sorry? Surely you mean Harry and Ted?"

Jess's stomach lurched. "You've seen them?"

"They were in the cell next to me. Sarah's cell. I should have got them out, too." Her voice was quiet. She opened her hand to reveal a set of keys nestled in her palm. Jess looked down at them, marvelling at her sister-in-law.

"You've got *keys*?" she gasped.

Ruth nodded. "I didn't know about Sally and Roisin. Sorry. I just saw Sarah and Martin, and heard Ted and Harry come in this morning. Were they with you?"

Jess stiffened. "No. But that doesn't matter now." She

remembered her promise to Ben. "Look, Ruth, we need to find somewhere safe to shelter and plan our next move. Now that we know where they are – and that you have those keys – we have the upper hand. But we don't want to waste it."

Ruth looked back at the house. "Aren't you going to go straight in there and get them?"

Jess put a hand on Ruth's arm. "It isn't as easy as that. We need to be able to get away. All of us. We have no idea if anyone's injured."

Ruth looked at her. For the first time, Jess noticed a yellowing bruise on her cheek.

"Did they hurt you?"

Ruth closed her eyes. "I don't want to talk about it."

Jess pursed her lips, not pressing her.

Ruth took a deep breath. "Jess," she whispered. "Did Ben know them? The man called Robert? Did he do something to him?"

CHAPTER TWENTY-NINE

After his first encounter with Robert in detention, Ben had started to drift away from his loose group of school friends, spending more and more time with his new pal. Over time, a couple of the others had followed him, becoming part of Robert's group without anything ever being acknowledged. Bored by looming exams and the inevitable futile search for a job, he'd neglected his studies and started to miss the odd day, not enough to get him into trouble with Sonia but enough to provide the thrill of rebellion.

At first they'd hung around the local shopping centre, whistling at passing girls and muttering amongst themselves on benches, laughing at the glares they got from adults. Jayden, one of the boys who had transferred groups with him, had a good line in impressions and he would mimic the people who passed them once they were safely out of earshot, mincing past the bench, contorting his face into hilarious expressions and adopting imagined voices that make the boys collapse into a pile of laughter and gangly limbs.

As exams drew closer the new group shrank again, leaving just him and Robert. Robert had no intention of getting any qualifications and skipped every day of GCSEs, but Ben was too cowed by Sonia's nagging and too worried about his future to risk missing them. But on those days when he had no exams in the afternoon he would join Robert for a celebratory rampage around town, relief at getting through one more exam making him throw caution to the wind and risk shoplifting in the shopping centre or trespassing on the railway lines to daub obscene graffiti for the entertainment of the evening's commuters.

On the day of his last exam, he careered out of school. Robert was watching from the other side of the street, standing in the shadow of a tree.

Ben sped across the road towards him, ignoring the shouts of the boys behind, inviting him to join them in the pub. He grinned as he approached his friend. An afternoon in the Dog and Duck was tempting, but he hadn't brought a change of clothes and knew he wouldn't get served in his uniform. So when Robert raised an eyebrow and turned to lead him along the street, he followed.

He found himself tripping over his feet to keep up with Robert's determined stride. When Robert suddenly came to a halt, he crashed into him, nearly sending the two of them tumbling to the pavement.

"Stop it!" hissed Robert. "Don't be a dumbass." Robert was into Americanisms, that week.

Ben mumbled an apology then looked around. They were on the edge of an industrial estate about two miles from the school. A single road snaked its way up a low hill, with feeder roads leading off. At the far end was a high fence with electric wire buzzing across the top. As a kid he'd come here often, riding his bike around the quiet, unkempt roads and cycling away as fast as he could every time someone called hello from the units that flanked his makeshift racetrack. At the far end was an open area where trucks loaded up mornings and evenings. This was a great place to practise tricks, twirling his bike on the tarmac to get up enough speed to lift his wheels off the ground. At the weekends, when there were no cars, he'd arranged makeshift ramps, dragging sheets of metal and abandoned planks of wood into piles and whooping in delight as his bike flew through the air.

Today was a Friday and the place was starting to empty. Robert pulled him into a ditch behind a litter-strewn hedge and put a finger to his mouth as they watched workers leave one by one in their cars, calling to each other to enjoy their weekends. *Fat chance*, thought Ben. These idiots would all be heading home to identical boxes with screaming kids and nagging partners, the prospect of a football match or film on TV the greatest excitement the weekend had to offer. He thought of himself in the same place in ten years' time, shackled by a job and family, and shuddered.

"OK," whispered Robert. By now there were just a few scattered cars left: shift workers, security guards or keen bosses staying on late, hands in the till maybe. "You see that unit up there? With the red sign on the roof?"

Ben followed Robert's finger. At the far end of one of the short, dead end roads that flanked the main drag was a unit two or three times bigger than most, with a large red sign dominating its roof. *Arley Logistics*.

Ben nodded, hearing his heart thumping against the quiet of the afternoon.

Robert threw him a confident smile. "We're going to steal from it."

Ben's eyes widened. He looked back at the building: surely it would have a state of the art alarm, even a security guard. "Steal?" he breathed.

"Scared, are you?"

Ben shook his head. "But what if there's a guard? An alarm?"

Robert's smile grew. "Don't be stupid, dumbass." He gave Ben a gentle slap on the back of the head. Ben winced but smiled, knowing this was the expected response.

Robert looked towards the building again, his eyes narrow. "I've been watching it," he said. "There's one man in there at this time of day. All the others have headed home now, see?" He gave Ben a patronising smile and Ben nodded again. "He comes out at 4pm, obviously doesn't want to get home early to his adorable wife and kids. Can't blame him. But this is the best bit."

Robert lowered his head towards Ben so that their foreheads were touching. Ben could hear the two boys' breath mingling in the confined space behind the hedge.

Robert gave him another slap. "He comes out with a cash-box," Robert told him in a low voice. "Bold as brass, idiot. Carries it under his arm."

"Has it got cash in it?" Ben whispered.

"*Has it got cash in it?*" Robert mimicked. "Yes, of course it's got damn cash in it. It's a cash box." Another slap. Ben's head was starting to pound as much as his heart. "And we're going to take it from him. When he comes out we'll run up and grab it."

"But it can't be as simple as that, can it? To rob someone?"

"Let's see, shall we?" breathed Robert, nodding towards the building. Sure enough, a stocky man was emerging, his buttoned-up suit straining against his gut. Under his arm was a large red cash box, its colour echoing the sign on the roof.

Ben scanned the roads. Two cars sat outside nearby units, but there was no sign of life. "What about those cars?" he asked. "What if someone comes out?"

Robert grabbed his arm, pinching the skin under his blazer. "Don't be stupid," he said. "I've been doing my research. Casing the joint. They won't come out for ages."

Ben swallowed.

"Time to go, coward. Now!" Robert hissed, tightening his grip on Ben's arm and heaving him up to standing, pushing him through a gap in the hedge. Dragging him across the concrete towards the man.

Ben stumbled on a broken patch of road, loosening Robert's grip on him. Robert scrabbled to catch hold of his blazer but Ben fell backwards, landing on his back. He felt a jolt through his head as it slammed into the concrete.

He closed his eyes. Behind his eyelids the world was orangey-red, like a sunset. He could hear ringing in his ears and feel the hard scratch of gravel on his neck. When he opened his eyes there was nothing except a bright patch of blue sky above him.

There was a shout in the distance. "Hurry up, dumbass!"

He eased himself upwards, fighting nausea. He managed to prop up on his elbows and, blinking, saw Robert running away from him, towards the man. The man had stopped. Ben could hear shouting but couldn't make out the words.

The world went quiet. He let his head fall back. Above him was the sky again, flanked by the low branches of a tree. Somewhere, a bird sang. So at least his ears still worked.

He rolled onto his front and pushed himself up, rubbing at the back of his neck. He turned to face the spot where he'd last seen Robert, and the man beyond him. He blinked, struggling to focus in the sunlight.

He gasped. Across the brown space, nearly at the door of the unit, was a hunched figure standing over another shape lying prone on the ground.

Stumbling, he advanced towards the two figures, whose forms merged and separated in front of his swimming vision. As he drew closer, he recognised Robert's face turned towards him. Robert was standing over the man, the cashbox blown open on the floor next to them, notes and coins scattered across the ground.

The man was still, his limbs splayed out in a way that made Ben want to heave. Spreading across the concrete around him was a dark patch. The man's face was turned towards him, his neck bent back at an unnatural angle. His mouth hung open.

He let his gaze move back up towards Robert, slowly taking in the hunched form. Robert bent over the man, one arm extended. In his hand, a knife glinted. The sleeve of Robert's denim jacket was torn but it was patched with darkness too, darkness that looked too much like the pool of black on the ground.

"Hey! What's going on?"

A woman was running out of a print works. The woman advanced on Robert. She wore ink-flecked jeans and a dark shirt with a rainbow logo on the chest pocket.

As the woman approached, Robert turned on her, snarling. She froze, staring at him. Not breaking eye contact, she pulled a mobile phone from her trouser pocket and lifted it to her ear.

Robert turned to him and dropped the knife. "Ben!" he called, his voice suddenly that of a boy.

Ben turned towards the entrance to the estate. And ran.

Martin approached Sarah as she rubbed her foot. He swallowed the lump that was rising in his throat.

"Don't come near me," she snapped, her eyes slits. She dragged a hand across her face and took a breath.

He stopped at the edge of the sand, looking across the beginnings of the scrubby dunes towards her.

"Sorry," he muttered. Behind him a seagull cawed out a greeting which was echoed by another.

"What others?" she repeated. "What else haven't you told me?"

He sighed, lowering himself to the ground. He knelt, ignoring the damp of the sand through his trousers. His face was level with hers. "There were – are – two other women, as well as you and Ruth. I don't know their names. But they were taken at the same time as you, from your village."

"Were they in the other rooms? In that outhouse?"

He nodded.

"How come I never saw them then? Never heard them?"

He shrugged. He hadn't seen the other two women since leaving the boat, and could only assume that they'd not been let out of their cells, or that he hadn't been around when they had. He closed his eyes, imagining what they might be going through back there. What Robert's reaction to Sarah's escape might be, and how he could take it out on the others.

"We have to go back for them," she announced, pulling herself up, wincing as her weight fell onto her foot. He reached out as she stumbled.

She glared. "Don't touch me."

"Sorry."

"Where do they keep the keys? How are we going to get them all out?"

He sat back on the sand, its cold seeping through his torn jeans.

"I don't know whether that's such a—"

"What are you, some sort of coward?"

He frowned. "No, I just—"

A heavy spot of rain landed on his arm. He looked up to see that the sky had clouded over. Dark dots clustered on the sand, growing to become wet patches.

"We can't go now," he said, standing up. "Let's shelter in the hut."

She looked from him to the huts. The rain was starting to

soak through her shirt. She gathered her arms around herself and nodded.

“OK,” she said. “But only until the rain stops.”

He nodded and started running for the hut, the sludgy sand trying to swallow his feet. He turned to see that she was struggling. He went back to her.

“You’re not going anywhere on that foot,” he said. “Let me help you. Please.”

She scrunched her face up then nodded tersely, reaching up to him. She let him take her weight as they hobbled towards the hut, the rain turning to hail.

CHAPTER THIRTY

Jess held her breath. Behind her, Toni's breathing had slowed.

"They knew each other," Jess whispered. "At school."

Ruth's face turned grey. "And? What did Ben do to Robert? He hates him, you know."

Jess sighed. "I don't know all the details. Ben didn't..." She raked her fingers through her hair, cursing the younger version of her brother. "Look, we need to get you home. Get the others home. I think it's for Ben to tell you about Robert." Ruth said nothing. "Ruth?"

A nod. But Ruth had stopped smiling. "OK. So what do we do now?" she asked.

Jess looked back at the farmhouse, then at the keys in Ruth's outstretched hands. *We'll send word*, she'd promised. Ben would be worrying. And Sarah was out there somewhere, with Martin...

"It is tempting to go straight in there, get the others out," she said.

Ruth's face brightened. "Before the men come back!"

Toni was at Jess's back, a hand on her shoulder. It was cold, even through the woollen jacket.

"Bad idea," she muttered. "We shouldn't go in there without some sort of a plan. And we promised we'd send back word."

Sanjeev approached them, panting. His eyes flitted between her and Ruth, the house, and the beach beyond the field.

"Ted and Harry are here," he said. "That means the boat. We need to secure it. Get some rest, think about what to do next."

Jess sighed. "You're right," she said, as Zack came running up behind her. She hadn't noticed that he'd gone.

"Huts," he panted. "There are huts, at the beach. We can shelter there."

Jess nodded, looking past him along the rough field.

"We have to move fast." Ruth was staring back at the house, shivering. Four men came around its side, heading for them. Robert, Bill, and two younger men Jess didn't recognise.

Jess grabbed Toni's arm, then Ruth's.

"There's no time," she snapped. "Run, now!"

The five of them turned and ran up the field, stumbling on the rutted ground. Zack was already halfway towards the beach. Jess let go of Ruth's arm and tried to imagine the field was an unsullied running track, to ignore the bumps in the soft earth.

Behind, there were angry voices; she pushed them out of her mind.

"Whoah!"

The men's shouts were drowned out by a sudden clap of thunder, followed by Sanjeev's cry. Not breaking stride, she scanned the sky. Up ahead, it was an inky blue-grey, smudged with rain clouds. Huge drops fell on her upturned face. Just ahead of her Ruth was running. The shower would do Ruth good. Jess hadn't had the heart to tell her how badly she smelled.

As she reached the end of the field, her feet growing heavy with mud, there was a cry from ahead, where Zack was at the beach.

"The huts!" he called. "And a boat!"

She felt her chest fill and bit her lip to suppress her own answering yell. Now she could send back word, to Ben. She could only hope the boat was in a seaworthy state, and that the rain would let up.

She risked a look behind her. The men were struggling across the field, sticking to the mud. She allowed herself a small smile then picked up her pace.

"Into the huts!" she cried, as Sanjeev reached the dunes with Toni. Zack was already on the beach, sprinting for the boat; she would leave him to inspect it. Next to her, Ruth was matching her pace, wheezing with the effort.

"We've made it," she gasped. They'd outrun the men.

Sarah huddled in a corner of the hut, flashing him wary glances. He hung back, not wanting to startle her, but desperate to explain himself.

She was breathing heavily, her cheeks flushed. She raised a fist to her nose and held it there as she sniffed, trying to compose herself. He waited for her to speak.

"OK," she breathed. "Tell me everything. How you took us. Who else is here. What you've done to the others."

"I haven't seen the others, I—"

"Stop lying to me!"

She was on her feet now, hands on her hips. "You were in the boat, weren't you? When you took us?"

He said nothing.

"Tell me, Martin," she pleaded, her voice cracking.

He swallowed the lump in his throat, and nodded.

"I'm sorry," he muttered.

She grasped at her hair. "I don't want to hear your puny apologies! Just tell me."

He closed his eyes and cast his mind over the events of the past few days. The fog in his head cleared as he understood what he had to tell her. *Robert*. She had to know about the hold Robert had over him, the type of man he was.

The first time Martin had clapped eyes on Robert, he had been lying on the cold concrete floor of a deserted car park somewhere outside Sheffield.

Looming grey shapes swam before his eyes, indistinct patches of blurry nothingness. He had no idea where he was. As he dragged himself into consciousness, he pieced together what he could remember.

He had been making his way north, in search of a place to live, maybe Scotland or the Pennines, away from the floods in the south and east. He wasn't sure how long he'd been on the road; two weeks at least. Two weeks in which he'd travelled not much more than he might have managed in two days back when public transport was functioning and the roads weren't blocked by water, police roadblocks or crowds of refugees.

He could remember a group of boys, around his own age, gathering in front of him in the roadway. He blinked, recalling their shimmering shapes with the sun at their backs. He squeezed his eyes shut to try to remember more but nothing came. Just rough, angry shouts and a sharp pain in the back of his head.

He lay still, knowing that his attackers could still be near. He could hear the sound of breathing nearby.

Wait, he told himself. *Take your time, get your bearings. Maybe then you can lash out, get away.*

He let his head slump back onto the tarmac, feeling the rough ground meet the spot on his head where he had been hit. His hair was matted and his skin cold. Was that blood he could taste? He moved the tip of his tongue around his mouth, feeling his teeth, making sure they were all there. All present and correct.

He resisted the urge to bring his hand to his face and check his jawbone. He tensed his jawline and moved the muscles a little. Everything still worked.

He took a few breaths, not too deep. His chest hurt with each rise and fall and there was a sharp pain under his ribs. Once he was confident he could breathe normally he let out a long slow breath through pursed lips.

"Wake up, my friend."

He stiffened. The voice was male, with a lightness that spoke of comfort and enough sleep, not of long days and nights on the road. He brought his arms up to his chest, ready to protect himself.

The man laughed. "You don't need to worry. You're safe now." He muttered something, but not at Martin. *How many other people are here?*

Martin opened his eyes. The man standing above him was lean, with three-day stubble and blue eyes. He wore a neat leather jacket over jeans and a white shirt.

Martin blinked, letting the surroundings come into focus. Past the man's shoulder, he could make out four more silhouettes. He pulled his arms up to protect himself, waiting for a repeat of the previous night.

"Don't hurt me, please," he whimpered.

The man put a hand on his chest and Martin flinched.

The man laughed. "I'm not going to hurt you, you fool." The stranger was smiling, his white teeth incongruous next to the stubble. *Could he believe him?*

"Come on, get up now. There's a good lad." The man grabbed his hand. Martin was too tired to resist. He allowed himself to be pulled up to standing. Groaning at the pain that seared through his body, he was led across the tarmac and lowered to sit in an abandoned car seat. He let himself melt into its comfort.

"So," said the man. "How d'you get here then?"

"I was beaten up," he murmured. "Must have been dumped here."

The man laughed. "Well, I can tell that. But who by? And why?"

Dread shot through Martin as he remembered the rucksack he'd been carrying, the cash he'd managed to steal two days after leaving his parents. He'd crept into an empty cottage at night and helped himself to food and more, leaving a note for the owners in his shame.

He scanned the car park: no sign of the rucksack. He slumped down into the seat.

"They took my stuff," he said. "Rucksack."

The man exhaled. "Ah. No surprise there then."

Martin nodded and closed his eyes. *What was he going to do now?*

The man crouched down so he was level with Martin. "I'm Robert," he said. "What's your name?"

"Martin."

"Where you from, Martin?"

"Down south. Near the coast. Nowhere you'd know."

He wondered what had happened to his parents, if they were still in that house. If they were still alive.

Robert nodded. "You got any skills?"

"I worked on a farm. Know my way around machinery, and livestock."

Another nod, slower now. "Good."

There was a pause. Martin's vision was clearing now and he could make out the other figures approaching. Men.

"Today's your lucky day," Robert told him, folding his arms across his chest. "We're looking for an empty farm to make our own. We'll need someone like you. Will you join us?"

Martin smiled, wincing. "Yes." What else was he supposed to do? He had no belongings and nowhere to go.

"Good. Now before we get moving we'll need to deal with those thugs who attacked you."

Robert held out an arm and some other men appeared, dragging a couple of boys over, their hands tied behind their backs. Martin's attackers.

Robert pulled a knife from his pocket and leaned in to the closer of the two boys, placing the blade against his cheek. He turned to Martin.

"Are these the ones that hit you?"

Martin blanched, staring at the boys. The one closest to Robert was whimpering and the other stared at the blade, his eyes wide. Martin smelt urine.

Robert was smiling at Martin now, twisting the knife gently against the boy's face. Firm enough to pucker the skin but not to pierce it. Martin swallowed hard.

He nodded.

"Good. Take them away, lads. Sort them out."

"No!" cried one of the boys. He was rewarded with a fist in his gut.

After a while, Martin heard screams from a way off, followed by silence. He shut his eyes. He was safe now, at least...

CHAPTER THIRTY-ONE

SARAH STARED AT HIM. HE HADN'T TOLD HER EVERYTHING, but maybe what he had said was too much. He moved towards her but she shook her head tightly and he pulled back.

"Look," he began, but was interrupted by a thud against the wall of the shed. He stepped over to the window. Outside was Sanjeev, with a man and woman he didn't recognise. They hadn't spotted him but were huddled by the door to the hut, the woman tugging on the handle. Sarah gasped and stood up.

"Who is it?" she asked.

He blinked. "The villagers. They've come for you," he said, his heart heavy.

Ben and Clyde stood outside the boathouse and watched as the boy sprinted off towards the beach, not so much as glancing back at them.

Clyde let out a long, whistling breath.

"Jesus," he said. "What on earth came over Colin? Has he

any idea what'd happen to us if the world knew we'd started locking up their kids?"

Ben continued watching the boy run. Beyond his retreating figure, the sea was changing colour, ominous breakers topping darkening waves. He glanced up at the sky, also growing dark. "Rain coming."

Clyde followed his gaze.

"Uh-huh," he grunted, folding his arms over his stomach. The boy skirted a sand dune, disappearing from view. "Let's just hope he's scared of getting into trouble," Clyde continued. "Then he won't tell anyone."

Ben's chest felt hollow.

Clyde shrugged and started for the boathouse.

"Let's get shelter, man," he said, then stopped.

The bike was still lying on the ground, its wheels spinning madly in the rising wind. Clyde leaned over and pulled it upright, facing the beach.

The two men looked from each other to the bike and back again. Ben had a flashback of flying along country lanes as a teenager, legs thrown out either side of the saddle as he passed under puddles of dappled sunlight that glittered down on him through overhanging branches.

"I'll put it in the boathouse," said Clyde. "Keep it dry."

Neither of them suggested who they would be keeping it dry for.

Ben shook his head. "It's not secure. I'll take it back to the village. We can store it in the hall."

"Fair enough. I'm getting indoors."

The rain was coming heavily, great spots of water peppering the sand.

Ben shivered as water tricked beneath his collar. Why hadn't he put on a coat? Ruth would have reminded him to.

"Best get back to the boys," he said, turning for the village. Clyde shrugged and headed for the boathouse.

He shook his feet to dry his shoes a little then mounted the bike. The sensation of riding it was both strange and immediately familiar, and made him feel brighter than he had in days. He allowed himself a smile as he sped to the village square, not caring that his shirt was plastered to his skin.

The square was deserted, with no lights showing from the windows. He hitched his sleeve up to see his watch: nine thirty. There would normally be people moving about now, getting on with their tasks for the day. But the rain hung over the village like a shroud. It bounced off puddles, splashing up over his shoes and soaking through his socks. He held his arm out and lifted his face to the sky, enjoying the cool of the rain on his cheeks.

A voice called his name. He glanced over at his house, expecting Sheila to be waiting for him in the doorway. But the building was dark, the upstairs curtains still drawn and no light showing through the window in the front door. No surprise: the power would be off at this time of day.

"Ben!"

There it was again, a woman's voice. His heart quickened. *Ruth?* He climbed off the bike, looking around.

"Ben, over here!" He turned to see Dawn standing in the front door of the Evans house, her body in shadow.

Dropping the bike and shaking himself, he ran towards her.

"Dawn!" he panted. "Sorry, I thought it was—"

She gave him a tight smile: she understood. He blushed and she pulled back into the house, beckoning him in. He hesitated, startled. He'd never been inside this house.

Inside, the layout was identical to his own but that was where the similarity ended. The only objects in the kitchen were a toaster and kettle. The sink was empty, with no waiting dishes, and there were none of the items pushed against the wall that there were at home: spice pots, old tin cans holding cooking utensils, a makeshift bread bin.

The living room was even more spartan. The only sign of human habitation was on the coffee table: a solitary mug and a book placed squarely next to it, its edge parallel with the table's edge and a bookmark peeking out.

She spotted him looking around and followed his gaze to the coffee table, blanching.

"Sorry about the mess," she muttered, swooping down to transfer the cup to the sink and the book to a nearby bookcase. On one shelf was a row of books, sorted alphabetically by author. No ornaments or photos. Nothing personal.

Her eyes darted around the room, searching for anything else out of place.

"Has there been any news?" she asked.

He frowned and shook his head. "Sorry."

Her shoulders slumped. "Oh."

He cleared his throat. "I'd best be getting along," he said. "The boys."

As he reached for the door knob he felt the air stir behind him. A hand brushed his shoulder. He flinched and she pulled it back as if she had touched hot coals.

"Do you miss her?" she asked.

He faced her. "Of course I do. Every minute," he replied, his voice strangled.

She nodded. "That's good," she said.

He stiffened, considering what to say, how much he was ready to know about Ted. She shrank under his gaze, like Sean when he was in trouble.

"I'm sorry, I really need to get back," he said, and pushed the door open, not waiting for a response. As soon as he was outside he pulled the door shut behind him and leaned on it, his head swimming.

Do you miss her? she had asked. But it was more than that.

Ruth's absence was like a part of him had been cut away, like a creature was on his back. Whispering in his ear: *It's all your fault*.

In front of him, the boy's bike lay in the grass, speckled with raindrops. The rain had stopped now and the village was brightening, the contrasting brickwork of the houses glowing in the heavy orange light that only came after a storm. He could smell the moisture in the grass as the sun warmed it: a heady smell that made him think of his old life, of parks and freshly mown lawns, of walking past damp privet hedges on his way to work.

He strode over to the bike and picked it up, suddenly determined.

"I don't understand. So you're saying he helped you escape?" said Jess.

Sarah had asked that only Jess and Ruth come with her to the third hut along. She wanted to talk to the two of them in private. Back in the first hut, the others were with Martin.

Sarah smiled. "Yes." She bit her lip. "He got me out of there. He's not like the others."

Beside her Ruth was silent. Her features had set like iron as she'd listened to Sarah recounting her escape from the farmhouse.

"It wasn't his idea to take us," Sarah garbled, stumbling over her words, her eyes shifting between the other two women. "Robert made him go along with it."

Ruth gave an involuntary sound. Her skin was pale and damp. Jess reached out and placed a hand on her knee. "You OK, Ruth?"

She gave a tight nod. Jess looked back at Sarah.

"This is what he told you?" she asked.

Sarah nodded again. "I didn't believe him at first," she said. "But he explained."

Ruth folded her arms across her chest.

"He's going to help us," Sarah continued. "He knows the area, and the farmhouse. He can help get the others out, and get us home. We found your boat."

Jess raised an eyebrow. "Our boat?"

"The village boat. It's further up the beach. That's how you got here, isn't it?"

Ruth turned to Jess.

"No," said Jess. "We didn't bring the boat. We walked."

"You *walked*?" Ruth exclaimed. Then she fell back, remembering something. A shadow passed over her face. "Of course," she said.

"Ted and Harry came in the boat. They took it," said Jess.

"My dad's here?" whispered Sarah. Her cheeks had lost their colour and her voice was quiet and childlike.

"Mm-hmm," nodded Jess. "Ruth's seen him."

"Heard him," corrected Ruth. "They've got him and Harry locked up."

"Oh." The life left Sarah's face.

"It's OK," said Jess. "We're going to get them out. Ruth's got keys."

Sarah stood up, her voice breaking. "Don't, please don't," she wailed. "I can't face him!" Sarah pushed past Jess, heading for the door. Outside the rain had stopped.

Sarah turned to them, her hand on the door. Her face was creased and she was close to tears. "I need to see Martin." Then she pushed her way outside.

Jess stared at Ruth, open-jawed.

CHAPTER THIRTY-TWO

RUTH STARED AT THE DOOR TO THE HUT, TRYING TO GET her breath back. She knew Ted was volatile, but surely his presence shouldn't send Sarah running into Martin's arms?

Jess smiled at her. "You OK?" she asked, in a voice that made Ruth suppose she looked anything but.

She nodded, her lips pursed. "I'll be fine," she replied. "Aren't you going to go after her?"

"Yeah. But I'm worried about you. I'm sorry to say this but you look terrible. What did they do to you?"

She shook her head. *Not now.* She blinked the tears away. "Let's focus on getting home, shall we? And on getting the others out."

The door rattled as Sanjeev knocked on it, entering without waiting for a reply. Jess rose from her squatting position on the floor.

"Sanjeev," said Jess, putting up a hand to stop him speaking. "Sarah went to find Martin, I know. Is she with him?"

"She came barging in when we were trying to get him to tell us what happened. They took off together. They've headed inland."

Ruth frowned. *Surely they hadn't gone back to the farmhouse?*

"OK," said Jess, breathing slowly. "Well, he helped her escape so surely she'll be OK with him."

"No." Ruth swallowed and pushed herself up so she was level with the others. "He's not what you think he is."

Jess pushed both hands into her hair. "Jesus," she breathed. "This is all I need."

"Sorry," muttered Ruth. "But Martin isn't to be trusted."

"What?" asked Jess. "He got her out. Why can't we trust him?"

Ruth closed her eyes, stilling her hands. "We just can't." She touched the dent on her finger where her wedding ring had been. "Jess, when am I going to see Ben?"

At the mention of Ben's name Jess span towards Sanjeev.

"We need to get word back to Ben," she said.

Sanjeev nodded. "I can start walking back."

"No. We've got the boat now. Take that. Tell the village what's going on, let Ben know Ruth's safe, and send someone back to get us."

"OK." A pause. "Shall I take Ruth with me?"

Ruth felt her body lighten.

"No," said Jess. "I'm really sorry Ruth, but you're the only person we've got who knows their way around that farm. We need you with us."

Ruth's shoulders slumped.

"Is that OK, Ruth? Will you help us get the others?"

Ruth pushed down the lump in her throat. "OK," she whispered.

"Thanks. Come on then."

Ruth looked around the hut. She was desperately in need of rest, but knew they were relying on her.

"Come on. We need your cool head," said Jess, reaching out a hand. Ruth ducked away and out of the door, Sanjeev giving her a passing pat on the back. She flinched. She couldn't face touching anyone. Only Ben.

Jess headed for the other hut. The rain had stopped now and the sky was clearing. She looked inland for signs of Sarah and Martin. Nothing.

Sanjeev was right behind her, striding across the damp sand. But Ruth hung back, shuffling across the sand.

As Jess approached the other hut the door opened and Toni emerged with Zack.

"How's the boat?" she asked.

"Good," replied Zack. "More than able to get home tonight." He smiled at her, his eyes intense. She gave him a nervous smile back.

She looked out to sea; the water looked calm for now and the dark clouds above were moving northwards. But the sun was already setting – they didn't have much time.

"OK," she said, brushing sand from her hands. "We promised the village we'd send word and that's what we're going to do. San's going to go. How quickly can you get the boat ready?"

Zack shrugged. "Half an hour?"

"Good."

Zack turned back to the boat.

Jess looked at the others. "Let's get some rest. Then we'll head back to the farmhouse when it's dark."

"Should he go on his own?" said Toni. "Sanjeev, I mean?"

Jess looked from her to Sanjeev. She had a point.

"OK. Can you go—"

Toni frowned. "I want to be here for Roisin."

Jess sighed.

"What about Zack?" said Toni. "He can go."

Jess looked at Zack. She'd come to rely on him; his presence made her feel safer. He was moving around the boat, tying up ropes.

"No," she said, We'll need Zack's strength."

"San should stay here," murmured Ruth.

Jess turned to her. "Ruth, you can't go instead."

Ruth shook her head. "Not that. Look at the sky." She pointed out to sea. "It's getting dark. It's not safe, going that far in our tiny boat."

Jess followed her gaze out to sea. The sky was turning a yellowy grey. She thought of Ben, waiting for them. Of his anger at her.

"I promised Ben," she said. "I can't go back on that. We've taken the boat out at night before, it'll be fine."

Toni opened her mouth to protest but Sanjeev put a hand on her arm. "No problem," he said, and hauled himself up to walk over to the boat.

CHAPTER THIRTY-THREE

THE FARMYARD WAS TOO QUIET.

Jess looked up at the farmhouse, its blank upstairs windows reflecting the moonlight. The curtains were drawn. It looked so normal, as if the events of the last week had never happened.

She looked over her shoulder. Behind her, Toni and Zack flanked Ruth, who was shaking. Jess wondered if it would have been wiser to leave her back at the huts. But with Sarah and Martin still missing, they had no one to watch over her.

She heard a scratching noise. In a ramshackle kennel under the house's back windows, a dog was curled up. She put a hand up to warn the others, then motioned towards the dog. It was asleep.

Zack approached silently. She shivered. "Shit," she whispered. "What do we do? Can we drug it? Knock it out?"

He put a hand on her shoulder. "It's injured," he replied. "Look."

She shielded her eyes from the moonlight, and focused on the dark shape. Zack was right; its paw was bandaged.

"Still," she whispered. "We don't know..."

"It's OK," he whispered. "Look at the kennel. The wood."

She edged forwards, daring to approach the dog. The base of the kennel was dark with blood.

"And there's a chain," Zack whispered. "It's not going anywhere."

"OK," she conceded. "But we need to be quiet."

"Where is everybody?" he whispered.

She stopped. She was level with the door to the outhouse now, Toni and Zack next to her.

She took a few deep breaths, her heart thumping, and turned back to Ruth. Her sister-in-law was still a way behind, level with the side of the outhouse. She was staring at a door in the wall. The stink of human waste filled the air. Jess had held her breath as they passed, her eyes watering, but Ruth couldn't tear her gaze away.

She gestured towards Toni then pointed at Ruth. Toni nodded and went back to her, a hand in front of her mouth to keep her from gagging.

As Toni reached her and touched her arm Ruth recoiled, whimpering. Jess froze, waiting for someone to hear, to pounce. But there was nothing. She sighed and walked back to Ruth.

"Ruth," she whispered. "The keys."

Ruth stared at her, her eyes full of panic. "I can't go in there," she moaned.

Jess put out a hand.

"That's OK," she said. "Give them to me and I can open it. You can stay out here."

"Don't leave me," Ruth whispered, her eyes pleading.

Jess looked at her, thinking. Wishing Sanjeev was still with them. But he had gone hours ago, headed out to sea in the hope of getting home before dark. Sending him off like that hadn't been easy. But the sea was still – and she had promised Ben.

She looked at Ruth. It wouldn't be fair to take her in there, but Jess couldn't stay out here. Then she remembered she didn't have to do it all herself.

"Zack, can you stay with her?" she asked.

Ruth felt as if her mind were caving on in her. The smell of that toilet, the sounds of the owls in the trees beyond the field where she had watched Sarah escape, the moon illuminating the farmhouse that loomed over them. It was too much.

As they pushed through the hedge and the smells of the farm rushed at her, she had felt her legs weaken, and it was all she could do to follow the others, to stop herself collapsing to the ground. As they passed the toilet she had stared at it, trying to remember the determined woman who had slung her own waste into it not much more than twenty four hours ago, the woman who had thrown herself out of the window away from her attacker.

Zack smiled nervously at her as Jess left them. She returned his gaze, resisting the urge to reassure him, to lie about the effect this place was having on her.

"You OK?" he whispered.

She shook her head, her lips tight. She could feel beads of sweat breaking out on her forehead and a hot ball of nausea was rising from her stomach. Her knee throbbed.

"OK," he said. "Let's just stay here. Sit down, maybe?"

She shook her head. If she let herself relax now she might never get up again. She looked past him at Jess and Toni.

"Don't worry," Zack said, his teeth flashing as he offered her a reassuring smile. "I'm going to stay out here, stay with you."

She nodded.

"They're going in," whispered Zack. "In there." He gestured towards the outhouse and she felt a cold wave sweep through her. "I'll stay out here with you, keep a lookout. I won't leave you."

She smiled at him, wishing she had the strength for a thank you. Jess and Toni made their way towards the locked door, casting anxious glances about them as they did so. She let her legs give way and sank to the ground, cradling her head in her hands.

CHAPTER THIRTY-FOUR

JESS SWALLOWED AND PICKED A KEY, CAREFUL NOT TO rattle any of the others on the key ring. She bent down to insert it into the lock and turned.

Nothing.

She pulled it back out. Behind her Toni shifted her weight.

She worked her way through the keys, making sure to take them in order. On the third attempt, the key turned.

"Yes!" she hissed. Toni gave her a congratulatory thump on the shoulder. She pushed at the door, waiting for a scrape or a squeaking hinge. But it was quiet.

She looked back at Toni, unable to suppress a grin. Toni smiled back. Her breathing was coming fast and her cheeks were flushed.

Jess eased herself upright and crept forward, reaching out in the darkness. The only source of light was the open doorway behind her, and the obscured moonlight was barely enough to see by. But as her eyes adjusted she began to get a sense of her surroundings.

They were at one end of a narrow corridor, flanked on one

side by a row of four doors and on the other by the outside wall. The floor was concrete and the walls were pale in the dim moonlight that cast a blue haze through the solitary window in the outside wall. There were vague patches on the walls, damp interspersed with the jagged edges of peeling paint, and as her eyes adjusted further she spotted dry white flakes on the floor.

She looked at the doors. Ruth had described the layout: she had been behind the closest door, at Jess's elbow, then Ted and Harry in the next cell. That meant that Sally and Roisin must be behind the other two doors.

She turned back to Toni and waved a hand along the corridor; they would start with the farthest door and work backwards.

They crept along the corridor to the last door. Jess gave it a quiet knock then put an ear to the wood. Could she hear breathing?

She moved her mouth to the door and spoke through it.

"Hello? It's Jess. Jess Dyer. We've come to get you out. Who's in there?"

The door shuddered with the weight of someone landing against it on the other side. Jess held her breath, waiting.

"Hello? Jess? Are you Jess from the village?"

Jess smiled. "Yes," she replied. "Who's that?"

"Sally Angus," came the reply.

Jess felt Toni's body slacken beside her. She leaned into the door.

"Hi Sally," she said. "Give me a minute and I'll let you out."

Toni had moved along the corridor now and was in front of the second door, her mouth against the wood. Jess could hear a voice from inside. Toni gasped and turned to Jess.

"It's Roisin!" she exclaimed. "We have to let her out."

Jess nodded at her. "Sally first. Keep talking to Roisin."

Toni pushed a clenched fist against the door. "Are you OK?"

Roisin said something Jess couldn't make out. She focused on Sally's door, working her way through the keys again. Inside, Sally was silent.

Toni grabbed her arm, almost making her lose her balance. "Roisin's hurt. Let her out. We have to get her, now!"

Jess frowned at her. "Shhh. Please. I've almost got this one. Roisin's next."

"No."

Jess peeled her eyes away from the lock and stared at Toni. *This isn't like you*, she thought.

"Toni, please. Let me do this."

Toni put her hands on her hips. "Roisin's younger. She's hurt. Let her out." A pause. "Please."

Jess clenched her teeth. She almost had Sally now, but maybe if Roisin was injured...

"OK."

She glanced at Sally's door and pushed past Toni to stand next to Roisin's door. Toni mouthed a *thank you* but Jess just glared at her. All of the captives were important. Then she caught herself, realising she would have prioritised Ruth if she'd still been here.

"Let me out, please," wailed Roisin.

Jess bent to the lock, willing herself to focus. The key she had used for the outside door was still pinched between her thumb and forefinger, so she knew which one not to use. She crouched down and looked at the lock: it was similar to the one she'd already opened. That helped.

The second key she tried slid in and turned, the door shuddering on its hinges as she pushed it open.

The first thing that hit her was the smell: the dull scent of an unwashed human being in a confined space, mixed with the sharp tang of urine. Under it was a heavier, metallic scent – blood?

Roisin sat hunched against the wall, her face streaked with dirt and her thick brown hair matted. The thin sweater she wore was torn, the sleeve almost hanging off, and her grey skirt had an unmistakeable bloom of stale brown blood on its front.

Jess looked into Roisin's face, her mind creased with worry. What had they done to this girl?

Toni stumbled into the room, falling on Roisin. "Oh my god! What have they done to you?"

Roisin gave her a weak smile. "I'll be OK."

Jess reached out a hand. "Come quickly," she said, and pulled the girl out. She came easily, her frailness nothing against Jess's strength.

She clutched Roisin's arm as they fell into the corridor. "You're not the only one imprisoned here," she explained gently. "We need to get the others out too. Then we'll get you all away from here."

The girl stared back at her, unblinking. Toni put an arm around her and Roisin huddled into her, trembling.

Jess turned back to the other cell, wondering what was going through Sally's mind. She tried the key that had opened Roisin's door. It worked.

Sally was behind the door and fell out as soon as Jess pulled it open. She looked in a better state that Roisin. Her face was dirty and there was a thin cut on her cheek that was starting to yellow, but there was no blood.

Jess gave her a nervous smile. "You OK?"

Sally blinked and nodded. "Is Mark here?"

Jess frowned. *Mark?*

"My fiancée."

Jess remembered Mark Palfrey, pestering her to bring him

along with them. After Toni's outburst on seeing Roisin, she was grateful she hadn't listened.

"He's back at the village. Waiting for you." She paused. "He sent his love."

Sally's face broke into a smile. She was pale and blonde, and suddenly pretty when she smiled.

Next to them, Toni was muttering into Roisin's ear.

"We need to get a move on," Jess said. "Just one more door."

She felt a knot form in her stomach as she approached the third door. She pulled out the key again.

"Harry? Ted? You in there?"

There was relieved laughter inside. "Yes. Who's that?"

"Jess Dyer. I'm with some of the others. We've come to get you out."

She slid the key in the lock.

"Jess Dyer?" said another voice, its tone sharp. "Where's my girl?"

She took a deep breath, the key motionless in her hand. She couldn't tell him the truth. "She's OK. She got out already. I left her on the beach, in a hut, to wait for me. She's OK."

She closed her eyes as she turned the key and pushed the door open, hoping the lie wouldn't show on her face. Inside, Ted and Harry were both kneeling behind the door. Harry looked tired and pale while Ted had a pinched, angry look to him.

"Those bastards took my girl," he snapped. "Thank you for getting her back for me."

She bit her lip, unable to meet his eye.

"Come on, quick," she said. "We need to get back to the beach."

Ruth watched as Jess and Toni disappeared through the door to the outhouse. Images crowded in on her. Her stinking cell; Robert's lips on her hand; the moment he had struck her; the look on Martin's face. Somewhere behind them all, struggling to fight his way through, was Ben. Hovering at the edge of consciousness, seeping through everything she'd been through in the last few days. Keeping her from tumbling over the edge.

A sudden image of Sean and Ollie flashed behind her eyes. She shook the picture from her head; she wasn't ready for them yet.

She'd thought she'd be able to come back here, that the presence of mind that had got her away would let her return unharmed.

She was wrong.

Zack was a few feet away from her now, pacing the farmyard. Without Jess he seemed smaller, less solid. But she appreciated his staying with her, and was glad of his silence.

Zack stopped pacing and shrank into the wall next to her, staring towards the end of the outhouse. She looked from him to the hedge and back again.

"What is it?" she whispered.

He shrugged. "Not sure."

He raised a finger to his lips and she looked back towards the hedge, listening.

There. The crack of a twig underfoot, and a muttered curse from beyond the end of the wall. She heard the pigs stirring in their sty, disturbed.

She stared at Zack, her body cold. He grabbed her by the arm, and they stumbled into the middle of the farmyard, Zack casting about for a hiding place. For a moment she thought he was going to push her towards her cell, but then he seemed to think better of it.

"In here," he whispered, pointing at the kitchen door.

She shook her head, imagining what – who – might be in there, but he pulled her with him, not caring that she was stumbling over her own feet.

The kitchen was dark, hideous shapes looming at her out of the gloom. She could almost feel the breathing of the sleeping men upstairs, or maybe it was the building itself exhaling.

"Here, sit down," said Zack, scraping a chair across the tiled floor. She felt his hands on her shoulders, guiding her into it. She pulled herself in, trying to shrink from his touch, to hide from the room. When finally she was seated and he let go, she let herself breathe again.

She heard Zack walk across the room, towards the farmyard. *Don't leave me.*

She dragged herself upright, wiping her face, and stared at Zack silhouetted in the doorway. He turned back and smiled at her, then his gaze shifted past her and she saw his body tense.

She turned towards the doorway that led to the house. And screamed.

The corridor was crowded now. Toni was all but carrying Roisin, Ted and Harry were like coiled bags of energy and Sally shuffled behind them all. Jess pushed past them all to the open door. She peered round it into the farmyard.

There was no sign of Zack and Ruth.

She looked at the farmhouse. The back door stood open.

Harry put a hand on her arm. "Everything alright?"

She shrugged her shoulders. Where were they?

A scream rent the air, coming from the farmhouse. Her heart raced: it could only be Ruth.

Harry tightened his grip on her arm, keeping her from

bounding across the farmyard. “Look,” he said, his breath rising.

A shadow was crossing the yard; a tall, thin man’s shape outlined by the moonlight. He was pushing a bike. She pulled back, staring into Harry’s lined face.

She peered round the doorframe, feeling Harry lean over her to see. It was strangely reassuring.

The figure moved towards the house, then leaned the bike against its back wall and paused at the open door. Suddenly the door was illuminated, the man’s outline caught in its yellow glow.

She squinted, not trusting her eyes. She looked back at Harry, whose mouth had fallen open.

“What’s he doing here?” he whispered.

CHAPTER THIRTY-FIVE

ROBERT STOOD IN THE HALLWAY, FRAMED BY THE KITCHEN door.

He smiled at Ruth, panting. His face was red and beaded with sweat. It was the first time she'd seen him look anything other than immaculate.

In front of him, a knife to her throat, was Sarah.

Ruth reached out towards Sarah. She pulled her hand back as Robert adjusted the knife in his grip. Sarah, who had been staring at Ruth, closed her eyes. Her cheeks were ashen and her clothes even dirtier than before, with fresh tears in the fabric of her blouse.

Nobody spoke. All Ruth could hear was her own laboured breathing and the shuffling of Sarah's feet against the tiles as she struggled to gain her footing. Robert had lifted her in the air, and the tips of her shoes danced across the floor.

Finally Robert broke the silence. "Good evening, Mrs Dyer," he sneered.

She willed herself to meet his gaze. Her stomach was churning now.

She started to get to her feet but froze when Robert

yanked Sarah's head back, his fingers entwined in her knotted hair.

"Sit down," he snapped. Sarah stared at her, eyes pleading.

Behind her, she heard Zack move. Robert's gaze slid to him.

"And you can stay right where you are."

Zack shuffled back into place behind her. Robert adjusted the knife, making Sarah grimace, and he looked back at Ruth.

She took a deep breath and willed her voice not to betray her.

"Where did you find her?" she asked. She thought of Jess and the others in the outhouse. *Please don't follow us in here*, she thought.

He chuckled. "She was along the beach. Hiding in a ditch. Did you abandon her? I would expect better of you."

Ruth frowned. "Where's Martin?"

Robert's face broke into a grin. "Oh you know about that, do you?" He laughed again. "Of course, you watched their daring escape, didn't you?"

She said nothing, holding his gaze. She looked at the knife. At his hand.

"But of course," he continued, anger in his voice. "You were all in it together ,weren't you?"

She said nothing.

"Why did you betray me like that," he urged, "when all I wanted was the best for you?"

She swallowed. "You didn't answer my question," she said.

"Question? I really don't think you're the one who should be asking questions right now."

Sarah gasped as he tightened his grip on her shoulders, holding the knife across her body. Ruth looked at her, torn between protectiveness and anger at Sarah's naivety. *Martin*, she thought. *Bastard.*

"Did Martin bring you back here?" she asked.

Sarah gave a tiny shake of her head. "No," she whimpered.

Ruth pursed her lips and placed a steadying hand on the table, terrified she was going to fall off the chair. She took a few deep breaths.

"But since you were wondering," said Robert. He was looking over his shoulder into the hallway.

"Bill?" he called. "Bring the little traitor in here."

Robert stepped further into the room, dragging Sarah with him. Bill pushed past them, pulling Martin in. Martin's hands were bound with twine that glinted blue in the dim light, and there was a dark shape around his eye, a bruise.

"The prodigal son returns," announced Robert, beaming at Martin. Martin ignored him, focussing on Sarah. She started sobbing.

Robert waved his hands around the room expansively. "Well this is nice, isn't it? All of us back home together."

Martin made a lunge for Robert, pulling his hands up, but was jolted back by Bill, who had the other end of the twine.

"Bad boy," said Robert. "You behave yourself."

Martin spat in his direction. Robert laughed. "You missed! So..." He looked back at Ruth. "Seeing as you're back for good now, I think it's time you knew a few home truths about your beloved Mr Ben Dyer."

Ruth felt her heart pick up pace.

Robert pushed Sarah onto the chair opposite her.

"Stay there," he breathed into her face. She squeezed her eyes shut.

He stood behind Sarah, the knife still in his hand, so that he was facing Ruth across the table.

"I imagine you'll want to know what your husband did to me."

"Are you talking about me?"

Ruth shot her head towards the back door as the light flicked on.

There, looming in the doorway, was Ben.

CHAPTER THIRTY-SIX

JESS STARED AT THE SILHOUETTED FIGURE IN THE farmhouse door. Tall and thin, with scruffy hair. Stooping as he ascended the steps into the house. It was Ben alright.

Harry was motionless next to her. "What the hell?"

She screwed up her face, holding in her anger. Why had Ben followed her? Didn't he think she could lead this group, get Ruth back? And how had he got here? He must have left right after them, to have caught up so fast.

She scanned the farmyard, wondering if he was alone. She looked at the bike, leaning against the farmhouse. Had he cycled here? Whose bike was that?

"Typical bloody Ben," she muttered.

Harry looked at her, shocked. "Huh?"

She glared at him. "I told him not to come but here he is. He never trusts me."

Harry frowned. "I don't think it's like—"

"What do you know? I've known Ben all my life and this is just the sort of stunt he'd pull. He's going to fuck this up for us. Big time."

"Jess," protested Harry. "Go easy on him. He just wants to get his wife back."

"I love Ruth," she replied. "Yes, I was pissed off when all of a sudden she had to leave London with us, but she's Ruth, and it wasn't her fault. I came here to get her back, and I don't need Ben butting in."

Harry blinked. "I don't think you're being fair on him."

"Will you two shut up? Someone's going to hear you!"

They turned to see Toni behind them, frowning. Roisin leaned against her, breathing heavily.

"Look," Toni continued. "Whatever the problem is, can you park it till later? We need to get out of here. Look at Roisin, she's a wreck."

Jess looked around the group. Roisin wasn't the only one who looked bad. Both Ted and Harry were pale, with deep circles under their eyes, and Sally's skin had whitened in the moonlight.

"Sorry," Jess said, blushing.

"I know," said Toni. "Look, I'm getting Roisin out of here. I'll take her back to the beach. Sally too. We'll wait for the boat. And there's food we left in those huts. Look at her: she needs it."

"OK," said Jess, resisting the urge to turn and see what Ben was doing. *Has he seen me?*

Toni frowned. "Where's Ruth?"

Now she notices. "I don't know. But Ben's here. He's gone into the farmhouse."

"*What?*"

Jess nodded towards the open doorway. Ben was still silhouetted in it. Toni pushed past her and whistled.

"Shh," hissed Jess. She looked at Roisin and Sally again. "Take them. Go back to the beach. I'll deal with Ben."

"Sure?"

"Sure."

Ruth stared at Ben. Across the table Robert tensed, tightening his grip on Sarah and pulling the knife to her face. She stared at it through lowered lashes, her chest rising and falling.

Ben looked from Robert to Ruth and his face lifted. "Ruth?" he whispered. "How are you? What have they..."

He turned back to Robert, a shadow dropping over his face.

"You took my wife, you bastard," he said through gritted teeth.

Ruth blinked. "The boys, Ben? Where are the boys?"

"Well done, super sleuth," grinned Robert, ignoring her. "She's mine now."

"Yours?" cried Ben. "Yours? She's not yours and she never will be."

"You haven't answered my question," Ruth said quietly. "About the boys."

Ben looked back at his wife, and stepped towards her.

"Stop!" shouted Robert. "No one moves!"

He twisted his wrist and a spot of blood appeared at the tip of the blade, on Sally's cheek. She gasped.

Behind Ruth, there was the sound of struggling.

"Leave her alone!" shouted Martin. "What did she ever do to hurt you?"

Robert smiled at Martin, cocking his head to one side. Sarah looked across the table, trembling.

"Shut up, boy," Robert sneered. "She's just a silly girl. You should have had her when you had the chance. You owe me, so just keep your mouth shut and remember where your loyalties lie."

"I don't care about any fucking loyalties! I love her!"

Sarah's eyes widened.

"Ha ha! I love it! Don't be so stupid, Martin. You just want to shag her." He lifted the knife from Sarah's face and brushed it through her hair. "I can't say I blame you either. If it weren't for my lovely Mrs Dyer here I'd be rather tempted myself."

Ruth froze, looking at Ben. He turned to Robert, his cheeks red.

"What are you on about? What have you done to her?"

CHAPTER THIRTY-SEVEN

Robert laughed. "Oh, don't worry, Dyer. I've far too much respect for her." He paused. "You have no idea what you did to me, do you?"

Ruth could hear Ben's breathing, his voice rising in pitch.

"I did nothing and well you know it."

"Nothing! You ran off like a frightened child, leaving me to face the music. I went to prison because of you."

"It was nothing to do with me. You went to prison because you stabbed that man. And all for a poxy cash tin."

"If you'd been with me instead of hiding in the bush, that would never have happened."

"Never have happened? You didn't have to do it, you know. No one told you to."

Robert pointed to his temple. "Ha! But that's where you're wrong, you see. It was the voice, wasn't it? The one that tells me what to do when I'm stuck, or in trouble."

Ben snorted.

"Watch it, Dyer," Robert admonished. "Don't mock. It told me where to find you, didn't it? And your beautiful lady wife here."

Ruth shivered.

"Don't talk bollocks, Robert," said Ben. "I don't know how you found us, but—"

"Be quiet!" Robert thundered. "Just stop arguing with me! You lost the right to do that when you shopped me to the police."

Ruth looked at her husband. *Get rid of him, Ben,* she thought. *Sort it. Apologise, if you need to.*

Ben stiffened. "I didn't."

Robert pointed his blade at Ben. "Don't lie to me again."

Sarah's body relaxed as the blade left her skin. She looked over at Martin.

Ben shrugged. "You don't have to believe me. But it's true. I lied to them."

Robert froze. "No, you didn't! You told them everything!"

Ben shook his head. "No. There were other witnesses, remember? In the unit opposite. They saw what you did. They told the police."

"Liar," breathed Robert.

Ben shrugged again. "Believe it or don't."

"I've spent years looking for you," hissed Robert. "Thinking about how I'd get you back. And now here we are. You, me, and the lovely Ruth. I found you, I tricked you and I took her."

Robert looked at Ruth, a smile playing on his lips. She flinched and looked at his shirt pocket. Could her ring still be in there?

Robert pointed the knife at her, waving it in the air. She felt Ben tensing in the doorway, heard his intake of breath. Robert looked back at Ben.

"She's my revenge, don't you see?" he said. "Taking her from you."

As Toni headed towards the side of the house with Roisin and Sally, Jess turned to Harry.

"Can you go with them?" she asked. "Take Ted. I need to get Ruth. Deal with Ben."

Harry grimaced. "I think we should stay with you. We don't know where those men are."

She pursed her lips. "I'm perfectly capable of dealing with this."

He shrugged. "Sorry," she said. "That came out wrong."

There was a cry from across the farmyard. She turned to see Toni bending over Roisin, who was on the ground.

"You're right," said Harry. "We'll go." He blushed. "The boat's on the beach." A pause. "We brought it here."

"I know," she said. "But it's not there now. Sanjeev took it back home, but I'm hoping he'll be on his way back by now, or that somebody will."

"Eh?" Harry looked puzzled.

She shook her head. "Long story," she said. "But there's huts there, on the beach. And food. Take her there, and I'll find Ruth." She looked back at the house.

"OK," he said. He pushed past her and headed across the farmyard. He turned back.

"Ted? Come on!"

Jess shivered, remembering Ted standing behind her. She shrank back as he passed her in the doorway, muttering something under his breath.

Oh hell, she thought. Sending Ted to the beach with Harry meant that he'd find out that Sarah wasn't there.

But he'd have to know eventually. She said nothing, but let him cross the farmyard to the others. Toni was on the ground now with Roisin.

Harry stopped and turned back. "Let me just check there's no one here," he hissed, and disappeared around the house.

Ted hurried after him. He stopped next to Toni and lifted Roisin into his arms. Jess was surprised by his strength.

She looked towards the farmhouse doorway. Ben was still standing there, gesticulating. Ted stopped and looked at the door, Roisin groaning as they slumped to a halt.

Jess froze. Ben was moving, disappearing into the house. Beyond him, Jess could just make out a figure, sat at a table. Sarah – and someone else. Behind her, a shape she definitely recognised.

Robert.

She heard a thud and looked back to see Roisin, crumpled on the ground. Ted had dropped her and was running for the farmhouse door.

CHAPTER THIRTY-EIGHT

Ben looked from Robert to Ruth, anger rising in his stomach.

"What did he do to you?" he whispered.

She shook her head. In the harsh overhead light her skin was sallow and her hair seemed to have thinned. Ben felt an urge to cry.

"Nothing," she whispered. "Not really."

He turned back to Robert, who tightened his grip on Sarah. She gasped.

"Leave her! This is nothing to do with her!" cried Martin.

Robert sighed and looked at Martin, contempt darkening his face. "Oh please be quiet, you stupid boy." He drew the blade lightly across Sarah's forehead. A line of red formed, blood dripping into her eyes.

Ben looked at Ruth, more closely now. A bruise was blossoming on her cheek. Her hands look scarred, and there were scratches on her arms. Her T-shirt was torn.

"What did you do to her?"

Robert laughed. "Oh calm down, please. I haven't done anything, not yet. But now she's back she can leave her cell, and join me in the main house." He gestured up the stairs, towards the bedrooms.

Ruth whimpered.

Robert looked around at them all, smiling. "Not just me," he said. "Martin, it's not too late, you know. Now you're back we can keep your girl here. Have her, if you want. If you don't mind sharing. I'm sure Bill won't mind..."

Ben looked at Martin, still tethered to Bill like a dog. Bill clenched his fists, while Martin stared at the floor.

"No," said Bill. "We're not all like you."

"What?" exclaimed Robert. "But I let you have the pretty one, the one with the blonde curls."

"Sally. I know," replied Bill.

"Well, what stopped you then?"

Bill stared at Robert, his upper lip trembling. "Didn't you hear me? I'm not like you. The others aren't either. Why d'you think none of them are here?" He gestured towards the doorway. "They're all upstairs, keeping out of it."

Robert's eyes glittered. The blue was just as bright as it had been when they were at school. "Such a hypocrite. Of course you're like me, and you know it."

"No," said Bill.

"Nor me!" shouted Martin, struggling against his bindings. "I never touched Sarah!"

Ben looked past Martin, to the kitchen counter. Behind him, next to the sink, was a block of knives. *If he could just...*

He was disturbed by sobbing, and looked back at Ruth. She was hunched over the table now, her head in her hands. Her body shook.

Forgetting Sarah, he stumbled towards his wife and folded his arms around her, muttering into her ear. She stiffened and he loosened his embrace.

"Ruth," he whispered. "He can't do anything to you now. Let's go home."

She shrugged her shoulders, pushing him away. He stared at the top of her head, confused.

"Sarah!"

He looked up to see a man rush through the door and hurl himself at Robert. He lunged for Robert's hands, trying to pull the knife from them. The blade slipped. Sarah screamed and clapped a hand to her eye.

"Leave my daughter alone, you bastard!" the man cried. *Ted?*

Sarah raised her head, blood seeping between her fingers. "Daddy?"

Martin stepped forwards. "Sarah!" he cried. But she ignored him, her eyes locked on her father.

Ben tightened his grip on Ruth. Robert and Ted were scrabbling at each other, Ted desperately trying to snatch the knife. There was a shout as they hit the wall and pulled themselves upright again.

Ben let go of Ruth and lunged forwards, trying to grab Robert, but he was out of reach. As he straightened up, Robert pulled back, the knife dark in his hand. Sarah screeched something unintelligible.

Ted fell to the floor, blood darkening his chest.

CHAPTER THIRTY-NINE

Jess ran to the spot where Ted had dropped Roisin. Toni knelt next to her, shaking her.

She crouched next to Toni, putting a hand on Roisin's cheek. She was cold and her eyes were closed, dark lashes brushing her cheeks as if asleep.

She lowered her face to Roisin's, to check if she was still breathing. Toni held her breath.

Jess exhaled and relaxed. The warmth of Roisin's breath, though feeble, brushed her cheek.

"She's OK," she told Toni, who was pale herself.

She pulled back to let Toni stroke Roisin's face with her fingertips.

"Roisin? Wake up, sweetie."

"She going to be alright?" Harry was behind them, a hand on Jess's arm.

She shook her head. "I need to get Ruth," she said, not sure if Ruth's skills were up to this. She looked towards the door. Ted had disappeared inside and there was no sign of Ben.

She flinched as a scream came from inside the farmhouse,

jolting Roisin and almost sending her tumbling to the ground. Jess reached out to lift her again and then saw the state of her skirt in the growing light.

She froze. "What is it?" asked Zack.

She suppressed a whimper. "Her skirt," she whispered. "It's soaked in blood."

Toni stiffened and let out a low moan. Harry's breathing slowed.

"Oh hell," he said. "What are we going to do?"

She gazed at Toni, feeling helpless.

Toni looked back at her, her eyes brimming. "Get Ruth. Now."

Jess pushed herself up, her legs protesting. She shook herself out. There was another scream from the farmhouse.

She glanced at Harry, wide-eyed, then ran towards the open door.

Martin listened as Robert and Bill argued, shocked. As Bill's anger grew, his grip loosened on the twine holding Martin's wrists. He pulled a hand away to remonstrate with Robert, his finger jabbing at the air. The twine grew slack.

Martin pulled on it. Amazingly, Bill didn't pull back.

He looked at Sarah across the table. Dried blood lay on her cheek and her fingers were pushing at her forehead, smeared with blood. She pulled her hands away from her face and looked back at him. She smiled and his heart soared.

Ruth was bent over the table, her head on her arms.

Suddenly a man tumbled through the door, screaming Sarah's name. Robert cried out and the man fell on him.

Martin freed his hands and scanned the room, looking for a weapon. He pushed past Bill, reaching out for the knife block next to the sink. He plunged his hand between the handles and pulled one out at random, drawing it in front of his face.

A chef's knife. Perfect.

There was a scream behind him and he spun to find Robert standing over his attacker. His knife was raised in his hand, dark with blood. Sarah shot up from her chair and pushed past Robert, throwing her body over the man on the floor.

"Daddy!" she cried.

"I love you, Sarah," Martin whispered. Then he leapt over the table and hurled himself at Robert, keeping his own knife concealed.

Robert turned towards him. "You bloody idiot," he sneered.

As momentum carried Martin over the blood-smeared table he hurtled towards Robert. His leading shoulder barrelled into the other man, sending him thudding against the wall, and he brought his concealed hand forward to lunge with the knife.

"No," he replied, his voice steady. "Not any more."

"Martin, stop!"

He looked around to see Sarah staring at him, her eyes wild. He leaned back, attempting to halt his momentum.

It was no good. He carried on going until he almost hit the wall, Robert's body stopping him in his tracks. The two of them were eye to eye. He felt heat spreading on his chest and looked down. His arm was stuck, the knife still in his hand, plunged into Robert's neck.

CHAPTER FORTY

Jess thundered through the door, grabbing at its frame to stop herself tripping over Ted, who lay on the floor. Jess dropped to her knees, her fingertips recoiling at the sticky warmth beneath her hands. Next to her, Sarah was wailing and clutching at Ted's head. She looked up at Jess.

"Help me, Jess," she pleaded. "My dad."

Jess put her hand on Ted's chest, prodding gently. The wound was to the side, beneath his armpit. Hopefully he would survive it.

"Jess!"

Ben was kneeling beside an ashen Ruth. He had his arm around her shoulders and was rocking her. She was unresponsive, staring ahead.

Jess pushed herself up to see what Ruth was looking at. Martin and Robert were locked together, Robert sandwiched between Martin and the wall. Robert was making a spluttering sound that made Jess heave. Martin's hands were on his neck and blood poured between his fingers.

"What the—?" she exclaimed.

Martin turned towards her, letting go of Robert who

slumped to the ground. He grabbed the table to steady himself. His hands slid through the blood on its top as he eased round to Sarah.

"I'm so sorry, I'm so sorry," he cried, kneeling and pushing an arm around her shoulders. She didn't react, but bent over her father, her hands on his wound. She pushed against him with her fists, whimpering.

A faint smile lit up Ted's face. "I'm sorry, love," he whispered.

"Help me stop the blood someone, please!" she cried. Bill and Zack moved towards her, crashing into each other. Bill dropped to the floor next to Ted, putting a hand to his chest. He stood up and moved quickly to a drawer next to the sink. He pulled out some cloths and took them back to Ted. Sarah pulled away, giving him room to fashion a tourniquet.

Sarah watched, sobbing and wailing *Daddy* over and over.

"Jess! Hurry, please!" Toni was calling to her from outside. She took a deep breath and looked again at Ruth. *Can you help Roisin?*

But Ruth was in no state to help anyone. She lifted herself from the table and eased round to where Robert lay on the floor, edging past Sarah and Ted, close enough that Jess could hear her sister-in-law's breathing. Ben stood up and watched her.

Ruth stopped as she reached Robert. She looked back to Ben. "What you said about him... Was it true?" she asked.

Ben nodded.

"You lied for him?"

Another nod. Ben closed his eyes briefly but then opened them again, meeting his wife's steady gaze.

"He killed someone?"

Ben closed his eyes. "The man died two months later. Robert went to prison."

She looked from him and then down at Robert, whose

legs were spasming. Jess pinched her nose and took a deep breath.

"He wanted to rape me," Ruth said, her voice calm. Jess clenched her fists.

"He was going to make me live with him," Ruth continued. "But instead he did this." She touched her cheek. Ben reached out a hand, but she shook it off.

"Bastard," she said, and drew up a foot. Everyone except Sarah stopped to watch her.

She clenched her teeth and pushed the foot down onto Robert's chest, twisting it as it made contact. Blood spluttered from his mouth onto her jeans but she didn't flinch.

She bent over, reaching her hand towards his chest. Jess drew back, her heart in her throat. Ruth pulled Roberts's shirt pocket open and drew out a ring. She wiped it clean on her own grubby T-shirt and slid it onto her finger.

Jess looked at Ben: he was staring, holding his breath. His hand had gone to his own ring finger.

Robert's eyes widened. Ruth straightened up, her face expressionless. She twisted her foot again. His eyes rolled back and he stopped moving.

Jess put her hands to her mouth as Ben rose from his chair, the scrape of its legs on the floor breaking the silence. Ruth turned to him, shaking, and finally allowed him to hold her.

CHAPTER FORTY-ONE

JESS LOOKED OUT OF THE BEACH HUT WINDOW, LISTENING to Ruth's voice behind her. Roisin was stretched out on the raised bench, wrapped in a blanket they'd taken from the farmhouse. Her clothes were piled on the floor next to them, the heavy smell of stale urine mixing with the metallic tang of blood.

"You're going to be OK, my love," Ruth murmured as she cleaned Roisin's skin, lifting sections of the blanket as she worked. It was cold and they wanted to keep the girl covered.

"Is she?" asked Toni. She was perched on the bench next to Roisin, clasping her hand.

Ruth looked up and nodded. "The bleeding's stopped. It's not as bad as it looked – the urine made it look like there was a lot more."

Jess sighed and looked outside. Ben was leaning on the hut's wall, waiting for his wife. He stared out to sea, fidgeting with his wedding ring. Watching him, Jess made a decision.

She picked her way across the hut and pulled her rucksack from the pile of supplies in a corner. Ruth ignored her, focused on her patient.

Deep inside the rucksack, hidden in an internal compartment, was the tin. Sonia's tin. She pulled it out, smoothing her fingers across its hard surface. For a moment she tightened her grip on it, reluctant. But then she turned and held it out to Ruth.

"You should have this."

Ruth looked at the tin. She frowned and then her eyes widened as she realised what it was. "I can't," she said, her voice shaking.

Jess pushed it into her hand. "Yes. You'll wear them. I don't." She pulled in a breath. "And I need to let go."

Ruth bit her lip, looking into Jess's face. "Are you sure?"

She nodded, and closed Ruth's fingers around the tin. Ruth smiled and pocketed it, then moved back to Roisin.

The door opened and Ben all but fell inside. "The boat's back."

She felt her body fill with relief. She looked out of the window: sure enough, their boat was heading for the beach. Zack and Harry ran to the water's edge, waving their arms wildly. Zack was laughing. Behind them, Sarah sat on the sand next to Ted, who'd refused to come into the hut. Bill's tourniquet had worked and the blood had stopped. Sarah and Ted sat a few inches apart, not touching. Sarah kept glancing back towards the farm, probably wondering if Martin would appear. He'd stayed behind with Bill to bury Robert. Jess shuddered at the thought of it.

She flashed Ruth a look and then ran outside, following Ben. They joined Zack, jumping up and down in the shallows. A silhouetted figure waved back.

She turned to Ben and hugged him. "Oh, thank god." He pushed her away, holding her at arm's length. He was pale and unsmiling.

"Well done, sis," he said. She swallowed the lump in her throat.

"Thanks."

He nodded, blinking back tears.

The boat approached slowly, its engine becoming louder against the sound of the waves. Harry came up behind them, pulling Sally with him. She'd been silent since leaving the farm. Jess wondered what had happened to her, in that cell. What she would tell her fiancé.

The boat's hull dragged onto the sand and Clyde jumped out. Jess felt her spirits lift.

"Clyde! We're so pleased to see you."

He winked at her. "Hello gorgeous." She let herself smile back, spotting Zack watching them. She laughed and Clyde's face fell.

Zack and Harry ran to the boat, joining Clyde in pulling it onto the beach and tying it to a rock. She followed them, wrapping Clyde in a hug. Zack moved in and grabbed her hand. She let him hold it, feeling it warm her own.

"Is Sanjeev OK?" she breathed.

Clyde's shoulders heaved. "He's fine." He looked around the others.

"Everyone here?" he asked.

Jess looked back. Ruth was emerging from the hut, she and Toni supporting Roisin between them. Sally stood at the edge of the water, shivering. Ben was behind Ruth, and Zack was next to her, still holding her hand.

"Yes."

"Stop! Wait for me!"

She looked up to see a figure advancing from the dunes: Martin. Sarah stood up shakily and after glancing at Ted, ran towards him. They hugged and Ted spat into the sand.

"I'm not going with that little shit," he muttered.

Jess bit her lip, resisting the urge to tell him just how grateful he should be.

"It's fine," she said. "We won't all fit anyway."

Clyde nodded. "I can come back again."

"Thanks. Roisin, Sally, Sarah and Ted need to go back first. Take them, with Ruth. I'll wait here with Ben, Zack, Toni and Harry." She paused. "And Martin."

Sarah and Martin were with them now. Sarah mouthed a *thank you* to Jess and crossed to her father, pulling him up by the arm. He leaned into her and muttered something unintelligible.

Clyde, Zack and Harry helped the first group onto the boat. It wasn't easy; there were more of them than the boat was built for and Roisin needed to lie across Ruth, Sarah and Sally's laps. Ted brushed off Harry's attempts to help him.

"Leave me alone, mate!" he snapped. "I'm fine by meself."

Harry shrugged, smiling. Ted was going to be fine.

As the boat headed out to sea, Jess drew back towards the huts. "We may as well take shelter," she told Ben.

He followed her, Zack falling in with them. Martin stayed outside, staring out to sea. Toni stood at the edge of the water, her arm shielding her face.

In the beach hut Ben slumped onto the bench, pummelling his legs.

"Haven't ridden a bike for years," he said. "Felt good."

Jess smiled.

"I didn't mean anything by it, you know," he said. She frowned. Zack was next to her, listening quietly, his hand brushing hers.

"Following you," Ben continued. "I knew you'd get her. But it was something Dawn said – I just had to find her. I couldn't stay behind another minute."

She brushed his sleeve with her hand. "I know. She'll be home soon. We all will be."

"What are you going to do about him?"

She looked out of the window at Martin. Could she accept him in the village, after everything he'd done?

"It won't be easy, persuading them to let him in," she said. "I'll need your help."

He nodded.

She took his hand.

"Ben?"

She turned to him. He looked tired and drawn. "Hmm?"

"We'll deal with it together."

READ RACHEL'S NEXT BOOK

If you enjoyed *Exile*, you'll love my next book, *A House Divided*.

Kira Sinclair is many things: loyal government minister, loving wife and devoted mother.

But when a terrorist attack threatens her family, and her government responds with laws that target her Muslim husband and children, she must betray her former friends and colleagues.

And when her son Samir reacts angrily, the state Kira was once part of becomes her enemy. She has to take drastic measures to protect her family and her freedom.

A House Divided is a tense political thriller exploring the extreme measures governments will take to protect themselves, and their impact on one woman and her family.

To read the opening chapters of *A House Divided* before its release in Summer 2018, join my book club at rachelmccollin.com/read.

Thanks,
Rachel McCollin

PLEASE REVIEW THIS BOOK

Did you enjoy this book?

If you did, I'd be grateful if you did two things:

1. Tell your friends about it. Give to to a friend or donate it to a charity shop so someone else can enjoy it.

2. Leave an honest review on Amazon.

3. Oh, and there's a third: buy my next book when it comes out! Sign up at rachelmccollin.com/read and I'll email you when it's released.

Thanks,

Rachel McCollin

ACKNOWLEDGMENTS

This book was inspired by my work at the Environment Agency and by watching the European refugee crisis unfold during 2015 and 2016.

Acknowledging the people who helped it grow from a series of scribblings in a notebook to a finished book isn't as easy as it sounds - who do you name first? If you accidentally miss someone off, will they hate you forever? So if there is anyone who contributed to this book and I haven't mentioned you, my sincere apologies. The error is due to my forgetfulness, not your lack of merit. Tell me next time you see me and I'll buy you a pint.

So, here goes...

Members of Birmingham Writers' Group gave me feedback on early drafts, some of which helped me make the book better and some of which gave me encouragement. And three intrepid members of the group read the whole manuscript before it was properly edited and provided invaluable critique. Thanks to Martin Sullivan, Heide Goody and Sophy Pople for being my beta readers, you'll be pleased to know I took out most of the flashbacks. Thanks to David

Croser-Drake for giving one chapter such fulsome praise that I felt it would be a crime to literature if I stopped writing. Thanks to Chris Garghan for his able leadership of the group and for inspiring me with his own flooding story, infinitely more haunting than mine. And thanks too to other members whose encouragement, example and friendship has helped me write more and better than I would have done otherwise, including but not limited to Mat Joiner, Alex Brightsmith, Iain Grant, Simon Fairbanks and Anna Stephens.

Other writers who helped inspire me to publish independently include Rachel Walkley and Evie Bradbury. I look forward to reading your books when they're published.

My editor Karen Ball pulled the book into shape and made it a much better piece of writing and of fiction.

On the research side of things, I was helped by Rob Ellis of the Environment Agency, who pointed me in the direction of flood maps and ensured (inasmuch as I would listen) that I kept to sensible predictions.

No acknowledgements page would be complete without a declaration of how wonderful my family have been and how they've patiently waited outside the door while I've written. In reality they occupied themselves while I escaped the house to go and write in a coffee shop. Thanks go to Jamie and Michael for putting up with me while I talk about floods, and nasty men called Robert, and the topography of the Yorkshire coast. My dad Malcolm has always encouraged me and told me my writing is better than I know it is, and my mum Carol inspired me in so many ways (I still have a tin with her rings in). And finally my husband Pete has tolerated me becoming a writing bore and provided childcare, pots of tea and occasional glasses of wine while I disappeared into my own head. It'll all be worth it, I promise.

Lightning Source UK Ltd.
Milton Keynes UK
UKOW04f1517120118
316035UK00001B/179/P

9 781999 878290